Threads of Her Braid

Tanya Zuñiga

To the women who've paved the way,
and to the ones who will come after, planting new seeds
and blossoming along the journey. May we all continue to claim
the space we rightfully deserve.

THE FIRST STRAND: The weight of the past.

Better Late Than Never

Más vale tarde que nunca

AURORA

I once heard that the soul of a story lives in its first breath. If that's the case, mine lives within the warm aroma of *pan dulce* lingering under a sunny sky, carries the echo of small-town *chisme,* and wears an old skirt turned into a dress—not because my mother was crafty, but because life didn't leave her much choice.

Huejosquite was a speck lost in Chihuahua. One of those places where secrets traveled faster than desert winds and everyone knew your business before you did. Where even the chickens probably knew more about you than you knew about yourself. And yet, my story? That was mostly a mystery to me. My mother's eyes would turn as sad as an old *telenovela* if I so much as hinted at asking questions about the past, so I didn't. All I knew was that there was a life before, and a life after my father's death, and the two hardly seemed to belong to the same family. It was like someone had ripped apart a book and rearranged the chapters without bothering to check if they still made sense.

But even if I didn't have all the answers, I had my mother, and I had my older brother, Segundo. And for a long time, they were enough.

I remember little about my father, just a feeling, a warmth that lingers in the gaps of my childhood. My earliest memories are filled with the weight of his absence more than his presence—my mother's sighs as she scrubbed laundry, the way she would pause at the door before stepping outside, as if bracing herself for the world's pity.

Segundo used to whisper stories about Papá to me at night, trying to shape a man I could never quite see, while I clutched my doll, Mary—the only physical tie I still had to him. Mary was my father's gift to me for my fifth birthday, the last one we got to celebrate together before he was unfairly taken from us in a crime that no one ever cared to investigate properly. Segundo, at only eight years old, did his best to keep our father's memory alive; he told me about the little workshop in our backyard, where Papá would let us play with his tools, about the strength in his hands, the way he built things with patience and love. But all I had were shadows of those moments, blurred and softened by time.

When Papá died, the world swallowed us whole. I don't remember crying—I don't think I understood enough to—but I remember the way my mother's body curled inward, as if she were trying to make herself disappear. The town whispered about her, not always cruelly, but never kindly either.

"*Rosa should have known better, marrying a man that dark,*" they'd say. "*Her parents warned her against it.*" Their voices oozed the certainty of people who had never suffered a real loss. "*It's tragic, but what did they expect? This country has its ways.*"

And my grandparents—her own parents—treated her as if she had dragged shame through their front door. They took us in, but not without resentment. Their house, though larger than the one we left behind, felt smaller. Just like the rest of the town, it smelled of dust and judgment, of conversations that stopped the moment my mother entered the room. Of adults so engulfed in gossip that they never stopped to think I had ears too. My grandmother, Lupe, never outright said it, but her eyes did: my mother was a burden, a widow with no prospects, no way forward except the one they begrudgingly gave her.

I think that's why my mother clung to me so tightly. Because in a world that had turned its back on her, I was one of the few things that was still hers alone. She would braid my hair every morning, her fingers moving through my curls with the kind of tenderness that could stitch a heart back together. At night, she would hum lullabies, even when I was too old for them. Every so often, she would hold my face in her hands and whisper, "*Tú y tu hermano son lo único que me queda.*"

Being all she had made me feel special when I was younger. Then, I grew up and understood the responsibility that came with being someone's lifeline. After her passing, singing "Arrorró mi niño" to my own children, and later, to my grandchildren, would always bring back my mother. That's why I kept singing it after they were too old for it too.

My mother never let me see her break, but I knew. I knew in the way she held herself too still when people looked at her too long. In the way she never let herself rest, as if stopping for even a moment would let the grief catch up to her.

"Do you think Papá still watches over us from heaven?" I asked her once, my small fingers tracing patterns on her skirt.

She swallowed hard, brushing a strand of hair behind my ear. "He loved you more than anything in this world, and I believe that kind of love is too strong to fade."

I never doubted that. But love wasn't enough to bring him back, and it wasn't enough to make Huejosquite a kinder place.

Still, we had our moments of happiness. We had each other. And for a long time, that was all we needed. But as the saying goes: every season changes; neither summer nor winter stays forever.

And so, here I am. Writing. Trying to make sense of a life that's been woven with the unexpected, in a body that doesn't quite feel like mine anymore, and on a deadline I never asked for.

To be honest, I never thought I'd make it to this age. Not because I thought I would die young—though, looking back, some of my choices might've made that a possibility—but because I never imagined growing this old. Growing up, I always thought people like me stayed stuck in time—forever running from their pasts but never quite arriving at their futures.

Now look at me. Seventy-something, though I shouldn't bother counting anymore. Not with the doctor's words still ringing in my ears.

"Stage two," he'd pronounced, his face careful, his tone too soft. "I'm sorry, Señora Aurora."

At my age, cancer comes with its own set of complications, so I'll do the one thing I've avoided my whole life: I'll tell my story. I always told myself it wasn't worth it, that I had locked it away in the past. But now, with a body that no longer obeys me and a clock that refuses to stop, I know the truth: it wasn't that I didn't want to tell it, I was afraid to remember it.

I'm not trying to turn this into some tragic telenovela. I'm not here for pity, either. Just . . . honesty.

Because the truth is, while I've carried more than my share of hurt, I've also done things. Things I can't undo. Things that still wake me up at night.

Perhaps, in some small way, this is my chance to find forgiveness.

Even if it's only from myself.

Huejosquite was small—did I mention that yet? However, it was small in the loudest way possible, full of people who talked as if they had something to prove, but mostly, they just wanted to know everything about you.

Take my friend Pepi's mom, for instance. Every morning, without fail, she'd be outside her bakery, watering the dirt. I don't mean she was watering plants or flowers—oh no—she was watering the dirt. Why? Who knows. Maybe she thought it would grow something.

But the way she did it? With that purposeful, slow movement, it was like she wasn't just tending to the earth. No, she was watching us. Watching everyone who walked by.

I could almost hear her thinking, *Let's see who's coming down the street today, and let's see how much I can figure out about them just by looking at the way they walk.*

And then, of course, there was Pepi.

I didn't like her at first.

She had this look in her eyes the second we arrived in town—a kind of self-assured look, like even though she was just a year older than me, she knew something I didn't. She was wearing this little yellow dress, and she just stood there, staring at me like she'd already figured me out.

"Hi, I'm Pepi," she said. "You're Aurora, right? My mommy said your dad died, so I should be nice to you."

Of course, evidence that she did, in fact, know everything about me wasn't the first line I wanted to hear. But when you live in a town as small as Huejosquite, either you make friends or you make enemies; there is no such thing as minding your own business.

Eventually, Pepi and I became thick as thieves. We were like *uña y mugre*, as everyone in town called us. And, of course, we argued about who was the *uña* and who was the *mugre*. Who wanted to be the dirty part? We were just kids, after all, playing silly games and trying to figure out how this whole *life* thing worked.

Back then, days were simple. Mom, Segundo, and I helped at my abuelos' convenience store, *Abarrotes Lupe*, named after my abuela, of course. By *helped*, I mostly mean Mom and Segundo; I usually just got in the way when I was eight or nine. Pepi would often come over, and we would stand behind the counter, pretending to be busy, but mostly stealing. Well, not *stealing* exactly—borrowing cookies from the back stock.

It was our little secret.

If you could call it a secret in a town where everyone knew everything about you.

The men held the ultimate power—fathers, husbands, uncles, and brothers—running the world like they were born with the right to it:

"Serve my food, and make sure it's hot when I get here."

"Why is the floor like this? Clean it before someone trips."

"The kids are making noise again. Quiet them down."

"Don't meddle in men's business. This doesn't concern you."

Yet, there was something about my abuela that commanded respect. The men might have been the ones who made the big decisions, but in our house, it was Abuela Lupe who ruled. She wasn't loud about it, but her authority? It was unmistakable. She didn't need to raise her voice. She didn't even need to move fast.

Her power was in the quiet way she held the room, the steady pulse of her presence that made sure everyone knew their place.

My grandfather was, of course, the one who'd raise his voice and give commands. But Abuela? She held power over us in the smallest, simplest of gestures—like how she'd take her time at the dinner table, and just by the way she looked at us, we knew not to get up before her.

She had her ways of clarifying that while the men made the decisions, we were never to forget who truly kept everything together.

No one would have ever guessed that my grandfather had swiped her from her home against her will when she was just fifteen and he was already in his mid-thirties. I bet he never expected that age difference would eventually come back to bite him in the butt.

By the time my abuela reached her late forties and my abuelo his seventies, the turnover of control in their relationship was clear. Thinking back, the only reason my abuela didn't divorce him was probably because divorce carried a social stigma—especially when started by a woman—and my abuela could've well been the spokesperson for what was socially acceptable. I don't imagine the law back then made it that easy for women, anyway. But Abuela Lupe was the matriarch, and she made sure everyone understood what that meant.

I recall a tense day at my grandparents' store. A recurring client showed up while I was stocking the small fridge on the back wall with sodas: Don Evaristo.

His shirt was halfway open, revealing a hairy chest, and his breath reeked of *aguardiente.*

"Doña Lupe," he slurred, struggling to stand up straight, "what will it take for me to get some groceries and pay you later this month? You know I'm a man of my word."

My grandpa just frowned from his chair near the counter, but he didn't intervene.

My abuela didn't reply immediately. She raised an eyebrow and took her time pouring herself a cup of coffee. Time stood still, as if the store itself was holding its breath.

"Evaristo," she replied finally, in a cold and collected tone that seemed to cut the air, "trust is not earned with words, it is earned with actions. You owe me three months of groceries, and your wife just stopped by yesterday asking for salt because there was none at your home."

He opened his mouth, but she raised a hand to stop him.

"I'm not interested in hearing what you have to say next. My store is not a loaning agency, and I'm not a charity worker." She stood up and placed her cup of coffee carefully on the counter. "If you come around again without the money you owe me, I won't be as polite."

Don Evaristo left, mumbling to himself.

As soon as the door closed, my grandpa let out a deep breath and turned to my grandmother. "Always with that attitude, just like a general."

Abuela said nothing. She just held his gaze firmly until, eventually, he turned away.

It was in those early days, in the cramped storeroom behind boxes of cookies, that I learned the art of pretending. Pretending to be someone I wasn't. Pretending that everything was fine. That nothing hurt.

But when you stuff your mouth with cookies and try to sing a song with the dignity of a walrus, pretending doesn't last long. The crumbs in my mouth would fall like tiny confessions, spilling out of me even though I didn't want them to.

Once, Pepi and I were playing our favorite game, *adivina la canción,* in the storeroom, our mouths so full of cookies from the Surtido Rico box that we could barely speak.

"*Como tu sombra iré . . .*" I sang, trying my best to belt out the love song. With my cheeks stuffed, the sweetness in my mouth muffled my voice. But I didn't care. It was our game, our little breath of freedom.

Pepi burst into laughter, gasping for air between her giggles.

"*Como tu sombra iré*... right?" she guessed between bursts of laughter.

"Yes! But that's not the title," I exclaimed, crumbs flying everywhere.

We wiped our hands on our dresses, trying to clean up the mess, when we heard Abuela Lupe's voice shouting from the front of the store, "Another mouse in the storage room!"

Pepi and I scrambled out of there faster than actual mice, still giggling like we were getting away with the greatest crime in Huejosquite.

We ran around the corner and almost bumped into Segundo and his friend Paco. They were hunched over dominoes, completely engrossed.

Pepi had been in love with Segundo since she could spell *amor*.

"I'm going to marry him one day, you know?" Pepi declared as soon as we were out of earshot, her voice dreamy and far away as she watched Segundo teaching Paco how to properly shuffle the tiles.

I'd laughed so hard my sides hurt. "You? Marry Segundo? You'd argue with him every day!"

"Not every day. Just when he's wrong," she had shot back, hands on her hips, her face serious. Then, with a softer tone, she added, "He's so patient, though. He's not like the other boys."

Just the day before, while we had been braiding each other's hair on my front porch, she had sighed deeply and whispered, "Aurora, do you think Segundo notices me? I mean, really notices me?"

"Of course he does! You live right across the street and make it a point to be outside when he is," I teased. "How could he not?"

"That's not what I mean," she muttered, flicking an invisible speck off her skirt. "Do you think he sees me like ... you know ... someone he could maybe like?"

Now, standing there, watching Pepi bite her lip and tuck a strand of hair behind her ear as her eyes darted toward Segundo, I couldn't help but smile.

I had big plans for Pepi to marry him someday. That way, we'd be family.

After all, we already thought of each other as sisters.

But me?

I hadn't realized until that summer—the summer I turned thirteen and got my first period—that I might just have a tiny crush on Paco.

He had grown into his gleeful brown eyes and shiny black hair. I didn't know what it was, but every time he looked at me, I felt my cheeks turn hot.

I tried to ignore it, but Pepi wasn't having any of it.

She elbowed me, a sly grin spreading across her face.

"You need a drool catcher, or are you fine?" she whispered, her voice full of mischief.

"*Estás loca.* I don't know what you're talking about," I tried to say, looking as serious as I could, but I was the worst liar in Huejosquite—probably the only bad liar in town.

That was one of the last times we played in that storeroom, laughing so hard our stomachs ached and our hearts felt light, like *papel picado* dancing in the wind.

Back then, I couldn't imagine things ever changing.

I was too young to know it, but dreams could sometimes cost more than we could afford.

My mother tried her best to carry us, her face a mask of quiet determination. But even then, I could see her cracks, the places where she'd folded herself to keep us whole.

One Step Forward, Two Steps Back

Una de cal, por dos de arena

PILAR

I often wondered what my mother's face looked like when she left us. Did it crack like mine when I tried to smile through her absence? Or did she wear the same mask my father forced me into? One of acceptance and silence.

"Do you ever think about Mom?" I asked Meño as I idly flipped tortillas over in the *comal* to prepare for dinner.

I knew Meño would say the same thing he always did—something practical. Something to close the conversation. But the question never went away. Even though I couldn't remember her, there was something about her absence that weighed heavier than any memory ever could.

It's funny how, after all those years, the question still felt like something that could get you in trouble.

But there it was, slipping out of me as naturally as the steam from the hot tortillas.

I hadn't really thought about Mom in weeks, months, maybe. But lately, all the talk at school had been about quinceañeras.

Of course, I hadn't brought it up with my friends yet. My two best friends, Julia and Ofelia, both came from those picture-perfect homes where mothers were a permanent fixture—laughing over breakfast, nagging about their outfits, hugging them for no reason at all.

So, you know, it wasn't like I wanted to play the eternal victim by casually bringing up that *oh hey, I don't even remember what my mom looks like.*

But there was this tugging feeling in me, like a little voice asking, *What would a quinceañera be like for me?*

And every time that thought crept in, I was sure my friends' moms would go all out.

Mine?

She was just a dead hope. I'd been too young when she left to even call her a faded memory.

Meño, who was, as usual, in the kitchen with me—mostly for moral support and chitchat rather than actual help—didn't miss a beat when I asked him.

"What is there to think about?" He pulled at the sleeves of his shirt like he was trying to escape some invisible trap. "She abandoned us. End of story. I wouldn't even do that to Solovino, would you?"

I shot a glance over at Solovino, our scruffy dog, who'd earned his name by showing up uninvited to our home and was now sitting at the edge of the kitchen, staring at us like he was waiting for a snack— maybe something a little more exciting than the scraps we gave him.

"Of course not. And that dog would find his way back from the furthest corner of the planet, anyway." I turned off the comal and leaned against the counter. "But do you ever wonder why? I mean, why didn't she come back? Why did she leave in the first place?"

Meño sighed, rubbing his face like he was trying to scrub away a headache that was older than me. "'Why' doesn't matter. We're here, she's not . . . And like Dad says, family sticks together no matter what. But you know I don't like to talk about it."

Family sticks together no matter what.

My father's favorite phrase. The one he repeated every time things got tense.

As if he deserved to be off the hook, no questions asked.

Like that was some magic trick that could fix everything.

But it didn't.

And I didn't even know if I wanted it to.

"You always say it doesn't matter." I shot back, lowering my voice as I stacked tortillas inside a cloth to keep them warm. "But it matters. It matters to me."

Meño rested his body against the doorframe. "What do you get out of thinking about it so often, Pilar? Mom left us. End of story."

"No. Not end of story," I insisted, turning to face him.

"You always say that we need to keep on, but tell me, how am I supposed to move forward when I don't even know how I got to this point?"

Meño crossed his arms, but I saw something in his expression that he rarely showed—weariness.

"I ask myself the same thing every single day," he admitted in a barely audible voice,

"and I always land at the same answer: because it is what it is. Because we weren't important enough to her."

I was stunned silent, digesting his words like moldy crumbs. Finally, I mumbled, "Maybe it's not that we didn't matter to her. Maybe she just couldn't figure out how to stay."

"What are you two talking about?" Dad's voice cut through the air unexpectedly, making me jump. He had appeared out of nowhere, like he always did, and made his way to the table, sitting down in his usual spot—the one facing the wall with that crooked picture of *The Last Supper* hanging behind him.

That picture had been there since I was a kid, and it was always off-center, but no one ever bothered to fix it.

Maybe because it reminded us of something we couldn't have—something perfect.

"Nothing," I mumbled, glancing down at the *tortillero* in my hands like it was suddenly the most interesting thing in the room.

"You're not bringing up stupid topics, right?" Dad asked, narrowing his eyes at me, his tone like a warning bell. "If you knew how to keep your mouth shut like a lady, maybe dinner would be ready by the time I sit down."

I could already hear the grumbling in his voice—the kind that stated: I've been working all day, I'm tired, don't make me angry.

"We were talking about someone from school, Papá," Meño quickly chimed in, covering for me like he always did.

I shot him a grateful look.

"Someone from school, huh?" Dad muttered, gesturing to the food with a jerk of his head.

"Well, don't let it get cold like last time. I want no more *incidents*."

I quickly slid the plate of *picadillo* and the *tortillero* in front of him, trying to look as innocently busy as possible.

Dad glared at the tortillas, then slammed one down on the floor with an angry huff. "All I ask is to come home to a nice warm meal, but you can't even do that, can you? No wonder . . ." His voice trailed off, but the weight of what he didn't say hung thick in the air.

My eyes burned with tears that threatened to spill out, but I'd learned long ago that in these situations, tears only made things worse.

So I kept them in check.

"I'm sorry, I'll warm another one up right now." My voice was quiet, like I was speaking to a stranger instead of my father.

"Leave it," he snapped, his voice suddenly softening into something that felt like it was meant to be kind, though it didn't quite make it.

It was, however, enough for Solovino to brave going for the tortilla on the floor and devour it in a single bite.

"Sit down. We're having dinner as a family."

We all sat down.

Dad. Me. Solovino sprawled at my feet. Meño.

And that picture of The Last Supper glaring at us from behind my father.

There we were—two kids and a father, trying to pretend like we were something that resembled normal.

"Women," Dad muttered, shoveling food into his mouth, his eyes not quite on us but on something beyond us, probably lost in thoughts that weren't ours to share. "Always making a fuss out of everything."

He shook his head, then smirked as he picked up another tortilla— one that, I swear, had been as perfectly warm as the one he'd thrown on the floor just a few seconds earlier.

After dinner, I went to bed, overcome with that strange, aching emptiness I always felt when Mom's memory crept up on me. The kind that had been my constant companion, though I'd tried to ignore it for years.

I lay there, staring at the ceiling, my thoughts swirling like a dust storm.

What would I have called her if she were here? Mamá? Mami?

I whispered the words in the dark, trying them out on my tongue, tasting them for the first time. They felt wrong, like clothes that didn't quite fit. My heart ached a little more with each silent "Mami" I mouthed.

Was it the name that felt off? Or was it the fact that there was no one to call anymore?

I felt the familiar sting behind my eyes, but I refused to let the tears fall. That's something I'd learned to do since I was small:

Don't cry. Tears fix nothing.

❀✧❀✧❀

The next morning, I woke up from a dream where I was standing near the Zócalo, window-shopping with Mom.She was holding my hand, and the sun was bright.

In dreams, she always looked perfect—smiling at me with those eyes that never seemed tired or angry or distant, like I was the most important thing in her world.

But then, just like that, she turned the corner and started walking away from me.

I wanted to scream, but my voice wouldn't come.

I reached out to her, but my feet wouldn't move.

I was stuck, sinking into the pavement, as if the city was swallowing me whole.

I woke up with my heart in my throat and my face soaked in cold sweat. On mornings like that one, the hole in my chest felt deeper than ever.

I forced myself out of bed, slid my cold feet into my light blue slippers, and tiptoed to the kitchen, hoping to have breakfast ready before Dad woke up. With his mood lately, it was better not to be caught off guard.

I knew I had to keep quiet about the other things, the ones that made my stomach twist.

Talking about Mom was like poking a sleeping dog—sooner or later, you'd get bit.

I set off to warm up the tortillas I'd precooked the previous night. The sound of the comal, in some strange way, provided comfort. As if the warmth flowing out of the food could somehow soothe the coldness I felt inside.

While the coffee dripped, I thought back to what my life without her had been like. Everything that had been lacking in my life, and everything that, without me realizing it, I'd also missed out on by not being able to ask her. It wasn't only the absence of her body, but the absence of her words. Her guidance.

All that time I'd been missing it, even if I hadn't been able to recognize it.

As the aroma of coffee spread throughout the kitchen, I felt a tightness in my throat that didn't allow me to breathe, but I suppressed it.

I couldn't let the tears overtake me. What good would it do me? No one would be there to notice if I let them fall.

No one was going to make me feel better.

With the cup of coffee in my hands, I made my way to the dining room, not wanting to think much about anything other than just keeping on, one step at a time. By then, I'd lost hope of anything changing for the better, but I forced myself to keep going. Not for me, but for those around me.

The only thing I could do was keep standing.

❀✧❀✧❀

When I heard Dad's footsteps in the hallway, I jumped. He was already awake.

"I'm going into work early today," he mentioned as he entered the kitchen. "I'll be home late. Got some meetings. Important stuff."

Important stuff.

Like the bar meetings that meant he'd come home drunk and mean, leaving Meño and me to pretend we didn't hear him stumble into the house.

But whatever. I could survive another night of that.

He placed a few pesos on the table. "Here. Go get some ice cream with Meño later."

The pesos meant something, even if I couldn't quite figure out what.

I paused for a second, then asked, "Dad, I've been meaning to ask . . . I'm turning fifteen in a few months, and I've been thinking, you know, since my friends are all planning parties . . . Could I maybe have one too?"

My voice trailed off, a careful whisper of hope, barely holding onto the last word.

He didn't look up at first, focusing on the coffee he was pouring, as if my question hadn't even registered. Then, he stopped, cup in hand, and gave me a long, sideways glance, like he was sizing me up.

"And who, exactly, do you think is going to do all the planning, Pilar?" he asked, setting his cup down with a loud clink. His eyes narrowed, filling with a familiar edge that always told me I should've stopped while I was ahead. "You think I have time to waste on that? That's a woman's job," he scoffed, shaking his head. "I'm not your mother, and I'm sure as hell not wasting my time on frilly dresses and

15

dancing."

I felt my face flush with embarrassment, but I forced myself to nod, to agree.

"You're right," I replied quickly, trying to sound grateful. "Thank you for offering to pay for the dress so I can be part of Julia's and Ofelia's court of honor. I know that's a lot."

"Exactly. It's more than enough," he muttered, his gaze fixed on some invisible point on the kitchen floor.

I could almost hear his thoughts spiraling into that place where he always got lost when he was in a mood like this.

"Das la mano y te agarran la pata," he muttered, not caring if I heard.

Then he was gone, his heavy footsteps echoing down the hallway, leaving me standing there with my breath caught in my throat.

I went back to the living room, blinking hard against the stinging in my eyes.

I *should* have known better than to ask.

I *should've* known that a simple question could flip the entire room upside down, could turn my hope into something that felt more like shame.

It was always like this with him. A few good days scattered between the tough ones. And then, like clockwork, he'd remind us of all he'd done for us.

"You should be grateful," he'd say, as if he'd ever let us forget. "A roof over your heads, food on the table, and a father who, let's face it, could've been worse."

He'd lean in, that same old look in his eyes, and add, "I never laid a hand on you, like some fathers would. Maybe that's been my mistake, why you've grown to be so ungrateful."

He'd say it like it was a badge of honor, like his restraint was something to be proud of.

"There are plenty of kids who don't have half of what you have," he'd tell us, fixing us with a stare that dared us to disagree.

I tried to remind myself of those good days, the ones where we'd laugh over dinner, or he'd let Meño and me stay up to watch a movie.

Those days felt almost like a dream now, something soft and distant.

Maybe it should've been enough—all the things he reminded us he did for us. I should've felt lucky to be at an excellent school, to have friends, to live in a pleasant neighborhood.

But every time I told myself this, it felt a little more like a lie.

Family sticks together, no matter what.

I could hear his voice in my head, the phrase he'd used so many times it was almost like a command. And yet, a quiet voice somewhere deep inside me whispered that something wasn't right. That this life—where I had to tiptoe around, watch my words, and swallow my dreams—wasn't what family was supposed to be.

How could family stick together unconditionally when guilt and obligation were the fragile glue holding us together?

He Who Walks with Wolves, Learns to Howl

El que con lobos anda, a aullar se enseña

FER

Family sticks together. That's what they say, right?

But no one tells you how to stick together when all you want is to peel yourself away like a Band-Aid that's done covering up wounds. When the people you love and look up to the most betray your family in ways that make you feel like your only option is to do so.

The line shuffles forward, sneakers squeaking against the linoleum floor, and I adjust the strap of my backpack on my shoulder. My stomach tightens as I glance at the long row of fluorescent lights on the ceiling. I don't know if it's my nerves or the artificial glow buzzing faintly above me that's making the room feel colder than it should.

As I stand here, a freshman in queue for my college ID—a physical symbol of an achievement my parents and I dreamed of together. This was supposed to be a fresh start. Now it's just a reminder of everything I don't want to become.

I glance at the other students in line, most of them chatting with their parents, friends, or siblings—people who came to share this moment with them.

The couple in front of me clutches each other like they're on the cover of a college brochure. I want to be happy for them. I really do. But mostly, I want to scream.

A girl a few places ahead is wearing a red shirt that reads *Future Legacy,* while the woman next to her is wearing a matching one that reads *Alumni Pride.*

The sight makes my chest ache. Just a few weeks ago, I imagined my mother standing next to me, maybe taking embarrassing pictures, fussing over my hair, or telling me to stand up straight for the ID photo.

But now, here I am, alone and angry, thinking about everything that's happened in the past few weeks.

❁✧❁✧❁

Up until a couple of months ago, during my senior year of high school, if I had to describe myself in one word, it would have been average. I mean, we're talking an utterly unremarkable, wouldn't-stand-out-in-a-crowd level of average. The kind where you could slip into a classroom and no one would notice you, but you're not invisible, either.

My high school was mostly Mexican-American kids, like me. We had the same accents when speaking English—the kind that slips in from speaking Spanish as a first language, the one that gives away that English came second.

I wasn't popular, but you wouldn't find me eating lunch alone in a bathroom stall, either. I had a decent circle of friends, and okay, maybe even a few brief, mostly PG-13, romances from sophomore to senior year.

None of the three lasted, but hey, I have standards.

College was always the goal. First in my family to go and all that, so it wasn't like my secret boyfriends being banned from even glancing at my house was a problem. I wasn't about to let a boy derail my plans.

And as my dad made clear with his usual stern look, "Once you move out, you can do whatever you want, but while you're under my roof, your focus is school."

Oh, sure, Dad. No problem.

And for the most part, I actually stuck to the books. Rebellion just wasn't my thing, and my mom always had my back if I needed to sneak in a little extra fun here and there—a true *alcahueta* as they say, as long as my priorities stayed straight.

Things took a turn, though, when I got to secret boyfriend number three (or *Three,* as he's now affectionately dubbed).

One morning, we planned to ride the school bus together, so I waited at my usual stop, anxiously picking at my freshly painted nails while I checked the time.

The bus driver, who I'd begged for just two more minutes, telling him that Three was on his way, peeked his head outside the door and gave me a look before saying, "I'm leaving now, with or without you."

I glanced at the clock. My dad wouldn't leave for work for another hour, and he'd seen me leave for school, so on a wild impulse, I ditched the bus and waited for Three, hoping he'd show up soon.

When he finally did—fifteen minutes late with zero apology—we walked to a nearby diner to kill time until I could go home, intercept the truancy call, and avoid a parental meltdown.

You know, typical teenage logic at work.

We were holding hands like we had all the time in the world. Stupid. Like the universe wasn't five seconds from kicking me in the teeth. The diner was packed—apparently, cheating dads and bad decisions get the early bird special.

In my peripheral vision, I saw a couple kissing. Now, I didn't know the woman at all, but the man? Oh, I recognized him alright. That thinning hair, slicked back and greasy, and, of all things, the little earring he'd recently added, which my mom and I had dubbed his *midlife crisis earring*.

There he was—my dad—with his hand resting way too high on her thigh for anyone's comfort.

And what did I do?

In fight-or-flight mode, I am, regrettably, a solid *flight*. Without thinking, I dragged Three out of the diner, tears already blurring my vision.

As if being a flighter wasn't bad enough, I'm also cursed with the tendency to cry when I least want to. It's beyond humiliating.

Between gasps of pure shock and mortification, I managed to explain to Three what I'd just seen.

"Do you want to go back and confront him Fer?" he asked, though his expression begged, *please don't*.

"No, we're already closer to my house than the diner, and honestly, I wouldn't even know what to say."

Confront my dad in the middle of a diner? Yeah, right.

I normally wouldn't have let Three into my house, but that day, I did. And sure enough, waiting on the answering machine was a message about my absence for the first period. I briefly considered deleting it but left it.

Go ahead, ask me where I was, I thought bitterly.

Three stayed with me for about an hour until, eventually, I asked him to leave. I really needed time to process alone. I spent the rest of the day in my room, not coming out when I heard my mom get home, and definitely not coming out later when I heard my dad get home.

When my mom knocked on my door telling me dinner was ready, I still didn't have a plan for what I was going to say or do, but I still made my way over to the dinner table.

"So, there was a message on the answer machine about you missing school today. Care to explain?" Mom asked, her voice carefully measured.

Dad raised his eyebrow at me but didn't seem surprised. He probably already knew.

This was an ambush.

"I was waiting for a friend and accidentally missed the bus."

"And then? You decided you could just skip?" Mom pressed.

She didn't sound angry—just disappointed. And that was worse. I'd always been an outstanding student, after all. Skipping school wasn't like me.

"Who was this friend?" Dad cut in. "We trust you to be smarter, Fer. If your friend is okay with being late, they're probably not the best influence."

"Wow. Big assumption, Dad," I scoffed. "You don't even know who he is, and you're already judging."

Dad's eyes sharpened at "he". Shit. I hadn't meant to let that slip.

"I know my own daughter. I don't need to know who your 'friend' is"—he made air quotes with his fingers as if a boy and a girl couldn't just be friends, never mind that he was right this one time—"to know that he was the reason you skipped school today! I've warned you that boys only have one thing in mind. They are bad influences."

"Well, maybe you don't know me as well as you think you do, Dad. After all, I thought I knew you too. Turns out I don't." *How far could his hypocrisy go?* My anger was growing exponentially by the second.

Mom, who had been silent until now, finally spoke up. "You got caught skipping school, Fer. This would be a perfect time to apologize, not to speak like that to your father."

"Fine, I'm sorry I missed the bus. And I'm really sorry that instead of calling one of you to give me a ride, I went to have breakfast at the diner near my stop instead."

I looked Dad in the eye.

He didn't flinch, but something in his posture stiffened.

"The diner?" Dad asked, not missing a beat. By his tone—too even, too controlled—I could tell he was panicking.

"You know what's funny?" I tilted my head. "That diner sure is more popular than I expected on a weekday morning. Wanna guess who I saw there, Mom?"

Mom frowned. "Who?"

Dad shifted in his seat. "We're talking about you missing school, Fer." His voice was firm, but I saw it—his face was red, and there was that protruding vein along his forehead, the usual telltale sign that he was furious.

I turned back to Mom. "I saw Dad." My voice wavered, but I forced the words out. "And he wasn't alone."

"That's not true," Dad said, too fast, too forcefully. "You don't know what you're saying."

My chest tightened. *How could he?*

I had no expectations of what the confrontation would be like, heck, I wasn't even sure if I was going to bring it up if they didn't confront me about my absence, but his accusation stung more than I could've expected.

How could he accuse me of lying, as if I were the one tearing our family apart?

My fingernails dug into my palms. "Are you seriously going to sit there and call me a liar?"

"He's not calling you a liar, Fer," Mom interrupted, her voice desperate. "But is it possible you made a mistake?"

Dad opened his mouth, then closed it again. Something flickered in his eyes—shame? Regret? He turned away, inhaling deeply before his shoulders slumped. "I—" His voice was softer now, almost broken.

That's when Mom's composure cracked. Silent tears flowed down her cheeks. She didn't look angry the way I was. She just looked . . . shattered.

"You promised me this wouldn't happen again." Her voice was so soft it was barely audible.

Again? So that wasn't the first time?

"I'm not a perfect man." Dad's voice trembled. "I made a mistake, but I love you. You have to believe me."

I laughed, but there was no humor in it. "A mistake?" I yelled. "You don't 'accidentally' hike your hand up someone's skirt in public! Your tongue doesn't 'slip' into some bitch's mouth by mistake!"

I didn't know whether the woman from the diner knew he was married or not. Maybe it wasn't her fault, maybe she didn't deserve my insult, but I was furious.

Mom wiped at her tears. "Fer, this is something your father and I should discuss privately." Her voice was so heartbreakingly calm; I knew right then and there, she was going to forgive him.

I got up and stormed off to my room.

❊❖❊❖❊

Saturday mornings usually meant all three of us were home. But when the need to use the bathroom forced me out of my room, I noticed Dad wasn't there.

Mom was sitting alone at the dining table, and by the way she looked up at me, I guessed she'd been waiting to talk to me.

When I finished in the bathroom, I tried to walk past her quickly and get back to my room, but she called out to me.

"Fer . . ."

I exhaled sharply. "Did you kick him out?"

She motioned to the chair across from her. "Come sit down, please. We need to talk."

I didn't move.

"Did you kick him out?" I asked again.

Mom sighed. "Fer, this might be hard for you to understand, but no. We talked all night. I don't think of a family as something you give up on just like that. I'm giving him a chance."

A piercing cold shot through me.

"It's not 'just like that'! I told you what I saw! Is this what you're teaching me? That this is okay? That I should just let people walk all over me?"

"It's not that simple, Fer."

I clenched my jaw. "Seems pretty simple to me. Please explain to me how it's not."

My mom opened her mouth to speak, but I cut her off.

"Forget it," I snapped. "You do what you want. Just don't expect me to sit at the same table with him and pretend I didn't see what I saw."

I turned on my heel and walked away, slamming my bedroom door behind me.

Since that day, I've replayed the scene over and over in my mind, imagining all the dramatic things I could've done at the diner.

Sometimes I dump a cup of water on their heads.

Other times I sit at the table next to them and stare until he notices me.

Honestly, there's probably no *right* way to handle catching your dad having a midlife crisis in the worst way, but I wish I could be a fighter, not the crying flighter.

What was one of the worst experiences of my life ended up being the start of the best days and even better nights for Three, who got to sneak into my room almost every night until graduation. If my dad could get away with sneaking around, well, then so could I.

A tap on my shoulder jolts me.

"Next!"

I rub the spot on the palm of my hand where I've left a mark from nervously digging my thumbnail in as I step up to the blue X marked with painter's tape in front of the camera.

I shift on my feet, trying to arrange my face into something that resembles a smile.

My lips twitch, but I know it's probably more a grimace than anything.

The girl behind the camera, Jenny—I gather from her name tag—instructs me to relax my shoulders.

She has a friendly but efficient tone that suggests she's been snapping photos all morning but somehow still cares enough to be nice. Her slim, sun-kissed look is straight out of a summer beach movie—not like the deep brown tone my family and friends have naturally.

"There you go," she says. "Alright, three, two—"

The shutter clicks before she finishes the countdown.

"Your ID is more than just a student number," she explains, handing over my shiny new card. "You'll also use it for printing at the library, and you can load funds onto it to use at campus stores."

"Cool, thanks!" I reply, taking the card from her.

"No problem! I wish someone had told me all this my first day," she adds, smiling again.

I return her smile and walk out.

On my ID, a fair-skinned face with brown eyes and a determined expression stares back at me. My wavy, light-brown hair falls across my forehead, my bangs doing whatever they please, as usual.

2008-2009 is printed right beneath my picture.

I take in the crowd around me one last time. A surprising number of white faces and blond heads—far more than I'm used to seeing.

This is definitely not my high school. This campus feels like a whole other world.

My stomach twists, half with nerves and half with excitement. For the zillionth time, I pull out the printed copy of my schedule and scan it as I head to the library, ready to take on my freshman year and leave my high school drama behind.

The shadow of my father's betrayal stretches over me, whispering that I'm destined to live in quiet acceptance just like my mother, but I'm ready to grab this opportunity by the horns.

I'll make college my fresh start.

If Life Gives You Lemons

Si la vida te da limones

AURORA

The chair is stiff.

Not uncomfortable exactly, but not the place I'd choose to sit for hours at a time. Still, I settle into it, adjusting the thin hospital blanket draped over my lap. The IV line is already in, a steady drip marking the beginning of my first round of chemo.

I haven't told my children yet.

Not because I'm hiding—not really. But because I want to see how I handle this first. I need to know what to expect before I find the right words to explain to them what our near future might hold for us. All I've ever wanted is to give them the happiest life possible. To shield them from any worry or struggle, and this . . . this is something I'm not sure how to soften for them.

I glance around the room, recognizing more than a few faces. A young nurse passes by, giving me a soft smile. I haven't seen her before; she must be new.

This is just another step, I tell myself. Another shift in the ever-changing course of life. After all, life is nothing if not unpredictable.

The proof of that is in the very building I'm sitting in now. I smile at the memory of the first time I was here for something that mattered: the day I gave birth to my youngest. How different it had all felt then —joyful, terrifying, overwhelming in a completely different way.

How quickly things change.

Now, as I wait, I may as well write a bit, put some of my thoughts down. If I'm going to tell this story—the one that led me here—I might as well use this time to do so.

❀✧❀✧❀

Summers in Huejosquite were always hot and dry, but the summer Segundo and Pepi finally started dating, it seemed to burn with a vengeance, as if the sun had decided to nest right over our town for good.

Every day seemed to drag on forever, with the endless chores at my grandparents' little store waiting for me like a stubborn stain on an old shirt. After I'd been forced to leave school to help more around the house and store, days had stretched unbearably long, each one slipping into the next, with only my afternoons with my friends and brother to break up the monotony. In the late afternoon, when the sun finally began to dip and the unbearable heat turned to something softer, Pepi, Paco, Segundo, and I would sit on the sidewalk, chatting away the hours.

One particular afternoon, Segundo and I had just finished stacking dusty cans and sorting sacks of flour at my abuelos' store when Pepi and Paco wandered in. Pepi arrived with her usual dramatic flair, rolling her eyes.

"The bakery was hotter than the devil's tail." She pulled at her collar, mopping her forehead with a mix of frustration and humor.

"I don't remember the last few summers being this hot," I muttered, blowing out a sigh. "And it seems like it only gets worse."

"That's because last summer you were just an *escuincla*, a runt, playing silly games and learning to blow your nose," Segundo teased, casting me a smirk that made me roll my eyes right back at him.

It was true, I thought. Things had changed since those days Pepi and I had sneaked into the storage room to play our own secret games. I had been growing up and, along with it, a certain affection for Paco had grown too, no longer a silly crush but something more serious, though I was barely sure what to call it myself. I wished Paco would realize I wasn't just Segundo's little sister or the *escuincla* he'd known for years. But if he noticed, he didn't let on; he just flashed that quick, familiar smile and suggested we go cool off by the river since the air promised a mild evening.

When we reached the river, Pepi and Segundo slipped off to sit beneath a tree, huddling together with a familiarity I envied. Paco and I stayed near the water, flicking stones into the river. He had always been the boy whose laughter carried through the air, warm and steady like the sun, but that day, something seemed to weigh on him.

"What's on your mind?" I asked as I flicked a small round stone into the river.

For a beat, he didn't answer. Then he sighed, his gaze fixed on the fading sunlight. "My parents."

I didn't understand at first. "They're alright, aren't they? Your mamá seems strong for her age, and she still makes the best tamales in town," I noted, trying to lighten the mood.

He smiled faintly. "She does, but they're slowing down. Papá too. They've worked so hard their whole lives, and now I see it catching up to them. They don't move like they used to."

I stayed quiet, sensing there was more he wanted to say. A breeze stirred the surface of the water, and I shifted my eyes back to the river, allowing him time to pull his thoughts together.

"My brothers and sisters . . . they've all left," he continued after a brief pause. "They've got their own families now, their own problems. They send what they can, at least some of them, but it's not enough. It's just me now."

I didn't know what to say. Paco was the youngest of seven siblings, by quite a few years too. He had been the *oopsie*, the *pilón* as his parents teasingly called him, and to be frank, they seemed a bit too old to still have a son Paco's age at home. Paco glanced at me, and for the first time, I saw the weight he carried behind his serene smile.

"I've been thinking about leaving too," he finally let out. "Going up north to work. It's starting to seem like the only way to help them."

His words left a strange ache in my chest. I wanted to tell him to stay, but I couldn't. Paco wasn't the kind of person who ignored his responsibilities.

"Anyway, it's just a vague thought for now," he added, alleviating the ache.

We continued to talk about this and that until eventually, Elena came up—Paco's cousin who'd been taken by a man on his way to the city. It was, sadly, not unusual for girls in our town to find themselves married off to traveling men passing through. Half the women in Huejosquite seemed to have left this way.

"Do you think she'll come back?" I asked, watching the water ripple as I skipped another stone.

"If by 'back' you mean to my uncle's house, I doubt it. She knows better than that." Paco's voice took on a rare seriousness. "If she tries, he'll likely send her right back to that man. Probably slam the door in her face and say she's not a señorita anymore."

"That's a hard way of looking at it," I replied. "Though I know my abuelos would throw a celebration if someone whisked me off—but I'm sure Pepi would kill anyone who tried."

I forced a little laugh, trying to lighten the mood, but a cold worry flickered in the back of my mind. I wasn't sure if my abuelos would welcome me back if I ever left. I knew they'd be overjoyed to have one less mouth to feed, and the thought gnawed at me.

On the way back, we walked Paco home first since it was the farthest. Pepi and Segundo lagged behind, their voices drifting toward us in the warm evening air. Then, as if the thought had been there the whole walk, Paco turned to me. "What do you think about your brother and Pepi? As a couple, I mean."

"Oh, I couldn't be happier." I didn't miss a beat. "Only thing is, let's hope my grandparents don't find out. They want Segundo to go work in the city, send back money, not get anchored here with a girl. But can I tell you a secret? Pepi and I have had their wedding planned for years."

I laughed, casting a quick, shy glance down at my shoes, wondering if I was giving away too much.

"Can I tell you a secret too?" he asked after a pause, the moonlight catching a bit of mischief in his eyes.

"What? Have you and my brother planned a wedding too?" I teased, trying to sound casual despite the way my heart hammered in my chest.

"No, but I have also liked someone . . . for a long time," he replied, his voice softening in a way that made my heart dip into my stomach.

The moment seemed to stretch out, and memories of María and Carmen, two of the prettiest girls in town, flooded my mind. My grandmother always talked about my fair skin and green eyes, as if those traits were her greatest achievement.

"You got that skin from my side," she would say, lifting her chin with an air of triumph as she ran her fingers across my cheek. "Your eyes too. Green, just like mine. You're so lucky. Maybe that way, you'll find a good match, someone who knows how to appreciate a beauty like ours."

I would always stay silent, trying to ignore how her words made me feel. Her pride didn't fill me; it weighed on me, as if my appearance was the only thing she valued in me. Though I never told her, I would have given anything to have Carmen's golden skin or María's big, warm eyes, which always seemed so full of life and kindness.

I looked away, afraid to meet his gaze and reveal my disappointment, painfully waiting for him to mention one of their names. The memory of my grandmother's words lingered, making me feel small when I already felt like I wasn't enough.

"Aren't you going to ask me who?" he prodded, his voice pulling me back to the present. I forced myself to look up, barely meeting his eyes.

"Who?" I managed to ask, hoping my voice didn't betray me.

"You," he said, just as we reached his house.

Before I could even respond, Segundo and Pepi caught up with us, and we all exchanged goodnights.

Walking home, my heart was a mix of elation and disbelief. His words played on repeat in my mind, each syllable warming me through and through, like the memory of sunlight on the coldest days. Not even Abuela Lupe's scolding for being late to dinner could pull me out of the warmth that night.

As I lay in bed, tossing and turning with Paco's words echoing in my head, sleep was nowhere in sight. I gave up, quietly tiptoeing to our old encyclopedia set in the corner of the living room and reaching for one of the volumes. I scurried back to my room, where I sat at the edge of my bed, flipping through its pages to quiet my mind. Most homes in Huejosquite didn't have any books beyond a Bible, but my abuelos kept these, I suppose, more for show than anything. By then, I'd already read them cover to cover a few times, though what I loved most were the pages on nursing.

Helping at my abuelos' store was hardly a glamorous job: dusting cans, arranging and rearranging boxes of merchandise. Those were mindless tasks better done in sneakers and casual clothing. How I'd always admired the clickety-clack of the shiny heels nurses wore, small but still managing to sound so important—*I'm a career woman, hear me come!* And their pristine white skirts paired with stockings. I couldn't imagine a job I'd love more than one in which I could help others while being so fashionably dressed.

The night my abuelos had announced school was over for me was one I'd never forget.

"She knows how to read and write. No point in wasting time when she could help out more at the store," my grandfather had declared, and Abuela Lupe nodded her approval beside him.

"Please, let her finish elementary school," my mother had pleaded, her voice quiet but steady.

"We're doing enough by having taken you in. Three mouths to feed is no small feat. It's time she does her share," Abuela Lupe replied sharply.

Abuelo joined in. "A girl her age has no place in school when her future lies in a husband and a home. A proper woman knows her responsibilities and values, not her books."

The sting of their words lingered even then, and it suddenly dawned on me, reading those same pages on nursing I'd read countless times before, that my dreams might be forever out of reach.

A soft creak broke the silence of the room and the loudness of my thoughts. I stiffened, the encyclopedia still open on my lap.

"I thought I heard footsteps. What are you doing up?" Mamá's voice was gentle, barely more than a whisper as she stepped into the dim glow of the oil lamp. She was in her nightgown, hair loose over one shoulder.

I hesitated before answering. "I couldn't sleep."

She glanced at the open book and sighed, sinking onto the edge of the bed beside me. "Again with the nursing pages?" Her fingers ghosted over the worn edges.

I nodded. "I can't help it."

Mamá traced a careful line along the spine of the book, lost in thought. "You've always been like this. Even when you were little, always a dreamer, reaching for something just beyond what the world handed you."

I swallowed. "Did you ever dream of something like that? Something just for you?"

She turned away slightly, as if considering whether to answer. "Before Papá?"

I nodded.

A small smile touched her lips, one that didn't quite reach her eyes. "Maybe one day, when you're older, we can revisit that conversation. But for now, my dreams don't matter, *mija*. My only goal is to make sure you accomplish yours."

I frowned. "But they do matter, Mamá. You should—"

She reached out, tucking a stray lock of hair behind my ear the way she always did when she wanted to soothe me. "Your father believed we could do anything, Aurora. Unlike most men in this town, he never doubted me, never doubted you. He saw a future where we didn't have to ask for permission to dream. That's why my purpose now is to make sure you get the chance to chase yours."

A lump formed in my throat. "I want to be a nurse," I whispered, afraid that saying it too loud might make it vanish.

Mamá smiled, squeezing my hand. "I know."

"And I want a love like yours and Papá's," I admitted. "Something real. Not just because it's expected of me."

Her gaze softened. "I think you already have someone in mind."

I felt my cheeks grow warm. Mamá always knew more than she let on.

"Do you think you'll ever remarry, Mamá?"

She exhaled, looking down at the book still open in my lap. "I don't think so, mija. This town sees me as a woman who should have given up by now. They think being a widow should mean my life is over, that I should shrink into the shadows and never rebuild. But I don't regret anything, Aurora. Not defying my parents, not marrying your father, not the sacrifices I've made. Because they gave me the two people I love most in the world—you and your brother."

I bit my lip, wanting to say something else, anything to make it easier, to erase the weight I knew she carried alone. Instead, I simply squeezed her hand back.

"Get some sleep," she murmured, standing. "Dream as big as you want, mija. No one can take that away from you."

With those words, she gently took the encyclopedia from me, then stood up and started towards the door.

"You're the person I love most in the world," I said softly.

The pages, as usual, had left me with visions of white uniforms and polished heels. I could see myself as a nurse, busy with patients, married to a man I loved, not bound to some stranger with money that would mean little to me.

Abuela Lupe always said that a girl's duty was to marry well and keep her family intact. But I wondered, what if the family was already broken? Was I meant to marry the pieces together or let them fall apart? I didn't know the answer, but I was starting to wonder if it was even my duty to try.

As I lay back down, staring at the ceiling, I held on to my mother's words. I might have been a girl in a town that expected little from me, but I wasn't ready to let my dreams slip away just yet.

Birds of a Feather Flock Together

Dios los cría y ellos se juntan

PILAR

My family had been in pieces for as long as I could remember, so scattered it felt impossible to put back together. But my friends? They were the glue holding me together.

The Saturdays I'd spend with my best friends, Julia and Ofelia, were like a breath of fresh air. We'd gather in one of our bedrooms, lost in a world of glossy magazine pages and oversized dreams. We could sit for hours, imagining ourselves in the latest fashion finds, curating the looks we wished we could own. My father and their parents moved in the same circles, frequenting the same polished social gatherings and enrolling us in the same private school, but it wasn't just circumstance that made us friends. There's this saying: *Dios los cría y ellos se juntan,* meaning that people with similar souls find each other. That's what it was like for the three of us. Drawn together by our similar tastes in music, fashion, and our shared fascination with American culture, we were inseparable, bound by the threads of our dreams.

"Did you see this one?" Ofelia asked, pointing to a vibrant red dress with a pleated skirt and white polka dots.

"Whoa, that one's going in the notebook," Julia replied, holding out the notebook where we glued our favorite clippings like they were sacred texts. Every page brimmed with dreams—high heels, wide skirts, and stylish dresses that we pictured ourselves wearing, strutting down streets we'd only seen in movies.

Ofelia started cutting out the dress, singing along to the scratchy English lyrics of "Twist and Shout." We barely understood a word, but that didn't stop us from shouting along.

"They say all English lyrics are about sex, so we're probably singing about it right now," Julia teased, her eyes gleaming mischievously.

"Who's 'they' and why were you talking to them about sex?" Ofelia shot back with a raised eyebrow, and we burst into laughter. Julia's face turned bright red. Redder, I swear, than the dress we'd just glued onto the page.

"If my great-grandma Lola could hear you," Ofelia declared in her exaggerated, mock-serious voice, "she'd be tossing and turning in her grave! Imagine her—fighting for women's voices, just so we could gossip about sex."

But Ofelia had a point. Her great-grandmother, Doña Lola, had been a fierce woman, a leader in *Las Hijas de Cuauhtémoc*, fighting for women's rights in Mexico. Ofelia was always proud of her, always reminding us of the battles her family had fought. I couldn't blame her —if it weren't for women like Doña Lola, I didn't know when, if ever, we'd have earned the right to vote. I was barely a toddler when women here could finally cast a ballot. It was a little ridiculous; there we were in the sixties, and yet at home, *1910 refused to let go.*

"I bet everything would be better if I'd been born in the US," I said.

Julia and Ofelia exchanged knowing looks.

"At least you'd have been born with the right to vote." It was like Julia had read my mind, or maybe she just knew where my thoughts always ended up. Women in the US had been voting since 1920, decades before us. Here, we'd been the last country in Latin America to make it official. To think that Mexican women didn't get to go to the polls until 1955 always blew my mind.

"And I bet their friends don't bat an eyelash singing about sex," I added with a wink at Julia.

"Oh, Virgin Mary, forgive her!" She laughed, rolling her eyes toward the heavens.

We went back to flipping through the magazines, gluing down every little piece of glamour we could find.

"Hey! We should start a page for quinceañera inspiration," Ofelia suggested excitedly, holding up a page of evening gowns.

For a couple seconds, I let myself drift into the music playing softly on the radio. Elvis crooned, "Are You Lonesome Tonight?" and his voice wrapped around me, filling up the empty places I rarely let anyone see. It was a strange thing, music, how it could make you feel so full, and yet, remind you of all the things you were missing.

Before quinceañeras became the apparent center of our universe, I hadn't thought about my mother in weeks, maybe even months. Growing up, my family had always been just my father, my older brother Meño, and me. There were other relatives, but my father kept us at a distance, saying they were conformists, people without dreams. He took pride in keeping us separate, saying we were going to "move up."

When I was small, I took that literally—I imagined a tall wooden ladder, even taller than the Angel of Independence monument, one that would take us high above the city. Up there, I imagined I would find my mother. I'd see her face for the first time, and she would tell me she'd spent all these years trying to find her way back. We'd hug, and I'd turn to Meño and say, "See? I told you she was looking for us."

But then, as I neared my fifteenth birthday, I knew better. The fantasies had faded, and the real world felt colder, lonelier.

It was Julia and Ofelia who kept me going, who became my family in ways my own couldn't. They stood by me through everything— crushes and heartbreaks, messy first periods and self-doubts. Julia had even defended me in front of our entire class when the stain in my pants had announced to everyone present that I had my first period, dragging down the girl who'd embarrassed me with a loud, cruel shriek of disgust. I'll never forget how she brought that girl down by her ponytail.

"You'd better pray you're bald the next time you so much as think of embarrassing one of my friends," she'd said, looking down at the girl lying at her feet, curled up like she was waiting to be reborn into a better person.

And Ofelia, kind and careful, had quietly presented me with my first bra, then made sure I was taken care of, always slipping me pads and other things she knew I'd need. They were like sisters, filling in the places that felt empty, like the warmth of a mother's love that I missed.

But lately, as quinceañera season approached, that ache inside me felt sharper. Julia and Ofelia would have their mothers carefully planning every detail for their big day. I knew I'd be smiling at their parties, putting on a cheerful face, but the truth was, I felt left behind, like I was watching them step into a world that wasn't mine.

"That's a great idea, Ofelia. Let's do it," I said, forcing a smile and doing my best to sound like the friend they deserved. The kind of friend they'd been for me.

My face hurt from the effort of it, but I held the smile anyway, hoping they wouldn't see through me. They didn't deserve to carry my sadness. I would be happy for them, at least. That's the least they deserved.

I was happy for them, I truly was, but there was a weight in my chest, a longing that pulled me down, that whispered all the things I'd never get to experience.

And in moments like that one, they whispered my deepest fears.

Maybe my mother left because she couldn't carry the weight of all of us. Maybe she didn't know how to stay.

And maybe my friends would one day realize I'd never been someone worth staying for.

The Early Bird Doesn't Always Catch The Worm

No por mucho madrugar...

FER

Staying. That's what my mom does best.

Staying in a marriage where she's not really seen, staying quiet while my dad fills the silence with someone else. Staying. But maybe just staying isn't always enough. I don't want to just stay; I want to move forward.

So, in an attempt to start this new journey off on the right foot, I walked the campus yesterday to make sure I knew exactly where every single classroom was. I carefully plotted my route, checked the building locations, and even mapped out my break time for coffee runs.

But true to form, I still manage to mess things up on the first day. I wander into the wrong class first thing. I sit there for a good ten minutes, feigning intense interest in whatever the professor is rambling on about, something involving "the effects of capital markets on emerging economies" or whatever, which, frankly, should tip me off right away, considering I'm here for a communications class, not a crash course in advanced economics. Economics classes are probably among the most irrelevant to the psychology major, or at least I hope they are because numbers and I have never been friends.

In what feels like the longest and most obvious exit of my life, I leave the room and make my way to the classroom across the hall. Luckily, there's a door at the back, giving me a semi-stealthy entry. As

I slide inside, I scan the room for any open seats and catch sight of one. It's the only seat left, right next to a girl with a checkered backpack and the most intimidatingly perfect hair I've ever seen in my life. Just my luck.

She glances up, moves her backpack off the chair without a word, and goes right back to her notebook, the model of a studious, unfazed college student. The fact that she's the only other Latina-looking student in the room just adds an extra layer of scrutiny I definitely don't need on my first day. Trying to be invisible, I slide into the seat and pull out my notebook as quietly as possible, convinced everyone is watching me anyway. My pulse is pounding in my ears, my hands shaking just enough to make it hard to write anything down. How I expect to one day be a psychologist when I can't seem to get a grip on my own emotions is a mystery to me, but my heart wants what it wants, and it's relentless in feeling what it feels.

To calm my nerves, I try to focus on anything other than my internal spiral. I glance at the board and snort under my breath. The professor has written the course name in huge, dramatic letters, ORAL COMMUNICATION 103, like we'd somehow stumble into the wrong classroom. Oh, the irony. In my head, I mentally tick it off on my "cliché list," which, yes, is an actual thing I keep running in my mind.

In every cheesy school movie, teachers write the course name on the board as if it's not painfully obvious why we're there. I always think it's a dumb little trope, but today, I have to admit it would've been a lifesaver just a few minutes ago across the hall. Maybe I'll submit my list to Hollywood and the top editorial houses someday as a public service. Like, hey, we know office coffee always tastes awful, no need to describe it as such. And the main character releasing the breath she didn't know she'd been holding? Come on now.

I'm still chuckling to myself when I notice my seatmate glancing sideways at me. That's when I realize I haven't even looked at her properly since sitting down. She's stunning—big almond-shaped brown eyes, flawless light brown skin, and that calm, unbothered confidence that people either radiate or completely lack. In my case, it's firmly the latter. There's a familiarity about her expression, a certain kind of easy poise I always think only exists in old movie stars or, I don't know, people who've actually mastered yoga breathing exercises.

I take out the nice notebook and the set of beautifully colored pens and highlighters that I bought as motivation to stop procrastinating, a promise I make myself at the start of every school year. This one is no exception, so I've placed all my faith in my pretty stationery to be the determining factor in my personal growth. This will be the year, Fer.

When I open my new pencil pouch, I realize the receipt is still in there. Seeing the date from a few months ago makes my stomach tighten. I remember that day, before the whole situation with my dad went down, when my mom had taken me shopping to prepare for my new life as a college student. We were both so excited about my acceptance letter that we hadn't even waited for me to be done with high school. I never could've imagined then that just a couple of weeks later, everything would change so drastically.

By the end of class, I've been so lost in my thoughts that the notes in my notebook leave a lot to be desired despite the pretty stationery. I really should let my dad and his midlife crisis stop taking up so much rent-free space in my mind. I put everything back in my backpack, promising myself that I'll focus more and take better notes next class.

"Do you, like, plan on making this a habit?" checkered backpack asks, one eyebrow raised in an amused smirk. "Because my backpack needs to know if it should start saving your seat every day."

It takes me a second to realize she's talking to me and even longer to come up with a response. To my horror, I realize I'm sitting there, mouth slightly open, staring at her like I've never seen another human being. Fantastic start, Fer. Really nailing it.

"Oh, um—no. Hopefully not." I try to laugh it off, pretending I don't feel like a total idiot. "I promise, I usually have my life together. I'm just, you know, having a . . . character-building day."

She laughs. This low, rich laugh that somehow sounds genuinely entertained rather than pitying, thank God. She extends a hand, her movements smooth and unhurried, like she's not about to make a mad dash for coffee between classes like the rest of us mere mortals.

"I'm Alex," she says, her voice as effortlessly cool as she looks.

Finally getting my brain to connect with my limbs, I take her hand, trying not to make it awkward.

"Fer," I reply, feeling marginally less like a freshman imposter, "and, uh, I'll make sure to RSVP to your backpack if I ever consider being late again."

She chuckles, giving me this slow, approving nod, making me feel like I've unknowingly aced a secret exam.

"Got it," she says. "I'll keep a seat warm for you, then. Cool earrings, by the way."

Automatically, my hands go up to my ears. I made the little button earrings myself, hand-painted them with acrylics last week in a burst of back-to-school creativity. But it's the first time anyone has actually noticed them, let alone complimented them.

"Thanks," I mumble, the word slipping out before I can think of something smoother to say. But she's already heading toward the door, blending seamlessly into the flow of students leaving the room.

I exhale deeply, feeling a ridiculous combination of relief, amusement, and the vague sense that I might've just met my first college friend. Turns out joy and grief can sit at the same lunch table. They just don't talk much.

Where There Is Love, There Is Pain

Donde hay amor, hay dolor

AURORA

Aura, Segundo's daughter, had the day off and brought him to visit me today. It had been a while since I'd last seen him, and I wasn't sure when the chance would present itself again, so I told him about my diagnosis.

I hadn't planned on breaking the news today, and I definitely didn't plan on giving the news to my niece, as much as I love her, before I did to my own children. But there they were, sitting across from me, Segundo with his familiar, steady presence. I let the words tumble out before I could overthink it. I asked them not to say anything yet. I need to handle it my way, in my time.

Aura reached for my hand, squeezing it gently. "I'll be here as much as you need me to be, *tía*. Whatever you need, just say the word."

Segundo nodded, his expression serious but kind. "You know I'm here too. Always. But you should tell your kids. These things . . . they're easier to get through when you're surrounded by the people who care about you. You've always carried too much on your own, Aurora, and that's not the way it should be."

I know he is right. He's always had a way of cutting straight to the truth. I want to tell them—I'm just not ready. Not yet.

I wish I could go to the river, let the water carry away my worries the way it used to when I was younger. The steady flow always made my thoughts feel lighter, the weight of the world a little easier to bear.

Sometimes, when I close my eyes, I can almost hear it again.

The river had a way of making everything quieter. Its steady flow softened the noise of my thoughts. And in the friendship I'd built over the years with Pepi and Paco, I found something I had never found in my abuelos' home: a sense of belonging.

On my sixteenth birthday, Pepi, Segundo, Paco, and I set off for the river. The sun was sultry, but there was a light breeze that made the journey feel like a small adventure. I couldn't contain my excitement as we walked down the dirt path that led from our house toward the water. Pepi, as usual, was carrying a small bag that she kept reaching into, her fingers working with a purpose.

"A surprise," she told me with a twinkle in her eye, but she refused to tell me anything more. She kept the secret well, but I could see by the sly smirks and the knowing glances Segundo and Paco exchanged that they were in on it too.

I tried to remain patient, but with every step closer to the river, my curiosity only grew. The teasing was becoming unbearable, and as we reached the riverbank, I couldn't help but ask.

"What's the surprise? You've been hiding it all day."

"Patience." Pepi grinned, and for a split second, she almost looked like she was enjoying my growing impatience. "No peeking!" she commanded as she pulled a small parcel from her bag and held it behind her back. "Turn around, close your eyes, and wait until we tap your shoulder."

I couldn't help but laugh at the absurdity. "Or you can just say 'turn around,' you know?" My words came out a little sharper than I intended, impatience bubbling up like a pot just shy of boiling over.

"Shh," Segundo added, his voice teasing but firm. "Just do as we tell you."

I was about to snap back, to tell him not to "shh" me like a dog, but I knew the longer I resisted, the longer it would take to get to the surprise. Besides, I was already in too deep, curiosity gnawing at me like an itch I couldn't scratch. I took a deep breath and turned around, the anticipation of the moment flooding over me. I could hear the faint rustling of paper and the shuffling of feet, but no matter how hard I strained my ears, I couldn't figure out what they were doing. My mind raced with possibilities—what could they possibly be preparing for me? Even I wasn't sure what I would've given myself, and that made the suspense unbearable.

Finally, a light tap on my shoulder startled me. Without a second thought, I spun around, eager to see what they had planned.

"¡Eeeeeas don as magaiiiias ge gancaba . . . !!" The trio burst into song, their mouths full of cookies, the crumbs flying as they sang the traditional "Las Mañanitas" with all the hilariously garbled lyrics only cookie-filled mouths could produce. The joy in their voices, muffled and ridiculous, filled me with laughter. The sight of them, mouths stuffed with cookies, trying desperately to stay in tune—it was too much.

"I thought those were the silly games of *escuinclas*," I teased, my eyes narrowing at Segundo after their impromptu performance, the last crumbs still tumbling from their lips.

"One is never too old to have fun," he responded with a grin, pointing at Pepi and Paco. "And with these two," he added, "the song would've sounded the same whether or not we had mouths full of cookies."

Pepi and Paco exchanged mock glares, trying to feign indignation, but it was clear none of us could keep a straight face for long. It was the perfect birthday surprise, full of the laughter and warmth only true friends could offer. In that whisper of time, surrounded by the people I cared for the most, I felt like the luckiest girl in the world. I could have cried with happiness, but not one of them would have let me live that down, so I smiled instead.

We all sat down on the warm ground near the riverbank, cracking open the bottle of Coca-Cola I guessed they'd "borrowed" from my grandparents' store. The sweet fizz of the soda and the cookies made the moment even sweeter as we passed the box around, laughing and chatting about everything and nothing at all. The late afternoon sun kissed my shoulders, drying off the sticky sweat from our walk to the river and warming my skin like the embrace of an old friend. A brilliant shade of orange colored the sky above us, fading into pinks and purples as the sun dipped lower on the horizon. I remember thinking that if I could spend the rest of my life sitting right there—by the river, in the same company, watching the sunset—it would be enough.

As the evening grew quiet, I caught Paco sneaking glances at me. When our eyes met, he gave me a quick wink. I felt my heart skip a beat, as if he were reminding me we had unfinished business, a conversation we still needed to have. In the couple of weeks since his confession, we hadn't had a single opportunity to be alone. It was almost as if my Abuela Lupe could sense my intense desire to spend time with Paco and she kept finding tasks to keep me away from him. I had hoped I'd be able to speak to him later, but the occasion never came. The entire afternoon brimmed with laughter and light, and not once did I find myself alone with Paco. But somehow, I didn't mind. It was just enough to be there with him, with all of them.

❀✧❀✧❀

The next morning, still caught up in the joy of my birthday and the lingering warmth of the night, I moved around the house in a daze. I swept the floors with a vigor I hadn't felt in weeks, and without being asked, I mopped them too. Then, as if possessed by a sudden burst of energy, I moved on to dusting every corner of the house. I felt lighter than air, still floating from the memories of the previous evening, with thoughts of Paco swirling in my head. I heard Abuela's voice from the other room.

"What's got into her?" she asked, clearly surprised by my sudden enthusiasm for housework.

Mom simply responded with a noncommittal "Hmm."

In the afternoon, we gathered at the table for a meal to celebrate my belated birthday. My grandparents' store closed early on Sundays, so my mother had chosen that day to bake me a cake and make my favorite dish, cheese entomatadas. The fried tortillas soaked in tangy tomato sauce, topped with sour cream and crumbled cotija cheese, were a taste of heaven. The Oaxaca cheese, gooey and stretchy, melted between the tortillas like magic, holding together the pieces of the dish as if refusing to be separated. I took my first bite and savored it, feeling the warmth and comfort that only food made with love could provide. But just as I was about to dive into my second entomatada, the sharp sound of my abuelo clearing his throat broke the magic.

"I spoke to my compadre Alfonso," he said, his voice cutting through the room. We all looked up at him, sensing the seriousness of the conversation ahead. He turned his attention to Segundo.

"He can use a hand in his growing business and has offered to house you while you work for him. I told him you'll be glad to do it. This is a great opportunity for us. You'll be closer to the city, and it'll be easier for you to make the trips to restock the merchandise for our store."

The room seemed to close in around me, and for a second, I forgot how to breathe. I looked at Segundo, silently hoping he'd say something to reject this sudden change.

"I don't want to leave, abuelo," Segundo replied, his voice thick with emotion.

"I'll do more around the store. I can even make trips for the merchandise on my own if you want to stop making them."

But Abuelo's reply was final.

"I already gave my word to my *compadre*. You'll be leaving next week."

The authority in his voice was undeniable, and usually, no one in the room would've dared to argue further.

"No, abuelo, please, I don't want Segundo to leave!"

The words escaped from me before I could stop them. My throat tightened, and tears blurred my vision. Mom placed a hand gently on my knee under the table, a quiet but firm signal to stop. My heart sank. I turned my face away, not wanting anyone to see the tears I was struggling to hold back.

Abuelo didn't reply, neither did abuela Lupe, they just carried on placidly eating their plate of entomatadas. I knew mom had stopped me in fear I'd get scolded too sternly, but what I got, the confirmation that at my abuelos' table my voice didn't matter and never would, was even worse.

The entomatadas suddenly lost all their flavor. I knew better than to leave the table before my Abuelos did, and I knew better than to leave food on my plate. So, we finished the meal in heavy silence. The meal felt like it lasted forever, but at the same time, it was gone too quickly. When we finally stood up from the table, I knew Segundo would tell Pepi the news that would break her heart. It was a juncture I didn't want to witness, but it was one I couldn't escape.

The possibility of continuing the conversation with Paco that afternoon, the conversation I had dreamed about for so long, seemed more impossible than ever. The news of Segundo leaving, of my best friend losing him, overshadowed everything. How could we even think of something more when the relationship of the two people we cared about most was about to be torn apart?

Abuela always said a woman's value is in what she gives to her family, but what could I give to my family when everything just kept getting taken from me? I didn't know. All I knew was that my father had already been taken from me, and I couldn't bear to part with my brother too.

A Friend in Need Is a Friend Indeed

El que tiene un amigo, tiene un tesoro

PILAR

My dad always said that family comes first, but it never felt like that in our house.

It was more like family came at a cost, and Meño and I were always the ones paying. That's why I was so grateful for Julia and Ofelia. They were a constant reminder of what belonging felt like without having to sink deeper and deeper into debt to earn it.

Even though my father had made it clear that my own quinceañera wasn't happening, I was lucky enough to be a part of their special days as a member of their court of honor.

For the past week, we'd been like a pack of frenzied hummingbirds, darting from boutique to boutique, inspecting satin, tulle, and lace until we couldn't see straight. It felt like we'd explored every inch of the shopping district in Mexico City, weaving through the bustling streets, stopping every few minutes to adjust our shoes or sip on cold bottles of Jarritos.

Today, we'd started at the crack of dawn, the minute the stores opened, vowing to finish by noon. Julia had been lucky and found a dress she loved at our first stop, which was great considering that her birthday was coming up first. But noon had come and gone, and here we were, sun dipping and all, still on the hunt for Ofelia's dress, as well as the dress style that the girls in the court of honor, including me, would wear.

We had agreed to wear the same dress to both Julia's and Ofelia's parties to make it simpler, but it was turning out harder to find a single dress that fit both their styles.

Our stomachs growled in unison, as if rehearsing for some makeshift mariachi band, and my feet were begging for mercy. But despite the exhaustion, Julia's eyes locked onto every boutique sign like they held the key to treasure.

"Just one more, please!" Julia pleaded, flashing those wide, hopeful eyes that were as impossible to resist as her mother's *mole* recipe.

"Only because you said please," I teased, letting out a sigh that wasn't entirely fake.

We pushed through the door of the boutique, the small brass bell above us chiming softly. The smell of fabric dye, fresh roses, and some powdery perfume I couldn't place hit us instantly. The shop was a little on the small side but packed with dresses in every shade and texture imaginable.

They hung on racks like jewels, twinkling under warm lights, each one daring us to try them on. It was the kind of place where you didn't dare to breathe too hard, like each dress was a work of art that might just crumble under a whisper.

"Look at that one! And that one! Oh my gosh, Pilar, can you believe this place?" Julia spun around, her arms already full of potential candidates.

I nodded, barely listening, my eyes scanning the walls.

And then, I saw it.

Or maybe it saw me.

A dress so beautiful, so perfect, it was as if it had dropped straight out of a fairy tale—or maybe the set of a whimsical film.

I blinked, half expecting it to vanish if I looked away. But it stayed, glowing softly, inviting me closer. My heart stopped, and for a second, I forgot where I was.

"Wow," I whispered, not sure if I'd actually said it out loud.

I took a shaky step forward, the rest of the world blurring as I got closer to the dress.

It was a soft white, as if woven from moonlight and mist, with a hint of shimmer woven into the fabric that caught the light in a way that felt almost magical. The top was formfitting, hugging the torso in a way that seemed both elegant and regal, like something meant for a queen. The neckline dipped between a heart and a V, just daring enough to be sophisticated but still so innocent.

I traced the line of it with my eyes, down to the waist where the skirt blossomed out like a flower in full bloom.

The skirt. Oh, the skirt.

It wasn't just poofy; it was cloud-like, airy, light enough that I swore if I twirled too fast in it, I might actually lift off the ground.

And the details. Tiny, delicately embroidered flowers bloomed along the neckline and scattered down toward the hem, like little silk petals falling in slow motion. They added just the right amount of sweetness to the look, making the whole thing feel like a dream.

The sleeves, though, were the real enchantment. They were fitted snugly to the elbow, then flared out toward the wrist in a way that felt almost ethereal, as if my arms might disappear into the fabric.

I'd only ever seen sleeves like this in magazines—magazines I'd pored over in secret, imagining myself in dresses like these even if they were far out of reach.

"It's perfect," I breathed, almost afraid to touch it.

I could see myself in it, gliding across the dance floor, each little flower bobbing as I moved. I imagined the crowd, everyone's eyes on me as I took my first steps into womanhood.

It was like a little piece of a dream, and for a moment, I could picture myself inside it, as someone important, someone who mattered.

"Do you want to try it on?" A voice floated over from behind the register, warm and inviting.

I looked up and saw a woman in her thirties standing there, watching me with a knowing smile. She leaned on the counter, hands delicately folded, her dark eyes sparkling as if she'd seen this scene play out countless times before—a young girl, heart set aflutter by a dream dress.

Her gaze moved from me to the gown in front of me, and her smile widened, a blend of tenderness and amusement.

I felt Ofelia's and Julia's eyes on me, somewhere between hopeful and hesitant, as if they knew the weight of what the lady behind the counter was asking.

I bit my lip, running my fingers just barely over the fabric.

"No," I said finally, forcing myself to smile. "No, it's too much. I'll find something simpler. I'm in search of something for the court of honor, but Ofe, you should really try it, it's so beautiful!"

It was a hard thing, letting go of that dress, walking away from something that felt like it could hold all my wishes. But maybe seeing one of my best friends wearing it would offer a bit of comfort. That dress was too beautiful to be left behind, waiting for someone else to come along.

"I think I'm done trying on dresses for today. I might pass out from exhaustion if I pull one more zipper," Ofelia said. "I've still got a few weeks left anyway. Let's focus on the *damas'* dresses instead, since we're cutting it close for Julia's party."

I forced a smile and turned away, pretending to be engrossed in the simpler gowns set aside for the court. The longing lingered in my chest, a quiet ache I had carefully tucked away ever since accepting I wouldn't have my own celebration. But seeing that dress brought it back, as though my secret wish had stitched itself right into the fabric.

"This one, that pastel pink with the matching parasol, it's perfect for you!" Ofelia squealed, shoving a light pink dress into my hands. "Try it, please! You'll look so beautiful."

I gave her a grin and took the dress, slipping behind the curtain. As I struggled with the zipper, I could hear their whispers drifting through the boutique.

"She'd look so pretty in that one," Julia murmured.

"I know," Ofelia replied, her voice soft.

I bit my lip. They were trying to keep their voices low, and I could tell they didn't want me to feel left out. But somehow, their pity only made the hollow feeling stronger, like I was missing out on a part of life I'd only get to glimpse from the sidelines.

Finally, I managed to zip up the dress and stepped out from behind the curtain, doing my best to smile as brightly as possible.

"Oh, look at you!" Ofelia exclaimed, clapping her hands together. "Pilar, you look like a doll!" She gestured toward the mirror. "Turn around, look at yourself!"

I gave a twirl in front of the mirror, spinning the little parasol and trying to picture myself at my friends' parties, dancing the waltz alongside them. It wasn't the dreamy white dress, but it was pretty, and the way they looked at me made me regain a spark of excitement.

"I like it," I said with a brief nod.

"Well, then that's it! This is the one!" Julia said, her eyes gleaming. "Now we can finally head back before we pass out from hunger."

We all laughed, the tension from earlier lifting a little.

"But," she added quickly, "we'll definitely come back this week with the other girls to take measurements and make the reservations."

We grabbed our bags and headed out of the boutique, our heads buzzing with ideas. As we walked down the cobblestone street back toward the bus stop, Ofelia spun to face us, her eyes twinkling. "So, we still agree on same style, different colors for the court of honor, right? That way we can wear the same dress for both Julia's quinceañera and mine. It'll look amazing in the photos."

"And you know what? The damas could even swap dresses between parties," I added, catching her excitement. "You know, mix it up a little."

"Exactly!" Julia nodded, looking thrilled.

"How didn't we think about that before?"

I smiled, imagining it, letting their excitement fill me up. They were so kind to me, wanting me to be part of their happiness, to include me in every detail.

As we neared the bus stop, Julia linked her arm through mine. "You know, Pilar, just because you're not having a quinceañera doesn't mean we can't celebrate you. You're still turning fifteen, after all."

I looked at her, touched by her words, and nodded. "Yeah," I said, smiling. "I guess I am."

Just then, the bus arrived. A group of guys, maybe in their early twenties, got off and handed us a flyer. I mindlessly accepted one that read *"No queremos Olimpiadas, queremos revolución."*

As the upcoming Olympics hosted by Mexico drew nearer, the excitement over our country taking center stage in such an important worldwide event seemed to grow in parallel with the political tension and the student protests around us. Flyers with phrases such as *'68, the year of the bought-out media* or *We don't beg for our rights, we demand them* seemed to sprout up all over the city. Along with them, it was not uncommon to find some type of advertisement for the Olympics: *Mexico, host to the world* or *Mexico, triumph is a collective effort.*

"Wasn't that Chava's friend?" Julia asked Ofelia.

Ofelia's older brother, Chava, had become increasingly involved in the student demonstrations against Díaz Ordaz's regime. Lately, he'd also been expressing his discontent with the upcoming Olympics and the way the government was handling the event.

In all honesty, we'd been so caught up with everything quinceañera-related that at first, we'd hardly paid Chava any mind. But the tension in the air seemed to grow exponentially by the minute, making it almost impossible to ignore what was going on around us—even if we didn't quite understand it.

Before Ofelia could reply, she was swept along by the crowd

boarding the bus. Julia and I hopped on the bus, and by the time we made our way back to Ofelia, we were back to giggling as we talked about flower crowns and parasols, plans and dreams that seemed as endless as the sky over Mexico City that late afternoon.

And for a little while, the ache in my chest faded, replaced by the warmth of my friends' laughter and the feeling of belonging as we rode home through the bustling streets. Julia and Ofelia laughed like the world was theirs to take, and at least in that moment, I loved having a front-row ticket to witness it.

The sky had turned a deep indigo by the time I stepped off the bus. My stomach tightened with every hurried step I took home.

I was late.

The excitement of the day, the dreamy dresses, the hushed whispers of political unrest that I still didn't quite care about—they had all swept me away, making me forget that tonight, Dad would be home for dinner.

I had planned to get home early, to have dinner ready before he returned from work, but now . . . now I was walking into trouble.

As I reached home, I hesitated for a moment outside the door. Upsetting Dad this close to Julia's quinceañera was a big risk. I'd never forgive myself for my stupid mistake if he didn't let me go.

Maybe if I hurried, I could at least start something before he arrived, make it seem like I had been cooking all along. Fake some sort of kitchen accident outside of my control.

But as soon as I stepped inside, the rich scent of garlic and cumin wrapped around me, and my breath caught.

I found Meño standing at the stove, flipping pieces of chicken in a pan, the golden-brown skin sizzling in the oil. A pot of rice sat covered on the counter, and a bowl of beans rested nearby. The table sat perfectly arranged, napkins folded, glasses filled with water.

I stared at him, my mouth opening, then closing.

Before I could say anything, the sound of my father's boots echoed outside. The front door swung open, and in he walked, his shoulders stiff from the day's work, his face lined with exhaustion.

He walked straight to his usual spot at the table, sitting down with a grunt.

"Smells good," he said as I walked over, placing the bowl of beans in the middle of the table.

I lowered my gaze, my stomach twisting.

Meño came up next to me, placing the platter of chicken next to the beans. "Wait till you take a bite. Pilar outdid herself this time."

My head snapped up, eyes widening.

"Sit down, Pilar. I'll bring the rice."

I looked at him and held his gaze in a silent thank you.

That night, like countless others, Meño had stepped in to avert chaos.

As I sat down, my fingers curled around the edge of my chair, steadying myself. Meño placed the last dish on the table, sliding into the seat across from me with the same ease he always carried, like this was nothing, like it was just another night.

I picked up my fork, glancing at him between bites, at the quiet way he handled things, the effortless way he smoothed over the cracks in our world before they could split wide open. He never asked for thanks, never expected recognition. But he deserved both.

I wanted to say something, to let him know I saw him, that I saw everything he did for me. That I knew he carried more weight than any seventeen-year-old should. He could easily let me take on all the chores Dad expected of me just for being the only female in the house, yet he'd never bought into Dad's strict view of gender roles.

The words of appreciation sat heavy on my tongue, unspoken. Instead, I made myself a promise. If it ever came down to it, I would do the same for him. One day, I would be strong enough to stand between him and the storm the way he always did for me.

Every Cloud Has a Silver Lining

No hay mal que por bien no venga

FER

Some people walk through life like they already own it. On campus, I can see it in their easy smiles and perfect outfits, their laughs echoing as if they've never carried a secret in their lives.

Here's the thing: it's only the third day of classes, and I already feel like a minor-league imposter. Growing up in San Ysidro, I'd been surrounded by people like me, Latino through and through. Now? I've counted just a handful of Latino students across all my classes combined. I'm still the same "average" girl, but apparently, average here looks . . . different.

Being first-generation sometimes means shouldering dreams that weren't yours to begin with but learning to make them your own. Now that this dream is mine, I am determined to make it come true—although I'd be lying if I don't admit that glancing at the people around me is already making my determination waver ever so slightly.

It's the second day of Oral Communication, my class with Alex, and for once, I wake up early. Like, absurdly early. So early that I don't even have time for my usual snooze-cycle ritual: alarm, snooze, roll over, repeat.

I arrive at class ten minutes early, which feels borderline heroic. I pick the same seat as Monday, plunk my backpack beside me, and immediately spiral into a low-level panic about the open chair next to me.

So I'm here, staring at my backpack planted on the desk next to me, wondering if saving a seat for Alex is one step too close to desperate. My anxiety grows with every student that trickles in. What if she doesn't even want to sit by me?

And then, like a slo-mo scene worthy of my mental cliché list, she walks in, right on cue. I hold my breath, practically willing her into the seat beside me. She's the only person here I've exchanged a single unprompted word with, and weirdly, I'm counting on her to anchor me.

Three steps go smoothly, and then—because apparently nothing in my life can happen without a twist—on the fourth, she trips. She catches herself right next to my desk as the professor starts the class. I grab my backpack off the desk, and she takes a seat.

"Smooth move," I murmur under my breath, and as I sit there, my inner smartass decides to make a quick appearance. I scribble a note and slide it over:

Do you always trip on your way in? Because my backpack wants to know if I should move it closer to cushion your fall.

She reads it, and for one horrifying second, I think I've gone too far. But then she smirks, looks over, and carefully mouths, *I like you.* I turn red. Like, heart-beating-in-my-ears red. What the hell is going on here?

After class, she starts to pack up, and I'm doing my best to act casual. I'm about as far from casual as a cat at a bougie dog show, but I'm trying.

"First year here?" she asks, as if she doesn't know she's about the only person who's spoken to me voluntarily.

"Yep," I reply, nodding. "You too?"

She grins, a little smugly.

"Second. Got your books yet?"

"Nope," I say. "The campus bookstore is my next stop."

She snickers. "Rookie mistake. Campus bookstore is a rip-off. You're better off at The Bargain Bear. It's just outside campus and way cheaper. I'm headed there anyway, wanna tag along?"

My heart does this embarrassing thing that's halfway between skipping a beat and breaking into a tap dance.

People keep telling me that, unlike high school, it's "totally normal" to see people studying alone here, but I've been dying to make at least one friend. I still have no idea what to do with myself during the long breaks between classes. Now that someone is actually inviting me somewhere, my brain's flickering like a faulty light bulb, barely able to string a thought together.

We make small talk on the way to the bookstore.

"So, where are you from?" she asks, her voice casual but warm.

"San Ysidro," I say. "I commute every day."

"Wow," she says, lifting her eyebrows. "That must not be fun, especially with the heavy San Diego traffic. I'm from the Bay Area, but I live off-campus with Charlie—my best friend from high school."

This would be a perfect opportunity to let her know that by *commute*, I mean public transportation—I'm nowhere near being able to afford a car—but I waited too long, and now it would be weird. So instead, I nod, managing a small smile.

"That sounds nice," I say, but something about the way she says *Charlie*, softly, like it's a name she's used to leaning on, lingers in my mind longer than it should.

The thought flits in before I can stop it: *What if their "best friend" situation evolves into something more now that they're living together?*

I tell myself it's none of my business, but the idea settles in anyway, catching me off guard with the strange way it makes my stomach tighten—like I've stumbled into a jigsaw puzzle with no cover art to guide me.

"That is so cool that you get to live near campus. I really wanted to live in the dorms, but the entire process was so confusing for me as a first-generation student. By the time I figured out my financial aid situation, it was too late to apply for the dorms," I explain.

"I'm sorry it didn't work out for you, but you can always try again next year," Alex offers with a soft smile.

"It was probably for the best anyway," I add. "I've been struggling to find a job that accommodates my class schedule, and I really want to keep being a full-time student. Plus, my FAFSA wouldn't have covered the entire cost of the dorms, and let's just say things are complicated at home right now, so I wouldn't want to ask my parents for financial help. I can't wait to find a job and move out of my parents' though."

I surprise myself with the ease at which I let out so many details about my life with Alex. I've been known to ramble, so I'm no stranger to oversharing, but this is not it. Something about her makes me feel safe to speak my thoughts.

"Ugh, I get that. It is so hard to balance work and being a full-time student. I didn't qualify for FAFSA, but luckily, I found a job near campus. I felt bad about my parents having to pay for my apartment."

"I was so scared I wouldn't qualify for FAFSA. We're right at the line where I wasn't sure if I'd get approved, but there was no way I could've afforded college without it either. And filling out the darn form was so complicated—I may have spilled more tears than I care to admit trying to figure it out. Anyway, sorry, I'm rambling. Where do you work?" I ask.

"Okay, I swear I don't get commission or anything—I work at The Bargain Bear, where we're headed," Alex says, and I think I can see her face flush.

"Ah! So I've been scammed by a saleswoman!" I say, laughing.

"Oh no! My jig is up!" Alex exclaims in mock exaggeration.

We both laugh.

When we arrive, I'm expecting some kind of cute used bookstore vibe, but The Bargain Bear is the exact opposite of cute. Books are stacked to the ceiling, and the whole place smells like a mixture of days-old coffee, dust, and old paper—a chaotic mess of textbooks, novels, and random office supplies.

And then there's Charlie.

He's tall and lean, with beach-bronzed, tousled hair and an amiable smile that exudes effortless charm. He's in a faded T-shirt that reads *Gay AF*, and as I read it, that weird, gnawing tension that's been building up since Alex referred to him as her best friend eases up.

"*Ya era hora, ¿dónde andabas?*" he teases Alex, raising an eyebrow as he reprimands her three-and-a-half-minute tardiness.

The smooth cadence of his words catches me off guard, considering the way he looks—definitely not what I expected to hear coming from someone who could pass for the cover of a surfer magazine.

"This is Fer, my new friend. And about that *Help Wanted* sign you asked me to post? I was thinking it might not be necessary after all. She needs a job more than anyone I know." She gives me a teasing look. Clearly she'd been planning this since I mentioned I was looking for a job,

"Late girl?" Charlie asks her, throwing me a mischievous look.

Late girl? *So I have a nickname?* She's been talking about me? I can't decide whether to feel embarrassed or weirdly flattered. I bite my lip to keep from smiling.

Charlie gives me a once-over and grins.

"So you're Fer," he drawls in a way that makes me instantly wonder how our one small interaction the other day made enough of an impression that she's already mentioned me to Charlie.

He nudges Alex, looking as if they're sharing some inside joke I'm now an honorary part of.

I feel a little less crazy for having saved her seat.

"So, wanna join The Bargain Bear circus?" Charlie asks. "We need help. The pay's not great, but once the first few crazy weeks are over, we practically get paid to hang out and do homework. That, and put up with Christmas music from the first of November—we just can't help ourselves." He winks.

I'm almost dizzy with relief, and maybe a little shocked. I've gone from nobody to Bargain Bear staff in under five minutes.

Charlie explains the "highly rigorous" sorting system (one color sticker for "slightly used" and another for "mildly abused"), and before I know it, I'm standing behind the counter, learning how to shelve.

I've stumbled into this little bubble of sarcasm and weirdness, and I'm not mad about it at all.

⌘✧⌘✧⌘

The door to Alex's and Charlie's apartment swings open with an exaggerated creak, and I follow Alex inside, clutching a bag of Jack-in-the-Box tacos we picked up on the way. It's small, cozy, but it's still a different world from my tiny dining room-turned-bedroom back home. It's hard to believe it's only been a week since I started working with Alex. Somehow, in just seven days, she's already started to feel familiar, like someone I've known much longer.

"Welcome to the humble abode!" Alex says, kicking off her shoes near the door. She tosses her keys onto the kitchen counter, the sound echoing in the quiet space. "It's not much, but it works."

I glance around, taking in the neatly arranged furniture, the framed prints on the walls, and the sleek espresso machine perched on the counter. Everything about this place is . . . grown-up.

"It's nice. Must've been hard work getting it to look like this," I say, trying not to let my voice betray the tiny pang of envy I feel.

Alex grins. "If it were up to Charlie and me, it would've been a lot simpler, and we'd probably have beanbags instead of actual couches, but my mom and dad helped us set it up. My dad is so over the top he even insisted on hiring movers. Said he didn't want me lifting 'all those heavy boxes.'" She rolls her eyes, but there's a warmth in her voice that makes it clear she didn't mind the extra help.

59

"Movers, huh?" I say, setting the tacos on the counter. "Fancy."

Alex laughs, pulling two glasses from the cabinet. She fills them both with water from the fridge dispenser and pushes the one that reads *Proud Plant Dad* my way. I glance around, checking for plants. There are none.

"Trust me, it wasn't my idea. But my mom likes to hover, and my dad's obsessed with 'making things easier' for me. He can be extreme. So, here I am, spoiled and caffeinated." She gestures toward the espresso machine.

I nod, smiling, but the words sink in like stones in water. *Making things easier.* The phrase feels foreign, like it belongs to a language I've never learned. My parents didn't have the luxury of making things that easy for me. They've done their best—scrimping, saving, rationing meals when the bills piled up—but that's different.

"Beanbags sound fun, but I gotta take your parents' side on this one. Those couches look pretty comfy, and the word *extreme* doesn't exist in my vocabulary when it relates to coffee. I just count myself lucky my parents were all about me coming to college," I say, trying to keep my tone light. "And even then, they couldn't believe I needed so many books. '*¿Pues qué tanto vas a leer allá?*'" I mimic my mom's surprise after seeing how much I'd have to pay for textbooks.

Alex chuckles, leaning against the counter. "Moms, right? Making their opinions known."

I smile, but I can't help adding, "Yeah, but movers? My parents could barely even chip in for my books this semester. My mom saved up just to get me transportation money. The rest is all financial aid." I shrug, trying to play it off like it doesn't matter, but my voice wavers slightly.

Alex pauses, her smile softening. "That's tough," she says quietly, and for the first time, her usual calm confidence seems to falter. "I guess I never thought about it like that. My parents just . . . I guess they struggled when they were younger, so now they try to do everything for me. I don't want to sound ungrateful—I love them for that—but sometimes I'd like a bit of a chance to do more things for myself, you know?"

"It's nice that they can do that for you, though," I say, not bitterly but honestly. "My parents try, don't get me wrong, but for them, college wasn't even in the cards. I feel guilty sometimes, like every dollar they spent on me could've gone to something more important."

Alex tilts her head, watching me. "That's not on you, though. If anything, it's amazing that you're here. You're making it happen."

"Yeah," I say, looking down at my hands. "But sometimes it's like I'm carrying their dreams too, you know? Like, I can't mess this up because I'm not just doing it for me."

There's a blink of quiet, and then Alex sets her glass down on the counter with a soft *clink*.

"For what it's worth," she says, her voice steady, "I think what you're doing is incredible. I mean, I might not get it—what it feels like —but even though I'm just getting to know you, I can see how hard you're working. And that's . . . badass."

I blink in awe of the sincerity in her voice.

"Thanks," I mumble, feeling a strange mix of gratitude and vulnerability.

Alex shrugs, her grin returning. "Now, how about we break into those tacos before they get cold? I'm starving, and the last thing I want is my parents bringing me a taco warmer for Christmas."

Her joke pulls a laugh out of me, and for a moment, the weight on my shoulders is a little lighter.

As we sit on the couch and dig into the tacos, I let myself enjoy the simple rhythm of our conversation.

Later, when I'm back on the trolley heading home, her words linger. I think about how her parents made sure she had everything she needed, how they've smoothed the path for her. My parents, within their possibilities, have tried to do the same for me.

I wonder if we'll ever be able to get back to what we had before.

The trolley hums beneath me, a steady rhythm that matches the beat of my thoughts. For once, the chaos doesn't feel so heavy. Maybe it's the sound of the wheels or the promise of tomorrow, but I feel lighter.

I lean my head against the window and watch the city lights blur together the rest of the way home.

Hope Is the Last to Die

La esperanza muere al último

AURORA

The first couple of days after chemo sure tricked me.

I thought it hadn't been too rough on my body, but after the third day, the symptoms began. An exhaustion that I can't seem to shake off took over my body, and I am constantly nauseous at the sight of food, but otherwise, I feel . . . okay. It is strange how, even though my body doesn't feel like my own, I am adjusting to the rhythm of it, how something that once terrified me is becoming just another part of my routine.

Aura stopped by in the morning, knocking on my door with her usual hurried energy, a grocery bag in one hand and her car keys in the other.

"I'm just dropping these off," she said, stepping inside and placing the bag on my kitchen counter.

"My mom made them—bland, easy-to-eat stuff. She figured you'd be sick of crackers and plain rice by now."

I gave her a tired but grateful smile. "Tell her thank you. I don't know what I'd be eating if it weren't for her."

Aura waved a hand, brushing it off like it was nothing. "Next time, I'll bring her with me. She really wants to see you, but I was rushing to work today, so I figured I'd just stop by on my way."

She hesitated for a second before adding, "And . . . thanks for letting me tell her. I don't think my dad and I could've kept it from her much longer. You know how she is."

I nodded, knowing exactly what she meant.

"I'm glad you told her," I said. "And I promise, this week, I'll tell the rest of the family."

Aura let out a breath, like she'd been holding all the tension of my secret with it. "Good."

She squeezed my arm before glancing at the time and sighing. "I have to go, but I'll check in later, okay?"

I nodded, watching as she hurried out the door.

Once she was gone, I sat at the counter for a moment, staring at the grocery bag she'd left behind. The weight of everything—not just the chemo, but the conversations still ahead of me, the way my family would react—settled onto my shoulders.

But then my phone rang. I glanced over at the answering machine. *Pepi.*

Her number on the screen was enough to pull me out of my thoughts, to remind me that life outside of my own worries kept moving.

"Can I come over this afternoon?"

She's supposed to come over in an hour. I haven't seen her in a few weeks, but hearing her voice today has brought back so many memories.

❁✧❁✧❁

Segundo's last week in Huejosquite felt like a blur, like someone had hit fast-forward on a week I desperately wished could last forever. Only a couple of weeks had passed since he'd left, yet his absence felt even sharper than I'd expected, like the surrounding air had thickened, pressing in from all sides. I missed him terribly, but I tried to keep my chin up for Pepi's sake.

The early afternoon sun cast soft shadows on the uneven, unpaved street where we walked, its warmth settling lightly on our skin—not too hot, not too cold, just that perfect in-between. A faint breeze rustled through the trees lining the road, carrying the scent of dry earth and distant cooking. The town felt unusually still, the usual hum of daily life reduced to the occasional distant voice or the scuff of our shoes against the ground.

"He promised you he'd come back as often as he can. You know my brother loves you, and he'll keep his word," I said, my voice softer than I meant for it to be. I wanted my words to lift her up, to sound like an unshakable truth, but somehow they felt hollow, fading as soon as they left my lips. And, if I'm honest, the words didn't fill the aching emptiness I felt either.

Pepi let out a shaky breath.

"He says he'll save as much as he can and he'll come back for me soon, but *soon* just doesn't seem soon enough."

There was a quiet devastation in her voice. Her face was wet with tears she didn't bother to wipe away, and I could almost feel each one as it fell, stinging with all the weight of longing and uncertainty.

I squeezed her hand, the only comfort I could think to offer.

"Sooner than you imagine, he'll be back for you, you'll see. Remember when we used to hide in the stockroom and plan your wedding to him?" I tried for a smile, hoping to bring a little light into the conversation, and after a fleeting second, I saw the corners of her lips curl up slightly.

"We were so silly back then," she said, with a half-laugh that still sounded a bit like a sigh. "I miss those days . . . Remember how your grandma would lose her mind, thinking there were mice getting into the merchandise?"

I laughed, a genuine laugh this time, picturing Abuela's frown as she'd inspect the half-empty boxes. "I can't believe we never got caught! Did she really think mice preferred the same cookies every time and even went for the same boxes?"

The memory warmed me, if only for a second, and Pepi laughed too, a sound that felt like a balm.

She looked at me, eyes still shining with tears but softer now. "Did you think back then that I'd really end up with Segundo?"

I raised an eyebrow, pretending to scoff. "Are you kidding? *Donde pones el ojo, pones la bala,*" I said with a wink. "If you could get me to like you after thinking you were the nosiest little pest I'd ever met, of course I knew you'd get my brother too."

I bumped her elbow, a playful nudge that finally earned me a smile from her.

She leaned against me, her voice small, almost timid. "Do you think your grandparents will ever be okay with Segundo and me being together?"

I wrapped an arm around her shoulders, pulling her closer. "I think

—no, *I know*—that when Segundo comes back for you, whether or not they're okay with it won't matter. And besides, we'll always be sisters, no matter what."

I rested my head against hers, feeling the warmth of her closeness, the bond we had stitched so tightly over years of secrets and shared dreams. I knew my abuelos would never agree to Segundo's relationship with Pepi for the same reason they hadn't agreed to my mother marrying my father, but I would never hurt Pepi's feelings by saying that aloud.

"Remember when we were around seven and thought we could outrun the moon?" I asked Pepi, in an attempt to lighten the mood.

"Oh, I remember. That was the day we discovered the moon didn't care where we went; it was stuck to us like glue. I shouted at it, 'Hey, why are you following me?!' so loudly that my mom came running outside, broom in hand, ready to swat whoever dared to trail her little girl." Pepi laughed, her eyes crinkling up. "She was ready to whack some stranger right in the street! I swear she thought there was a whole gang after us."

"And we panicked and started running in opposite directions, yelling, 'It's following me!' 'No, it's following *me*!' I thought we'd actually be able to shake it off." I shook my head, remembering how simple things had seemed back then. Our biggest worry was an overly attached moon.

Pepi's laughter softened, and she took a deep breath. "I know it's silly, but . . . there's something comforting about it, don't you think? Knowing that the same moon we're looking at right now is following Segundo too."

"That's not silly," I told her, putting a hand on her shoulder. "It's beautiful."

We both looked up at the moon again, quiet and thoughtful, until Paco's voice broke our reverie.

"Did you know the moon gives out candy if you ask nicely?" he asked, suddenly there behind us, looking up at the moon like he'd just revealed one of its best-kept secrets.

Pepi and I both jumped.

"What are you talking about, Paco?" Pepi asked, half-amused, half-skeptical.

"The moon," he said, as if stating the obvious. "If you ask it politely, it'll drop down a candy just for you. All you have to do is say, 'Moon, come, give me a candy!'"

Pepi raised an eyebrow. "Uh-huh. Right. I'm almost seventeen. Even as a kid, I never once fell for the idea that the Three Kings brought the presents."

"Well, suit yourself." Paco shrugged, though his eyes gleamed with a dare.

After a sigh, Pepi rolled her eyes and tried it. "Moon, come, give me a candy," she said, smirking.

Nothing happened, and she gave me a little shove. "See? Silly."

Paco snickered. "You have to say it like you mean it."

Pepi straightened, looking like she was about to scold a younger sibling, then faced the moon with complete earnestness and shouted, "Moon, come! Give me a candy!"

We stood there, a little embarrassed but waiting, just in case. And then, softly, almost too quiet, a little *plop* sounded right by her feet.

She gasped, bending down to pick it up. "A Gloria!"

Her face lit up with astonishment. Glorias were her favorite candies. Segundo had brought her one nearly every time he came around. The memory made my heart ache in the sweetest way, and for once, I thought of my brother without the usual sadness that crept in afterward.

Pepi nudged me, grinning like a kid. "Well? Are you gonna try?"

Paco raised an eyebrow, like he was waiting too.

I rolled my eyes, but I gave it a shot.

"All right . . . Moon! Come! Give me a candy!" I shouted, more than a little self-conscious.

Another soft *plop!* landed at my feet, and I jumped back, startled.

We all burst into laughter, the silliness of it lifting something heavy from my chest.

"Aren't you going to ask for one?" I asked Paco, still giggling.

He smirked, reaching into his pocket to reveal another Gloria. "I collected mine earlier."

"Cheater!" Pepi laughed. "You didn't even shout at the moon!"

"There's always next time," he said with a wink as he popped the candy in his mouth.

I took a bite of my Gloria, savoring it, then held out the rest for Pepi, who had already finished hers in record time. She eyed it for a second, then, like a frog, snatched it with her tongue, making us laugh all over again.

"I'll come by later this week," Paco said as we headed home that evening, his grin as easy as ever. "We can 'ask the moon' again."

Pepi pointed a finger at him, narrowing her eyes. "But next time, you have to wait to get your candy with us. Swear it!"

He raised a hand, feigning seriousness. "I swear. No candy without you two. Happy now?"

"We'll see," Pepi muttered, but her smile betrayed her satisfaction.

And so, over the next few weeks, Paco kept coming back, and every time, I'd stare up at the moon, waiting for that little *plop* by my feet. Once, the candy grazed my hair as it fell, and I laughed so hard my stomach hurt.

These memories, ridiculous as they were, felt like tiny, perfect gifts that held off the loneliness and longing we both felt. Sometimes, even when you know better, it just feels right to believe in these little bits of magic. That's what Pepi and I did, every time.

And every time we shouted up at the moon, I was more certain: I was head over heels for Paco.

If I could shout it off the rooftops, I would have, but given Pepi's and Segundo's situation, it didn't feel like the right time. I think Paco felt the same way because even though I could perceive love in the way he looked at me, neither one of us brought up our unfinished conversation about our feelings for each other.

Not All That Glitters Is Gold

No todo lo que brilla es oro

PILAR

The best moments were always the ones that felt like magic, little bursts of joy that made everything else fade away.

"I can't believe we're just a week away from my quinceañera!" Ofelia exclaimed, practically bouncing on the couch as a commercial break interrupted the movie we were watching.

We were having our final waltz rehearsal for her party later that evening. Although it was my birthday, I didn't mind having the rehearsal that day because the *Quinceañera* special was scheduled to air earlier that morning, and, of course, we had to watch it together.

Ofelia's mother had kindly offered to buy a cake so we could have a small celebration for my birthday with the rest of the court of honor before the rehearsal. So, Julia and I had arrived at Ofelia's house hours before the rest of the court of honor.

Julia's celebration had been two weeks earlier, and although I'd been a little bitter at first about missing out on my own grand celebration, the fun I'd had at hers had completely erased any resentment. Now, I felt nothing but grateful for the opportunity to celebrate my birthday among friends at Ofelia's house.

To my father's credit, he had never failed to come home with a cake for my birthday or Meño's, but he hated having people over. The only friends I could ever get away with inviting were Julia and Ofelia, and only when he was planning to spend the day out.

"I can't wait to dance the night away, but I'll miss having an excuse to spend every weekend practicing the waltz," I said, overwhelmed by nostalgia as I watched Ofelia twirl around, giddy with excitement.

"I'll miss having an excuse to spend so much time with Juan," Julia chimed in, grinning.

True to tradition, Ofelia was having fourteen *damas* and fourteen *chambelanes* in her court of honor. For symmetry's sake, we'd been paired by height.

Julia had gotten really lucky. She was paired with Juan, the cutest boy in the group, who looked like a young Javier Solís, the heartthrob of every teenage girl. With his dark, soulful eyes and the charm of a movie star, he was practically a walking, talking romantic hero.

I, on the other hand, was paired with Chava, Ofelia's older brother, who looked nothing like Javier Solís and definitely not like Jim Morrison or Paul McCartney, my two personal crushes.

Don't get me wrong, I absolutely adored Chava, and he had his own charm, but while I wasn't as close to Chava as I was to Meño, I had always thought of him as another older brother.

And to be fair, dancing with Juan, or any other boy closer to my age, would've been way more exciting than stepping on Chava's feet for the umpteenth time.

Just then, the television crackled to life with a bright, enthusiastic voice.

"México '68! The world is coming to Mexico City!" the announcer declared as footage of athletes flashed across the screen: runners sprinting on a track, divers slicing through water, and a gymnast sticking a perfect landing. "Join us for the games of a lifetime!"

The commercial's energy pulled our attention away from the conversation. The scenes on the screen momentarily filled the room with a sense of something bigger than us, something almost magical.

Ofelia would be the last of our classmates to have her quinceañera, and with most of the others' celebrations already behind us, the focus of everyone around us had shifted to the upcoming games.

I was too young to understand just how much weight the Olympics would carry that year or the political undercurrents surrounding them, but I could sense the buzz in the air, almost like it was an event we had to celebrate.

Mexico, hosting the Olympics—the first ones ever to be transmitted in color—was supposed to be the country's big moment on the world stage, and I felt part of something huge just by being caught up in all the glittering excitement.

"I'm so curious what it'll be like to watch the Olympics in color," I said as the black-and-white images of the Olympic venues filled the screen, looking so futuristic and shiny.

"If only people would wake up and care as much about what's happening around us as they do about the Olympics," came a voice from behind us.

Chava.

I hadn't noticed him join us in the living room. He leaned in, his face tense with frustration, his eyes glued to the TV.

"Why don't they talk about the student protests, the real issues, instead of feeding us this ridiculous spectacle?" He glared at the television as if daring it to answer. "The government's too busy with the Olympics to care about the people."

Chava had always been outspoken about his opposition to Díaz Ordaz's presidency and the way the government was handling the upcoming Olympics.

I'd overheard Chava talking to Meño about the vast sums of public money being poured into building Olympic stadiums while students protested against the regime, their voices growing louder every day. "They're spending all this money on stadiums and fancy ceremonies," Chava had said, his tone sharp, "while people are fighting for their rights, and the government doesn't even blink."

His words were passionate, but I had to admit I didn't really understand much of it. The more he spoke, the more it felt like something huge was happening outside my world. Something I wasn't ready for.

The idea of color broadcasts, the glamour, the spectacle still thrilled me. Politics? That was something adults talked about in hushed voices. But Chava's words echoed in my head, pulling me into a reality I wasn't sure I was ready to face.

The movie resumed, cutting through the tension, and for a moment, we returned to the flickering screen of *Quinceañera*, as if the world outside could be forgotten. By the time the credits rolled, most of the members of Ofelia's court, including Meño, had arrived for our last rehearsal.

❀✧❀✧❀

The last strains of music echoed through Ofelia's backyard as the waltz rehearsal ended. We bowed and clapped in mock applause, collapsing onto mismatched chairs while the boys scattered toward the refreshment table.

"Finally," Ofelia groaned as she pulled off her heels and tossed them into the grass. "If I have to hear 'El Vals de las Flores' one more time before my quince, I'm going to scream."

"It's not our fault you picked that song," Julia quipped, though her teasing smile softened the blow. "And don't forget, you still need to practice your curtsy."

Ofelia rolled her eyes, but the rest of us laughed, the weariness from rehearsal fading as the evening cooled around us. She looked radiant despite the heat, her hair pinned up in loose curls that framed her face. I leaned back in my chair, enjoying the hum of chatter and the glow of the setting sun. For a moment, everything felt right, easy, warm, alive.

But my eyes wandered to Ofelia's mother, who stood at the edge of the yard with her arms crossed. She wasn't smiling.

Her eyes flicked toward the open window, where the faint buzz of a radio filtered through. I caught pieces of the broadcast—words like *protests*, *tension*, and *security measures*—before Ofelia's father reached through the window and turned the volume down. His voice, low and tight, carried just enough for me to hear.

"Things are getting worse," he said. "Do you think we should even go through with it?"

Ofelia's mother shook her head, her lips pressed into a thin line. "We've already sent out the invitations. What can we do? Cancel? And look at her, she's so excited. We can't let her down."

I glanced back at my friends, but no one else seemed to notice. Julia and Ofelia were debating what hairstyle would best suit their dresses, while a few of the boys joked about sneaking a sip from the unopened bottles of cider meant for the big day.

It was Cesar, Ofelia's cousin, who broke the moment.

"Did anyone see all those flyers covering the wall near the mercado?" he asked, plopping into a chair. "All about the protests. 'Down with Díaz Ordaz' or something like that. The students are looking for trouble if you ask me."

Chava stiffened and turned to him, his eyes narrowing. "You think asking for basic rights is looking for trouble?"

"They're blocking the streets and making everything worse for everyone else," Cesar shot back. "You think that's helping? They should leave politics to the politicians."

Chava opened his mouth to argue, but Ofelia stepped between them, her hands raised in mock surrender.

"Can we not fight tonight, please? I have enough to worry about without adding a political debate to the mix."

"Fine," Chava muttered, sitting back with a huff. "Only 'cause you're asking." But the tension hung in the air.

The group quieted, and my attention drifted to the quinceañera shoes near Ofelia's feet. They gleamed in the fading light, their white lace trim delicate and perfect.

For a moment, I imagined Ofelia floating across the dance floor, her skirt billowing like clouds. But the image was fleeting, replaced by a prickling unease I couldn't shake.

The radio crackled again, louder this time, as the broadcaster's voice cut through the silence. "The government urges citizens to remain calm and avoid large gatherings in light of recent protests."

Ofelia's mother rushed to the window and snapped the radio off, forcing a smile as she turned back to us.

"Let's not think about all that nonsense. It's Ofelia's night soon. That's all that matters."

We nodded, some more convincing than others, and conversation slowly resumed. But I caught her father's silhouette, now inside the house, pacing, his shadow stretched long and restless against the wall.

❀✧❀✧❀

Chava and the entire conversation after the rehearsal had certainly piqued my curiosity about the student movement, but I still didn't understand what was so wrong with hosting the Olympics. Why would anyone protest that?

So on our way back home, I asked Meño.

"Whatever you do, don't bring this up in front of Dad," Meño warned, his voice low. "He and Chava are on opposite sides of this whole thing, and I doubt he'll let you keep hanging out with Ofelia if he thinks Chava's been filling your head with nonsense."

"So, which side are you on?" I asked him, still confused about what the Olympics and student protests had to do with each other.

"Don't worry about it," he said with a half-smile. "Someday, you'll understand. But for now, just focus on making sure you don't step on Chava's feet next week at the party, okay?"

"I only stepped on him once," I protested, but even I could hear the resignation in my voice.

I was growing tired of always being left with more questions than answers. Why were things so complicated? Why was everything happening so fast?

As Meño teased me about my dance moves, I couldn't help but feel like there was a world out there that I was on the edge of. One that seemed to shift under my feet, where the colors of the Olympics weren't the only thing that mattered.

Everything seemed to be on the verge of collapsing, and I couldn't grasp why.

A Leopard Cannot Change Its Spots

El leopardo no cambia sus manchas

FER

Sometimes the world shifts under your feet, but if you're lucky, you find places that are steady. At least for a while.

The past month and a half at The Bargain Bear, my steady place, has been a bit of a dream, mostly because I've gotten to hang out with Alex and Charlie, who it turns out are pretty cool. From my first week working there, I've felt at home with them, even when I had to ask a million questions about shelving. And honestly, I can't remember what life was like before I met them. They're like a little slice of comfort in this crazy new world.

My classes, though? Completely different story.

I've tried to convince myself that the first year of college, just like any other major life change, takes adjustment. But as the weeks go by, it only seems to get clearer how out of place I really am. It's not just that I'm the only Mexican in most of my classes; it's that everything about my life until now suddenly feels ... wrong in a way I wasn't expecting.

Hearing my white classmates talk about their high school experiences, their families, their futures—it's made me realize how much of a struggle my community has been through just to get by. Discrimination doesn't always show up with insults or direct attacks, I've learned. It comes as underfunded schools, getting just enough resources to scrape by but not nearly enough to actually get ahead.

We've been stuck in this loop of surviving, not thriving, and the worst part is that I didn't realize how deep it went until now.

It started as a quiet doubt, but now I'm questioning whether I'm even good enough to be here. I can't help it. I don't know if I belong in a place that's supposed to be for everyone but feels like it isn't.

And then, there's the culture shock. It's one thing to know you're different, but it's another thing entirely to feel it so sharply.

As I'm sitting in English class waiting for my essay to be returned, one I'm sure I've aced—writing has always been my strength—my mind wanders to something that happened just last week. I overheard a classmate telling two of her friends about a trip she made to Tijuana. It's not like I was eavesdropping, but I couldn't help but hear her talk about how "sketchy" and "unsafe" it was down there.

"I've never been south of here," one of them said.

"Yeah, I went to San Ysidro once," the other added, pronouncing it like she had no idea how to say it. *"San Yee-sidro."* Like it was some place completely foreign to her.

"It looks pretty ghetto," she continued. "I mean, no offense, it's just . . . unsafe. And when we stopped to buy water, the cashier could hardly speak English. It was like, all Mexicans there."

I sat there, my chest tightening.

I mean, I knew people had their stereotypes about places like mine, but hearing it spoken out loud like that was a whole new level of frustrating. Was it really that threatening to them? Did being Mexican automatically mean "dangerous" to them? I wanted to say something, to tell them I was from San Ysidro, that I knew that place better than they ever would, but I didn't. I just sat there, hoping no one would see how much it hurt.

And then, as their voices faded into the background, my mind drifted to something else—the San Ysidro massacre.

I couldn't shake the thought that it wasn't a Mexican who was behind it. It wasn't *our* people who were the threat. And yet, there it was, our town, our culture, being painted with the brush of danger and violence. Meanwhile, the Yellow Ribbon Memorial, which was still decorated with fresh flowers at least a few times a year, was a constant reminder that almost every adult in my small town had known one of the twenty-one people whose lives were stolen that day. The heart of my town was still hurting for them.

The disconnect hit me hard.

How could they not see that? How could they not understand that, sometimes, it was the people who looked like them causing the harm, not us?

But of course, I didn't say any of that. Instead, I just sat there, feeling more isolated than ever.

❁✧❁✧❁

Finally, Professor Johnson starts to call out names to hand back our graded essays.

This is my first college essay ever, an analytical piece on body image, and although I'm confident in my writing, I've still been on edge about knowing what grade I got on it.

When I see my classmates react to their grades, some look disappointed, but most smile, and I can't help but be a little relieved for them. I'm rooting for everyone, secretly hoping that this college thing isn't as impossible as it sometimes feels.

But then he gets to my row. And doesn't call my name.

I begin to stand up, thinking I misheard, but nope. Another name gets called. And then another. My stomach twists with that familiar mix of anxiety and confusion.

When he finally looks up and sees the few of us still sitting empty-handed, he says, "If I didn't call you, please see me during my office hours. We need to discuss your essay before I hand it back."

My heart sinks.

Why not me?

I glance around the room, trying to figure out if the other empty-handed students are feeling as lost as I do, but if they are, I can't tell. I wonder if they're freaking out on the inside too.

The professor moves on to talking about our next unit, but I can't focus on a single word he says. I glance down at my hands and realize I'm gnawing on my nails again—something I do when I'm nervous or stressed, which, apparently, is all the time now. I notice a small spot of blood where my thumb's been bleeding from where I bit it too much.

I try to tell myself it's not a big deal, but it feels like one more thing I've failed at.

One more reminder that maybe I'm just not cut out for this.

❁✧❁✧❁

I take a deep breath before gently knocking on Professor Johnson's half-open office door.

I don't know why he asked to meet about my essay, and over the past two days as I've waited for his office hours, part of me has dared to hope it's because he found it so impressive he wanted to know more.

But the nagging voice in my head tells me otherwise: maybe he's finally realized I don't belong here, that I'm not cut out for this place.

"Come in, take a seat." He gestures to the chair across from him.

As I step inside, I'm greeted by the sharp scent of coffee mingling with a faint hint of dust. It's not just the air in the cramped room that makes it hard to breathe—it's my nerves.

I sit down, hands clenched in my lap, feeling out of place in this world of towering bookshelves and complicated academic papers.

"Fernanda García, right?" he asks, and I nod. He flips through a stack of papers until he pulls out mine.

My stomach sinks as I see a D scrawled at the top.

Writing was always my strength. Or so I thought.

Now, I'm not sure I have one.

"English isn't your first language, is it?"

"No. Spanish is."

There's no judgment in Professor Johnson's tone, but my answer feels like admitting a fault.

He nods, as if confirming something he's noticed. "The way your essay is written, it made me wonder. Do you think in Spanish and then translate those thoughts when you're writing?"

I pause, thrown off. "I guess I do. I never really thought about it before."

He smiles, trying to be encouraging. "You have some beautiful phrases here, but it's long-winded. Spanish is a rich, expressive language. When something's translated from English to Spanish, it often ends up longer. In English, we like to get right to the point."

I nod, but his words sting.

I'd known my accent sounded different, that my speech sometimes carried traces of my roots. But I'd never realized my writing was "different" too, that my thoughts could come across as *foreign* on paper.

A wave of frustration rises up my chest, but I blink it back. Crying here would just make me feel smaller.

⊗✧⊗✧⊗

Growing up so close to the Mexican border, I was surrounded by people like me.

At the grocery store, at the pharmacy, the person next to me would just as easily greet me in Spanish as they would in English.

My parents raised me in this bubble where Spanish flowed naturally, where English was something I'd learned but didn't *live* in.

When my college acceptance letters arrived, there was this unspoken pride among my friends and family; I'd made it. I'd done what so few in our community had done: I was going to college. And not just any college—a four-year university. The first in my family.

But here, in this small office, I'm coming to realize what I'm up against. I don't just have to learn English the way it's spoken and read here; I have to change how I *think*, how I *structure* my ideas, how I *express* myself.

In my mind, I hear my mother's voice, her expressions, her advice all spilling over into my thoughts in Spanish, rich and flowing, with every word feeling necessary, every detail important.

How can I cut away those details, all that *feeling*? How do I learn to write in a way that's so different from how I *think*, how I *am*?

Professor Johnson means well, I know that. I see it in his patient smile, his gentle suggestions. But as he explains how to make my writing more direct, I realize he doesn't understand the depth of what he's asking.

For him, it's just a matter of technique.

For me, it's like asking me to change the language of my heart.

⊗✧⊗✧⊗

By the time I leave his office, I know that my high school GPA of 3.9 means nothing here. Getting into college wasn't the finish line—it was the start of a new struggle. I have to retrain my mind to move from the poetic turns of Spanish into the bluntness of English, the language that will either carry me through this journey or leave me behind.

I'd thought getting here was the achievement, but now I see I'm only halfway there.

Nothing Ventured, Nothing Gained

Quien no arriesga, no gana

AURORA

Pepi's visit yesterday afternoon did me more good than I'd realized it would. Having her here, letting myself get lost in our old memories, lifted some of the weight pressing down on me. Now, I'm ready to start calling my children to give them the news. Pepi has always been the sister I never had. I can't believe now that I once let years slip by without talking to her. I wonder how differently things could have turned out if I hadn't. But it's too late for what-ifs. All I can do now is continue to untangle my story.

It had been four long months since Segundo left, and time had crawled without him, like a slow parade of empty days. His absence had brought on a strange waiting that felt endless, like being stuck between where you're at and where you'd hoped to be. At the same time, it felt like only yesterday that he'd been there with us. He'd returned twice to bring us merchandise, and both times, Pepi and I had been thrilled to see him. And both times, I'd done my best to console Pepi as she cried when he left again.

"I know if he's saving for us, he can't keep spending his money coming back and forth," she said one night, her face streaked with tears. "But it's so hard having him far away, spending more time apart than together."

I tried to reassure her. "I know it's hard, Pepi, but he's keeping his promise. Without our abuelos taking every peso, Segundo's already saved more than he thought he could. At this rate, he'll be back for you in a year."

But without Segundo, it had become hard for me to see Paco. My grandparents didn't see any reason for a "decent young lady" to spend time with a boy unless marriage was in the future. Aside from stolen moments with the moon as our witness, Pepi always in tow, we were never alone.

One afternoon, though, when Pepi and I were alone in her family's bakery while her parents ran errands, Paco walked in, smiling faintly as he asked if he could borrow me for a few minutes. He led me outside, and as the sunlight splashed across his face, he looked at me with a seriousness that stopped my heart.

"Do you remember that conversation we were having the night before we found out Segundo was leaving?" he asked, his voice soft, a warmth creeping up my cheeks.

I nodded, my voice barely a whisper. "I remember." I'd been aching to tell him I felt the same way, but then Segundo had gone, and it had never felt like the right time.

"I meant what I said," he continued, his gaze piercing, "but I have tough news, and I wanted you to hear it from me first." He looked down, and I held my breath. "One of my uncles from Tijuana is working as a bracero in California, and some of my other uncles and cousins are planning to join him."

I'd vaguely heard of the Bracero Program, some sort of labor initiative inviting Mexican workers to American farms. Just the week before, I had walked past a small group of men sitting outside the corner store and talking about the Bracero Program with a mix of hope and skepticism.

"I hear they're offering good work in the States," one man had said, his face wrinkled from years of sun but his eyes bright with possibility. "Good wages for picking crops. Enough to feed our families back here."

Another man, younger, shifted uncomfortably. "I've heard it's not all it seems. They promise the moon, but how do we know they'll keep their word?" His tone was cautious, like he didn't want to get his hopes too high.

An older woman, leaning against the doorframe with her arms folded, chimed in. "It's not like we have many choices here. If they'll pay, if they'll take us, we go. Better than starving." She gave a shrug, like it was a reality she had long accepted.

I had stood there, listening, trying to understand what they were all hoping for. On one hand, it seemed like a chance for something better, a way to send money back home, a way to lift the burden. On the other hand, the doubts were evident in their voices. Doubts about what they were promised, what they had to give, and what they would truly get in return. But I hadn't realized what that could ever mean for us.

Now, standing by the river with him again, the memory pressed heavily against my chest, as real and raw as the moment he first said it.

"I'm going with them. I leave next week," Paco said, and with those words, my world shattered like a glass jar dropped on hard stone. "I can't ask you to wait for me," he added, his voice heavy with sadness, "but this will be temporary. And when I come back, I'll prove to your grandparents that I'm worthy of you. I hope." He swallowed hard. "I hope you'll think so too."

Although we'd never spoken openly about it, there were two things my abuelos cared about for marriages in our family: preserving our light skin and increasing our wealth. Paco and Pepi were two of the smartest, most caring, and most hardworking people I knew. Yet, their skin was at least a few shades darker than ours, and neither one of their families was wealthier than my abuelos—who weren't even close to wealthy either but seemed to be convinced that looking down on others was enough to fool everyone. Paco's words were confirmation that he'd known so too.

Tears blurred my vision as I answered, "I could never think otherwise. You have nothing to prove."

With a gentle hand, he reached up, cupping my cheek, and then he kissed me. Soft, barely there, like a promise just out of reach. Time seemed to freeze as we stood, pressed together, the world fading around us. For a few seconds, I knew happiness so complete I didn't know what to do with it, and for years, it would be the last moment of genuine joy I'd have.

After Paco left, life felt like wading through thick mud. Days were colorless, flavors dulled; even the laughter Pepi and I used to share had faded. She was the only one who truly understood, and we fell into a sad game, taking turns being the one to cry on the other's shoulder. One day she'd be inconsolable and I'd comfort her, and the next it'd be my turn to grieve and she'd remind me we'd get through this somehow.

But it wasn't just Paco. I felt trapped, lost in a life that didn't belong to me. My grandparents refused to let me pursue any education, calling it a waste of time for a girl. My only option seemed to be finding someone to marry and hoping he'd be kinder than my grandpa had been to all of us in his role as the patriarch.

That was life in Huejosquite: young girls swiped by older men, spirited away in the night, no one asking permission. We all knew a friend, a cousin, the friend of a friend it had happened to. But although I knew it was a real possibility, I never really thought it would happen to me or Pepi.

But then it did.

❁✧❁✧❁

If two things were true about Huejosquite, they were that men only left women alone out of respect for other men and that when a woman no longer had a male figure looking out for her, news traveled fast. One time we'd overheard jokes from Tito, a local boy, saying he'd "steal Pepi one of these days." Back then, Paco had told him to shut his mouth. Tito had raised his hands in mock surrender but laughed as he said, "Hey, if it isn't me, it'll be someone else." Without Segundo or Paco around, Pepi and I had known we weren't safe. Her father was always too busy running the bakery, and my abuelo had never been exactly a protective figure to me.

One afternoon, just a few days after Paco had left, Pepi and I had been running errands when we passed two men on horseback, strangers to us.

"Beautiful girls, these señoritas," one of them had said, his voice loud, pointed.

"A shame if someone were to steal one of them," the other had replied, chuckling.

Even though we were just a couple of blocks away from our street, their comments had made us feel vulnerable. It was so unfair how we couldn't even venture a few blocks away from home without feeling like prey waiting to be chased by a predator.

As we quickened our step, the realization that Pepi, usually so quick-witted and unafraid to clap back at anyone and everyone, also looked afraid made something in my stomach tighten.

When I got up the next morning, the streets of Huejosquite were barely waking up, stretching their songs into the sky while the sun painted soft, sleepy strokes of pink and orange over the horizon. My hands were chilly, shoved into the pockets of my apron to keep from shaking, but my stride was steady with the familiar rhythm of our routine—mornings at the bakery, afternoons at my abuelos' store.

The heavy wooden door to the bakery creaked when I pushed it open, and the smell of the dough for the bolillos hit me first. But something else reached me next, a sound I couldn't place at first. It wasn't the usual clatter of trays or Pepi's mother humming a familiar Amparo Montes or Agustín Lara bolero. The sound was muffled, sharp, broken. Like sobbing.

I stepped inside, and there was Pepi's mother, hunched over the worktable, her hands shaking as she pressed a flour-dusted cloth to her mouth. Her father was pacing near the oven, his face red and wild, muttering under his breath. The sight of them sent a chill down my spine.

"¿Buenos días?" I said tentatively, my voice sounding far too normal for what I was stepping into. They both turned toward me at once, their eyes brimming with something that made my stomach twist.

"Aurora," Pepi's father said, his voice tight, a vein pulsing angrily at his temple, "do you know Pepi's whereabouts? Have you seen her?"

"Pepi? No, I thought she'd already be here . . . " My words trailed off as Pepi's mother let out a wail. I rushed to her side. "What happened?"

"She's gone," Pepi's father said, his voice breaking for the first time. "Her window, it was wide open this morning. She left! That girl must have been sneaking out behind our backs. I should've known. She had been acting different, tense. She must've been seeing someone."

My heart sank. "Pepi would never do that!" I exclaimed, my words a mix of dread for the my best friend's unknown whereabouts and indignation at her father's baseless accusation.

"She wouldn't? Well, look around. She did!" He gestured to the entire bakery, so full of Pepi's absence. His hand trembled, and that's when I noticed the fear in his eyes. His anger was masking a greater fear. Something darker.

Pepi's mother looked up at me, her face streaked with flour and tears. "Are you sure of what you're saying, Aurora? Pepi has mentioned no one? Even in passing?"

Even in passing. Her question suddenly transported me to the previous afternoon. To the comments those men on horseback had said in passing. *"Pepi no se fue. Se la llevaron,"* The most painful words I'd ever had to pronounce in my life.

"What do you mean she was taken?" Pepi's mother asked, the question sounding as painful coming out of her mouth as the words I'd said to her.

"Pepi and I are like sisters. We tell each other everything. If there was someone, I assure you I would've known. Pepi didn't leave. She didn't sneak out for some forbidden love affair. She was taken." I proceeded to explain to them what had happened the day before, and the words tasted salty in my mouth, blended with the tears streaming down my cheeks.

The weight of it hit me like a punch to the stomach. I clutched the back of the chair Pepi's mom was sitting at, my knees threatening to give out. Images flashed through my mind—Pepi laughing in the bakery, her hands covered in flour. Pepi teasing me about my uneven braids. Pepi telling me her dreams of moving away from Huejosquite one day to study, to do something big with her life. A life that she wanted to build with my brother. All those dreams, gone in an instant.

Tears burned in my eyes. I tried to swallow them, to be strong for her parents, but they spilled out amid the sobs I couldn't contain either. "We have to look for her," I managed to get out amid sobs.

"Mi hija," Pepi's mom's sobs grew louder. "They robbed her of her dignity. What will people say?" she asked no one in particular, ignoring what I'd just said.

I looked to Pepi's father. His fists were clenched, but he didn't reply to my suggestion to look for Pepi either.

That's when it dawned on me—Pepi's parents loved her, there was no doubt about it, but that didn't mean they would take her back. The realization made the space we were sharing feel suffocating. I couldn't be inside that place a second longer. Without a word, I turned around and rushed out of there. I needed the comfort of my mother's arms.

I ran straight to my abuelo's home, where thankfully my mother was the only one still there.

When I broke the news to her, my mother wrapped her arms around herself as if shielding from the words. "We have to get you out of here, mija. You're almost seventeen, you're not a little girl anymore, and it's only a matter of time before someone takes notice."

"Where could I go?" I asked, a knot tightening in my stomach. "Why can't we go together?"

Her face softened, shadows darkening her eyes. "After your father died, my choices were to stay and let you work beside me or come here where your grandparents could help us. It wasn't what I wanted," she said, her voice laced with regret.

Mom squeezed my hand, her eyes full of fear and urgency. "Don't breathe a word of this to anyone until we know it's possible."

The thought of leaving terrified me, but I had no choice. It was safer to wait for him in the capital than to remain in Huejosquite.

The Calm After the Storm

Después de la tormenta llega la calma

PILAR

The day of Ofelia's quinceañera was supposed to be perfect. I never expected that I'd be terrified leaving home that morning. It was Saturday, September twenty-eighth, and I'd been counting down to that day for weeks. Julia and I had planned to meet up early. I had been looking forward to it all week—getting ready together was always the best part.

"We are still on for early Saturday, right?" I'd asked on Tuesday, as I adjusted the straps of my dress in front of Julia's bedroom mirror. I'd traded dresses with another girl from the court of honor so we'd both get to wear a different color, but that trade had required some minor adjustments to the dress.

"Definitely," Julia replied with a grin. "We'll do each other's hair and makeup, then ride with my parents to the church."

I smiled, already imagining the fun of it. "Sounds perfect."

Everything felt right until I opened my bedroom door and stepped into the hallway, and there he was, sprawled across the floor. My father.

His shirt hung open, half-buttoned and stained with vomit. The reek of alcohol was thick in the air, sour and sharp, mingling with the damp scent of urine pooling around his shoes. He was barely recognizable— his face sunken, mouth slack, like some tragic puppet tangled in its own strings. My stomach turned. He hadn't been like that in months.

I'd believed things might be changing. But, of course, his episodes never happened at the most convenient times. I tried to move silently, stepping over him as if he were a landmine that might explode at the wrong pressure. If I didn't leave right then, I knew he'd ruin everything. My heart pounded as I tiptoed away and reached for the door. But I wasn't fast enough.

"Where do you think you're going?" his voice cut through the silence, low and slurred. I froze, gripping the doorknob. The hope I'd held—that I could slip away undetected—drained out of me.

"Today's Ofelia's quinceañera, Dad," I said, almost pleading. "Remember, I told you I'd be going to Julia's?"

He let out a dry, bitter laugh and then started crying. "You were just going to leave your poor father on the floor like this? No doubt about it, you're that *cualquiera*'s daughter. Just like her."

His words hit me like a slap. It wasn't the usual string of curses, not the regular accusations of ungratefulness or complaints about his hard life. He'd never talked about my mother like that before, much less me. But now he did, as if her absence had left him entitled to every cruel insult he could think of. I was too stunned to move, too shaken to even breathe, until I heard the soft creak of the floor behind me.

Meño stood there, his face twisted with a fury I'd never seen before. Meño, always the calm one, the one who could make me feel safe, was suddenly a storm.

"What did you just call her?" he demanded, his voice low and dangerous.

In an instant, he was across the hallway, grabbing our father by his collar and lifting him to his feet. Solovino was right behind him, barking frantically as if trying to make sense of the chaotic scene that I couldn't quite make sense of myself. Our father sputtered, caught off guard, too intoxicated to fight back.

"Meño!" I cried, not in defense of our father, but for Meño. I couldn't let him turn into this, not for me, not for anything. He stopped, looking at me, the storm still in his eyes but softening as he lowered his arms.

Our father looked past Meño and fixed his gaze on me. "I'm going to shower. Mop up this mess. And you'd better not even think about leaving the house."

The moment the bathroom door clicked shut, I felt a numbness settle over me, like the weight of every silent morning, every angry word, every silent cry pressing down all at once. I turned to grab the mop, but Meño placed a hand on my shoulder, stopping me.

"You're going," he said firmly, his voice leaving no room for argument. "This day means too much to you."

But all I could feel was dread. "If he comes to the party, if he ruins it for Ofelia . . . I can't risk that." I also couldn't bear the thought of Ofelia looking for me, worrying, maybe even sending someone to knock on the door.

Meño looked at me, determined. "I'll take care of it. You just need to leave before he's done in there."

"But if he finds out I left . . ." My voice was barely a whisper, and the tears were threatening to spill over.

"I'll handle it, Pili," he promised, reaching out to give me a quick hug. "Now go, before it's too late."

His words held me together, barely, as I slipped out the door. I didn't look back.

Julia's parents greeted me with warm smiles, oblivious to the churning turmoil inside me. The second we were alone, Julia's face softened with concern.

"Pilar, what happened? You look like you've seen a ghost."

I tried to keep it to myself, to protect her from the shadow cast over me that morning. But the words spilled out along with the tears I'd been holding back all my life. Soon, I was pouring out everything, including my dread of my father showing up.

"We should tell my parents," she said without hesitation, her eyes fierce with loyalty. "They'll go over there and put him in his place, trust me."

"Julia, you don't understand." I could hear the hopelessness in my voice. "Your parents can't do anything. He knows too many people in law enforcement. They'd just get into trouble, and he'd ban me from seeing you. I can't lose you."

Julia bit her lip, her determination wavering. "And Meño?"

"I don't know what he's planning," I said, trying to sound brave, "but he's stronger than my father. He can take care of himself."

We talked it through as we got ready, falling into the motions of brushing and pinning hair, dusting cheeks with makeup—all the while, a different strength building between us. By the time we were on our way to the church, a strange calmness settled over me. But as we walked inside, my eyes couldn't help but drift to the doors. Every few seconds, I'd glance back, waiting, hoping that Meño would walk through, giving me that reassuring look that only he could give.

It wasn't until almost the end of the mass that I realized what Ofelia was wearing.

When we'd gone back for fittings, I'd urged her to choose the one I'd fallen in love with after I caught her staring longingly at it too. She'd hesitated, surely because she knew how much I'd wanted it for myself, but I'd insisted, pushing her to try it on, to feel how right it was for her. Watching her in that dress felt like glimpsing a fairy tale. She looked so radiant, so complete. And just because it could never be mine, didn't mean she shouldn't have it. I wanted her to feel beautiful, to have something perfect, something untouched by shadows. In that dress, she seemed to carry a piece of the happiness I couldn't find for myself. But that day, she wore a dress I'd never seen. This one had shorter sleeves and a neckline that framed her shoulders, like the one Maricruz Oliver wore in *Quinceañera*.

"When we were watching the movie last time, I knew I wanted a dress like that," she told me afterward, her cheeks flushed with excitement.

"You look beautiful," I whispered, "it's like it was made for you."

She gave a soft laugh but then tilted her head. "Why isn't Meño here?"

I'd prepared for this, hoping she wouldn't notice, but ready to lie anyway. "My father had a small accident at work," I explained, my voice catching slightly. "He had to take him to the hospital, but he'll make it to the party."

Her face softened, confusing my worry for Meño with concern for my father. "I hope he's all right."

The celebration continued, but my heart stayed heavy, waiting. And still, my eyes drifted to the door, wondering if Meño was holding his ground, if he was safe, and if somehow, someday, we could escape from the shadows that followed us.

❀✧❀✧❀

Ofelia's backyard had transformed into something out of a dream. Lanterns hung like stars in the trees, and every corner burst with flowers in every color imaginable, spilling out from pots and trailing from trellises as if nature itself had been in on the secret all along. Ofelia's mother had outdone herself, turning the place into a paradise of roses, bougainvilleas, and wild marigolds that seemed to glow in the soft evening light. I had expected nothing less from her. It was like stepping into one of those movie sets we'd seen in the magazines—only better, because this was real.

But nothing, not even all the flowers in Mexico, could outshine Ofelia herself. She sparkled, radiating pure joy in her quinceañera dress, the picture of elegance and grace. She looked like a princess from one of the fairy tales we used to read as kids, only way more glamorous and with that unmistakable Ofe spark.

I, on the other hand, must've looked like a nervous wreck. Usually, I'd have been devouring my plate of barbacoa, but tonight, I couldn't even take a bite. My stomach was churning with worry, my eyes glued to the entrance, hoping Meño would show up.

"Are you sure he's coming?" Ofelia asked, glancing anxiously at the clock. Julia was standing next to us, with her eyes glued to the entrance. The waltz should've started twenty minutes earlier, but we were still waiting.

"He told me he would. Let's give him ten more minutes. If he doesn't make it, I'll just sit out so the court isn't lopsided." I tried to smile, but I think it came off more like a grimace.

Just then, Julia's eyes lit up. I turned and spotted Meño walking in at last, though not in the matching chambelán suit like the others. He wore a suit, sure, but it was different. I waved, but he didn't notice me. Instead, he locked eyes with Ofelia's mother, and the two of them rushed into the house. My heart dropped. What was going on? Had my father done something to Meño? Had he ruined his suit? Or worse, hurt him?

I practically sprinted into the house, with Ofelia and Julia right behind me. My stomach twisted as I braced for some terrible scene in the living room. But instead, I found Meño and Ofelia's mother beaming like they were in on the world's best-kept secret.

"Do you want to tell her?" she asked Ofelia with a grin.

Ofelia's eyes shimmered with tears, and her voice trembled as she spoke. "Pili, we've all been planning a surprise for you. A gift. We hope you'll accept it."

At the mention of a gift, Meño set a big white box down in front of me. "From all of us," he said.

"A gift? For me?" I was confused. Weren't we all here to celebrate Ofelia?

"Just open it," Julia urged, smirking like she could barely keep the secret in any longer.

My hands shook as I lifted the lid. There, folded neatly inside, was the dress. The one I'd fallen in love with, the one I'd encouraged Ofelia to buy, even though part of me had secretly wanted it more than anything.

Ofelia took my hand, her eyes bright. "Your friendship means so much to us, Pili. We're not just friends, we're sisters. There's no way we could have a quinceañera without including you too."

Grabbing my other hand, Julia added, "We know you, Pili. We saw the way you looked at that dress. And even then, you put us first."

"That's why, when they asked me about pitching in to give you a quinceañera with Ofelia, it was an easy yes," Meño added, a little awkwardly, but his grin was warm.

"Mija," Ofelia's mother chimed in, "we know you deserve your own party. We can't offer that, but we can make sure you're celebrated. So, would you honor us by putting on the dress and letting us present you along with Ofelia for the waltz?"

My heart was pounding, and a million thoughts swirled in my head. How could I take some of the spotlight from Ofelia on her big day? But they'd gone to such lengths to get me that dress, and I didn't want to make them feel unappreciated by refusing. Ofelia read my hesitation and smirked.

"You know this isn't really a choice, right? Julia would have shared her own quinceañera with you too, but we decided to wait until now, since I'm the last one to have one. So, no excuses. Now, hurry and get dressed. We've kept the guests waiting long enough." Her tone was playful, but it had that undeniable mom-scolding edge.

Moments later, we were lined up, ready for the waltz. Ofelia was at the front, radiant in her dress with her chambelán beside her, and I was right behind her, in my own quinceañera dress, with Meño—who had traded spots with Chava—at my side. The rest of the court of honor followed in perfect formation.

Ofelia's mom took the microphone and clinked a glass to get everyone's attention.

"I'd like to thank everyone for joining us tonight," she began. The backyard quieted, and everyone turned to her. "We're here to celebrate my Ofe." She looked at Ofelia with shining eyes. "Sweetie, I couldn't be prouder of the young lady you've become." She paused, letting a few sniffles from the crowd break the silence. A few guests, probably noticing my dress, wore confused expressions, their brows furrowed. "And as many of you know," she continued, "there's another young lady we consider part of our family. She deserves to be celebrated just as much." She turned to me, her gaze warm. "Pilar, without further ado, let's welcome our two beautiful quinceañeras to the dance floor."

As the music started, I remembered the steps I'd watched Ofelia practice so many times, and in Meño's arms, I danced the waltz, letting every worry melt away—if only for a night. I allowed myself to feel like a true quinceañera, dancing under the lights, surrounded by friends. Loved. Celebrated. My father and all his shadows could wait until tomorrow.

Tonight was mine.

God Squeezes but Does Not Strangle

Dios aprieta pero no ahorca

FER

There are moments you claim, and then there are the ones that latch on and refuse to let go. My meeting with Professor Johnson has chosen the latter option—wrapped itself around my thoughts like static cling. It's hours later, and Alex and I are in the stockroom, half-heartedly sorting books under the dim flicker of fluorescent lighting.

She's talking, but I'm not really listening. Something about her neighbor's dog wearing sunglasses?

My brain's stuck somewhere between my D and my dignity.

"So, what do you think?"

Her voice slices through my spiral like a paper cut.

"Huh?" I blink. "Sorry—what was that?"

Alex pauses. Studies me. "You okay? You're kinda giving... haunted orphan energy."

I laugh, a little too fast. "Just tired. Got a lot on my mind."

"Uh-huh," she says, not buying it. "Is this about your meeting with Johnson?"

I blink. I only mentioned that in passing two days ago. She *remembered*?

And that's all it takes. Suddenly, the whole mess comes tumbling out—how I thought I nailed my essay, how that D slapped me across the face, how I feel like an imposter trying to translate myself into a world that doesn't want subtitles.

I admit that sometimes, I catch the tail end of pop culture references in class and laugh two seconds too late. That my accent sticks out like a bruise. That María la del Barrio isn't helping me pass comp class.

"Sometimes," I say, quieter, "I feel like I'm one bad grade away from giving up."

Alex leans against a stack of textbooks. She doesn't rush to speak. Just listens. And then:

"College doesn't know what to do with a badass like you yet. That's all."

It hits me like a glass of cold water and a blanket at the same time.

"Thanks," I say, heat prickling behind my eyes. "But you don't know how clueless I am. I didn't even know grad school was a *thing* until last week. I thought you just... kept showing up until they handed you a PhD."

She laughs—really laughs—and it's like hearing a song I didn't know I needed.

"You're not clueless," she says. "You're building from scratch. That's brave."

The air between us shifts. Thickens.

I don't know who moves first, or if we even *do*. It's like the air just decides to collapse the space between us. She leans in slightly. My heart stutters. My mouth forgets it has functions.

We are dangerously close to a moment.

And then—

BANG.

"OYE, FER!" Charlie bursts in like a confetti cannon made of chaos.

"Did Alex tell you the news?!"

I lurch backward so fast I nearly swallow a philosophy textbook. Alex practically levitates away from me.

Charlie grins, oblivious. "We were talking last night—and if you want, you could move in with us. No more two-hour commutes. Just good vibes and bad coffee!"

Alex looks like she's still deciding whether to die or teleport.

I lean back onto a shelf, clearing my throat, heart pounding. "Uh . . . tell me what?"

Charlie explains, "We were talking last night about how rough your commute is, and we were thinking . . . if you're interested, you could move in with us. Help with rent, have a shorter commute, no more worrying about getting home late."

Alex nods eagerly. "We know how much of a struggle it's been, and

I know you wanted to live in the dorms but couldn't make it happen. We'd love to have you around more."

I turn to Alex, half-wondering if she's changed her mind about having me close. But she just gives me an encouraging smile, eyebrows raised, like she's practically begging me to say yes. I can't believe my luck—two people who, without hesitation, want me around. Want to help make my life a little easier.

"Are you serious?" I ask, my voice breaking with gratitude. "That would be amazing. Having that time back would help so much. I just don't know that I can afford to do it right now," I say, smiling at Charlie, who, after all, signs my paycheck. "I appreciate the offer, though."

"We'll work something out. If you're interested, that's all that matters. We can discuss the details later," he says, grinning. "Rumor has it, the manager here's a softy and gives out hours pretty generously, anyway."

I laugh, blinking back tears. I can't believe how lucky I am. Just knowing I might have a way out of living with my father, that I could have even a little more breathing room, makes everything seem a bit more possible.

❀✧❀✧❀

The rest of the afternoon is quiet at The Bargain Bear. With the deadline to drop classes far behind us, the peak season of students buying textbooks has finally passed, leaving us with time to organize the shelves and share an occasional joke. Alex is sitting on the counter, flipping through a used copy of *Cosmo*. I'm sorting a stack of used philosophy books, trying not to think too much about how my performance in Professor Johnson's class still has my stomach in knots.

Charlie walks out from the stockroom, juggling a clipboard and a half-empty bag of gummy bears. "Why do I feel like someone just failed a midterm?" he says, tossing a gummy bear into his mouth.

Alex looks up, a sly smile tugging at her lips. "Fer failed nothing. She just had a little cultural critique session with her professor earlier."

Charlie frowns and turns to me. "Cultural critique? What does that even mean?"

"It's . . . a long story," I answer. "I'll spare you the boring details," I add, trying to downplay it.

But Alex, always the instigator, jumps in. "Her professor basically told her she writes essays like a poet. Which, apparently, isn't a compliment in academia," Alex explains, her voice laced with sarcasm.

Charlie pauses mid-chew, narrowing his eyes. "Wait, hold up. He criticized her for being . . . what? Too expressive?"

I sigh, closing the book I'm holding. "More like too Hispanic. He figured out I think in Spanish and then translate my thoughts when I write, which apparently makes it too wordy and emotional."

Charlie leans against the counter, frowning. "That's some . . . racist microaggression right there."

Alex laughs, throwing her hands in the air. "Thank you. That's exactly what I said."

"It's fine," I mutter, though it's really not. "I just need to figure out how to . . . adapt."

Charlie tilts his head, studying me for a moment. "Adjust? Like, shrink yourself to fit into a box someone else built? Nah. Screw that."

His words catch me off guard, and I can't help but smile, just a little. "Easy for you to say. You're not the one about to fail."

"True," he admits. "But trust me, Fer, you've got something most of these professors have never seen. Perspective. Don't let them snuff that out."

Alex hops off the counter and gives me a pat on the shoulder. "See? Charlie's basically a walking pep talk. I keep him around for moments like this."

Charlie grins. "Don't act like I'm not also the best manager this store has ever had."

"Best? You alphabetized the novels by color last week," Alex teases.

"Excuse me, it was an artistic statement," he fires back, raising his eyebrows. "But speaking of moments, let me tell you, Fer, you're not alone in dealing with that academic nonsense. I had a professor in community college tell me my art was 'too urban.' Like, what even does that mean?"

I blink at him. "You went to community college? When?"

He pops another gummy bear in his mouth. "For a couple of years. I was also living in my car at the time, so it was a sucker punch hearing that all my sacrifice to stay in college was probably for nothing."

"What?" The question escapes my mouth before I can even process what he's saying.

"Can you believe this guy? And he concealed it so well, otherwise my parents would've taken him in, no questions asked," adds Alex.

He shrugs, as if it's no big deal. "Yep. Me, my Corolla, and an air freshener called 'Ocean Breeze.' It wasn't glamorous, but it got me through."

Alex shakes her head. "Don't let him fool you. He's humble-bragging. Charlie has a full ride now to finish his art degree."

"Thanks to a scholarship and my blood, sweat, and tears," he says, his grin widening. "I worked every odd job you can imagine to save up. And yeah, my dad didn't exactly love all the art stuff. He wanted me to do something 'practical.' But if we drop the bullshit, my career choice was just too 'gay.'"

I frown. "What about your mom?"

"She was fine with it," Charlie says. "But she was also . . . distant. My mom's Mexican, from Jalisco, but she is not exactly the 'devoted Mexican mother' type. She was always out and about with her friends, yoga, brunch . . . you know, and I don't think she knew how to connect with me."

I pause, trying to process what he just said. "Wait . . . you're half Mexican?"

"Surprise!" he says with a mock bow. "The white-passing edition. I know, with me looking like this," he gestures to his sun-kissed yet light skin and his bright green eyes, "people don't look at me and think, 'Oh, Mexican.'"

I cover my eyes in embarrassment for having judged based on appearances. "All this time I thought you were a white guy who managed to learn perfect Spanish."

Alex smirks. "It took me a while to figure it out too. He's basically allergic to labels."

Charlie rolls his eyes. "I just don't like being put in a box. But yeah, it's . . . weird sometimes. Like, I get all the privilege of looking white, but it also makes me feel like I don't belong. Like I have to prove my Mexican-ness to people who think I'm lying or exaggerating."

I nod slowly. "I get that. Sort of. I mean, where I'm from, everyone's Mexican. San Ysidro might as well be an extension of Mexico. But here . . . I feel like I stand out for different reasons. Like I'm too obvious."

Alex nudges me. "You don't stand out. You make a statement. Big difference."

I laugh, shaking my head. "Man, this reminds me of what's going on in Mexico right now with the emos."

Charlie perks up. "Wait, what?"

"Oh, it's wild," I say, leaning against the counter. "Right now, punks and *cholos* in Mexico have declared war on emos. Like, actual war. There are marches. There was a whole segment on Televisa where a serious news anchor broke down the emo migration pattern, like they were an endangered species. There was this big confrontation in Mexico City and just when it seemed like the punches were gonna start rolling, this group of Hare Krishna showed up in white and orange robes chanting and mitigated the crowd."

Alex wipes away a tear that rolled down from laughing. "Honestly, that should be how all wars end. If you think about it, they are all just as stupid anyway."

Charlie shakes his head. "See? And you're worried about one professor thinking your essays are too emotional. Humanity has bigger problems."

Alex grins. "Like emo survival."

Charlie raises his gummy bear in a toast. "To Fer, the future poet-rebel of academia."

Their words settle over me like a warm blanket. "Thanks," I say, my voice soft but genuine.

"Anytime. Now, back to work, future essay-writing legend," Charlie tells me while casually tossing the last gummy bear straight into Alex's mouth like they've practiced it a million times.

THE SECOND STRAND: Weaving new paths.

What Doesn't Kill You Makes You Stronger

Lo que no mata, fortalece

AURORA

This morning I was flipping through the channels, not really looking for anything, just letting the images blur past. News, commercials, some game show with flashing lights and exaggerated laughter, more commercials . . . Then, a familiar face stopped me—María Félix, all sharp cheekbones and defiant eyes, staring back at me from the screen.

I set the remote down.

There's something about her—the way she carried herself, like the universe should bow at her feet. She didn't ask for space. She took it. The elegance, the confidence, the sheer force of her presence—it's mesmerizing.

And just like that, I was transported back to my first day in Mexico City.

Carmen wasn't working as a maid anymore. In fact, she was married and expecting her first child, yet thankfully she could still help me land a job. The only catch was that they needed me there within a week, or they'd hire someone else. Too afraid to make any mistakes that would tip my abuelos off that I was about to leave, I waited until the day I was leaving to pack up the things I was taking. I tossed into a bag a week's worth of clothes, my birth certificate, and just enough money to reach the address where I was supposed to meet Carmen. My hands were shaking as I reached under my pillow for my doll, Mary—the last physical tie I had to my father. I'd been so young when he passed, it pains me to admit most memories of him had faded by then. The one thing that could never fade, though, was the love and comfort that was still present when I hugged Mary and thought of him. *"Tú vienes conmigo,"* I told her.

I stealthily headed out with my mom to the bus station, where I would board the bus to Mexico City. Our goodbye was just a quick hug before I got on—not because we didn't care, but because we cared too much. A longer goodbye would've broken us both.

The hustle of the capital overwhelmed me the moment I stepped off the bus. If my memory doesn't fail me, it was March of 1950. The noise, the heat, the endless sea of people—I'd seen nothing like it. The *cocodrilos*, the city's old, rattling cabs, reminded me of giant lizards, crammed with people, their engines sputtering as they rattled down streets too narrow for their bulk. Everything was moving faster than I could keep up with. I had been traveling for hours, drained from the long bus ride and the unfamiliar air that felt thick in my chest. And beneath the exhaustion, a tight knot of panic twisted in my stomach. What if I couldn't find Carmen? Had I gotten off at the wrong stop? Worse—what if I'd gone to the wrong place entirely?

Stepping inside the cocodrilo and handing the driver the small, wrinkled piece of paper that contained my destination address made the reality of what I was doing sink in. The guilt of getting away, of escaping the destiny Pepi hadn't been able to escape, was almost unbearable. I felt the urge to throw myself out of the moving car, to run back to the bus and tell the driver that I'd made a mistake, that I needed to get back to Huejosquite.

It took every ounce of determination in me to remain seated, allowing the driver to take me to the place that would be the start of the rest of my life, away from everyone I'd ever loved. After what felt like forever, the cocodrilo finally stopped. The driver gestured for me to get off in front of a large house, painted a pristine white with a tall iron fence glistened in the midday sun. As I stepped off, my heart skipped a beat when I saw Carmen running toward me. She looked just like the last time I'd seen her back in Huejosquite—familiar and comforting, yet entirely different here in this city that felt so foreign and intimidating.

The knot in my stomach loosened as I made my way toward her. Despite not being close back in the small town, Carmen was all I had here. She was my lifeline, my only link to the world I had left behind. As I approached, Carmen wrapped her arms around me in a hug that was warmer than anything I'd expected. She pulled back with a smile that made the weight on my shoulders ease just a little. "You must be exhausted," she said, her voice soft but firm. "Come on, let me take you to where you'll be staying."

She took my bag, and we began walking down the street together. The city stretched out around us—towering buildings, cars honking as they weaved between one another, and streets crowded with people bustling with purpose. We walked for what, in my state of nerves and exhaustion, felt like a lifetime, and soon she stopped in front of a house nearly identical to the one where she had come from. It had the same gleaming white exterior, the same high fence, and the same neat little yard, but everything about it felt different—bigger, more polished. "We're neighbors," Carmen said with a small, proud smile, as if the simple fact that we were close by made this overwhelming place a little smaller.

Relief flooded me at the sight of the house, and my heart lightened at the thought that I wouldn't be entirely alone in this strange new world. The family I was working for, the Vegas, were well-off, but from the moment I laid eyes on them, they didn't seem particularly intimidating. Doña Constanza, probably in her mid-thirties, gave me a polite nod, while Don Eulalio, a man in his fifties, regarded me briefly.

"He was a police officer who retired when he inherited family money, but he is still very much involved with that crowd," Carmen had told me about Don Eulalio in a warning tone. It was common knowledge that corruption within that circle was a widespread issue, probably not the safest population for a young girl who was new to the city to be around. "I've heard nothing bad about Don Eulalio," she continued, "but if you want my advice, just try to keep your distance when he brings his friends around."

To my relief, the Vegas didn't even spare me a glance as they ushered me inside. Their two boys, Pedrito and Eduardo, walked past, the former offering me a curious smile, while the latter didn't even seem to notice me standing there.

As Doña Constanza showed me around, explaining where I'd be working, the house felt large and daunting, with rooms that seemed too clean and organized for someone like me. She guided me through the house, pointing out chores and routines, giving me instructions on how things should be done. "We're very flexible with the laundry," she said, leading me to a washing machine that was a marvel to me. At my grandparents' house, we didn't have such luxuries—just a washboard, where I'd spent countless hours scrubbing clothes by hand. "Just make sure there are no clothes on the line over the weekends. We like to enjoy the backyard without looking at a bunch of laundry."

"I'll make sure you don't have to," I said, trying to sound confident, though inside I was still trying to wrap my head around all the newness. Doña Constanza continued, her voice measured.

"You'll have Saturdays and Sundays off, unless we need you. We'll let you know if that happens." I nodded, trying to mask the wave of nerves threatening to overtake me. As a last stop, she pointed out my room. I was both eager and a nervous wreck at the thought of settling in for the night, my body aching from the long journey and my mind swirling with questions.

I stepped outside to thank Carmen, who was still waiting by the gate with a reassuring smile. "I know they're not the warmest," she said, her tone soft and understanding. "But they're not bad people. It's always hardest when you first come to the city, but you'll get used to it. Don't worry." Her reassurance was a lifeline, and I clung to it.

"Thank you for everything," I said, my voice faltering as the lump in my throat grew. The city felt so big, and the weight of being here alone hit me all at once.

"Don't mention it," she said, her hand gently touching my arm. "I go to mass on Sundays. Would you like me to meet you here so you can join me? I can show you around after, help you get to know the city a little, introduce you to a few friends."

I smiled—a genuine smile for the first time that day. "That sounds lovely." We agreed on a time, and with one last hug, Carmen left, wishing me luck and promising everything would get better.

❋✧❋✧❋

Sunday morning, Carmen was there, just as she had promised. We went to mass together, meeting two of her other friends, both girls from small towns, also working for families in the neighborhood. Afterward, we wandered the city, mostly window shopping and talking, our laughter echoing off the city walls, but never too loudly. Other than Carmen, the rest of us didn't have much money to spend, but we treated ourselves to lemon popsicles—cold and tart, perfect against the heat.

As we walked, I couldn't help but marvel at how impressive everything seemed. The city was so alive, so full of noise and movement. "I'm still in awe," I said, watching a man in a suit sip coffee at a sidewalk table. "Everything here seems so important."

Carmen's friend, who had introduced herself as Magnolia . . . or was it Martina? shrugged with a knowing smile. "At first, it's all big and shiny. But you get used to it. And then, nothing's as big or scary as it seems. Most people who come here don't go back home, you know?"

I chewed the last of my popsicle, my gaze wandering until a large cinema sign caught my eye. The letters, bold and black, announced *Doña Diabla*, starring María Félix. I barely noticed the crack in the sidewalk until I tripped and fell, hands scraping the ground as I tried to catch myself. Just as I hit the pavement, something—or someone— landed on my back. I felt heat rise to my cheeks as the man, who apparently had been as distracted by the sign as I'd been, scrambled to get up, muttering apologies and scolding the group of teenage boys laughing nearby. He extended a hand to help me up.

The boys' voices rang out. "*¡Cayó en blandito!*" He had a soft landing, they teased, their accents thick with city swagger. I could feel my face turning bright red as I gathered the last shreds of my dignity and stood up, muttering a thank-you to the man, who was already retreating in embarrassment. If that fall was indicative of how my time in the capital would go, I wasn't sure how much longer I could stay. But I was there now, and there was no turning back.

You Can't Teach an Old Dog New Tricks

El perro viejo no aprende trucos nuevos

PILAR

The music still echoed through the large courtyard of Ofelia's house as the quinceañera slowly wound down, reminding me that the time to face the consequences for having left that morning was near. There was no turning back. The mariachi band had packed up, but their final song, 'El Son de la Negra,' lingered in the air, its melody still looping in my thoughts. The sound of footsteps on the stone floor grew louder as people drifted toward the exits, reluctant to leave but knowing the night was drawing to a close. Meño had decided to wait for me outside as I lingered near the edge of the crowd, waiting for an opportunity to talk to Ofelia. The glow of the last fireworks was fading in the distance. The night had been a whirlwind—full of laughter, dancing, and the energy of a celebration so much bigger than my personal turmoil. But as the crowd thinned, the weight of everything I was avoiding came crashing down again.

I stepped out from under the long, colorful banners that hung from the eaves, the cool air of the late autumn night refreshing against my flushed skin. I found a quiet corner of the garden where the shadows of tall, palm-like trees seemed to embrace me. Closing my eyes, I let the faint sound of music drift over me. I knew it was time to leave, but I wasn't ready to face what awaited me at home.

My thoughts kept pulling me back to earlier in the day, the image of my father passed out drunk on the floor, ruining any excitement I'd had for the day. Meño had stepped in, like he always did, to handle the mess while I was forced to play the part of the compliant daughter, slipping out unnoticed, pretending everything was fine. The heavy silence of the house when I'd left in the morning gave way to the noisy celebration of the quinceañera, and for a few hours, I had allowed myself to forget. But the overwhelming sensation of being trapped in a cycle, of having to pretend, was still there, gnawing at me.

The final notes of the music faded, and I realized I was standing alone in the garden, my fingers clutching the delicate lace of my dress as I stared out at the city lights in the distance. For a moment, the world seemed both small and immense. Mexico City, with all its vibrancy, felt so far away from the tangled mess of my family's reality.

I heard the faint sound of footsteps and turned to find Ofelia approaching, her face glowing, a smile still lingering on her lips despite the night winding down. "Pili," Ofelia said softly, her voice quieter now as she came to stand beside me. "I'm so glad you came, glad I got to share this special night with you."

I gave her a small smile, trying to push away the bitter thoughts of my father. "I wouldn't have missed it for anything."

Ofelia leaned against the garden wall, eyes turning toward the fading lights of the celebration. "It feels like a dream, doesn't it? So much work, so much preparation, and then it's over in the blink of an eye."

I nodded, still lost in my thoughts. "I know. But I'm happy for you. You deserve all of this."

Ofelia glanced at me sideways, sensing something behind my distracted expression. "Is everything okay?" she asked, her tone softer now, more concerned.

I hesitated, not wanting to burden Ofelia on her big day, but the weight of it all pressed against my chest. "Yeah, just . . . I don't know. It's complicated."

Ofelia placed a hand gently on my shoulder, offering the same warmth that she always had. "You know you can talk to me, right?"

I let out a breath, trying to hide the tension on my face. Another night. Another mess. But Meño had promised to handle it. He always did. I should trust him—I knew that.

"I have to go," I said. "Meño has been waiting for me for a while now. I told him I wanted a moment to thank you for what you did for me tonight."

Ofelia nodded. "I get it. Just . . . true friends don't need to ask. They see the places you're too afraid to show. Whatever it is, remember to give yourself some grace. I love you."

I smiled, trying to reassure her. "I will. I promise."

The two of us shared a quiet moment before I finally turned toward the exit. The night air was cooling against my face as Meño and I silently headed back home.

When we reached home, it was eerily quiet. I stepped inside, Meño in tow, our footsteps soft against the tiles. When I passed my father's open bedroom door on the way to my room, I realized he wasn't home. It felt wrong, the emptiness of it all, but it was also a strange relief. I wasn't sure I wanted answers—I was growing tired of that cycle. The space where my father should have been felt vacant in more ways than one, but I wasn't sure if it was for better or for worse.

Three nights later, when my father returned, it was as if nothing had happened. His steps were heavy and slow, his face drawn with an exhaustion I hadn't seen in a while. But there was no apology, no explanation, just that same look of indifference.

Where were you? Part of me wanted to ask, but my throat was tight with all the unsaid words.

He shrugged, as if reading my mind. Then he slumped down onto the couch, his gaze distant. "I'm here now, and I'll be damned if I need to explain things in my own house. Let it go."

Let it go. It was always the same. The same cycle repeating over and over. Like being caught in a current, pulled under just when I thought I could catch my breath—no way out, no way to stop, no choice but to endure it. I wanted to scream, to demand more, but I didn't have the strength for it. Not then, and maybe not ever.

I stood there for a long moment, looking at him—the man who ruined everything over and over again. He had no answers, and even if he did, he'd never care to give me any. So, I left him there, alone in his silence, and walked away into my room.

Later, as I lay in bed, the events from that morning came back to me. The line my father had crossed by insulting me the way he did. The way his words had triggered Meño into a violent reaction. I was used to walking on eggshells, but that morning, things had escalated in a way that truly frightened me.

I knew one thing for sure: things would never be the same. But something had to give, or they would never change, either.

The Heart Has Reasons That Reason Cannot Understand

El corazón tiene razones que la razón no entiende

FER

Some things never change, and other times, change comes so quickly that it leaves you breathless, forcing you to adjust in ways you never thought possible. This is exactly what moving into the apartment with Alex and Charlie feels like.

Earlier today, my parents confronted me about moving out. The memory keeps replaying in my mind like a bad recording. "You're moving in with a guy?!" my father's voice boomed across the living room, his face a deep shade of red. His reaction was nothing short of what I expected and that's why I kept my moving-out plans to myself till this very day.

"And Alex," I said flatly, crossing my arms.

"And Alex?" he shot back, his eyes narrowing.

"She's my friend. That's all you need to know," I replied, my tone clipped. I wasn't about to explain anything more. He didn't deserve my effort.

"It's not proper," he said, leaning forward in his chair. "A young woman living with a man, and . . . "

I folded my arms tighter. "You don't get to talk to me about what's 'proper.' Not after everything you've done."

The room went silent. My mother's eyes darted toward him, then down at the floor. My father's jaw tightened, but he didn't deny it. "I don't want to argue," my mother said softly, her hands twisting the hem of her shirt. "Fer, we just want what's best for you."

"No," I said, my voice firm. "You want what's easiest for you. What makes you look good. There's a difference." I grabbed my bag and walked out before either of them could stop me.

Now, as I unpack another box in my new room, the room I'll be sharing with Alex, the memory echoes in my mind, each replay reigniting the anger simmering beneath the surface. Alex pokes her head in the room. "You okay?" she asks, leaning against the frame.

I swipe away an angry tear before turning to face her. "Yeah," I lie, forcing a smile.

She gives me a knowing look but doesn't press. "We're ready for the movie whenever you are."

"Thanks, be there in a minute."

As she leaves, I take a deep breath and glance around the room. Living here with Alex and Charlie feels safe, like a clean slate. But no matter how far I run, the anger follows. Anger at my dad, for what he's done, and at my mom, for forgiving him so easily.

How could they expect me to stay, knowing what I know? How can they expect me to live their version of "proper" when their own house is built on lies?

The thing is, I can't live under the same roof as my parents anymore, not after everything that happened. I can't keep pretending that everything was fine when all I see is her quietly accepting his mistakes, trying to keep up the pretense of a perfect family while he wandered off with another woman. Am I supposed to just let that slide? Am I supposed to stay in that house, silently watching her accept this distorted version of love, just so things can *look* okay?

Earlier, I'd heard my mother whisper-arguing in the room with him as I finished packing up, her voice strained: "She will have a female roommate as well, she's not just moving in with some guy." It felt like a slap in the face. Was she really defending me on this? Or was she just trying to avoid the judgment? It was as if her entire focus was on appearances—how things *looked*—when in truth I felt like I was suffocating in their carefully constructed "perfect" image of a family.

Once I'm done unpacking everything, I join Alex and Charlie in the living room. The three of us crowd around a small table, setting up a mini snack bar. For the first time in weeks, something like relief washes over me. It's such a simple thing, but for once, I'm away from my father's double standards and expectations.

"To new beginnings," Alex says, holding up her mug of coffee, the warmth from the mug mirroring the warmth I get from being here.

"Cheers," I say, tapping my World's Best Grandma mug against hers.

Charlie lifts his beer can, his expression mock-disapproving. "Cheers," he says, shaking his head at our "boring" beverage choice.

"What? Not all of us are living off booze and Cup Noodles," Alex teases.

"You two are like an old married couple," I say, grinning. "Don't forget to invite me to the wedding."

Truthfully, when Alex first told me she lives with Charlie on that first walk together to The Bargain Bear, I felt what I'm just now realizing was a strange pang of jealousy. I didn't really know why at first, but it had something to do with the way she said his name, with how evident it was they were so easy with each other. It made me feel . . . left out? But that feeling didn't last. Charlie is the kind of person whose impossible not to like: so warm, so friendly, and most importantly . . . so not interested in women in any way that is not strictly platonic. After meeting him, I knew there was nothing like *that* going on between him and Alex.

Halfway through our second movie, all three of us are fighting to keep our eyes open, so we decide to call it a night. Charlie heads to his room, and Alex and I head to our shared bedroom. The room barely fits Alex's full-size bed and my twin mattress, which I still need to buy a base for, but somehow it's cozy. It's *ours*.

"Do you mind if I play just one song?" Alex asks, her voice still a little too awake. "I can't sleep without music, and my earphones are busted. I promise I won't turn it up too loud."

"That's cool," I say, already drifting off into the comfort of our shared space.

A few seconds later, the soft, familiar sound of a song plays. It's a tune I recognize, yet the lyrics are not what I expected. Suddenly, I'm wide awake again.

"Nooo!" I exclaim, sitting straight up on my mattress. "You've got to be kidding me."

Alex looks at me, startled. "What? Please don't tell me you hate the Smiths. We can't be friends if you do."

"That's the Smiths?" I ask, in shock.

"You don't know the Smiths?" she asks, eyes wide with disbelief.

"I've heard *of* the Smiths, I guess, but if they performed in front of me, I'd probably ask for the name of their band after the show." I admit, suddenly feeling like I don't belong to this world of music either.

Alex bursts out laughing, clutching her chest. "Not knowing them is worse than hating them! I'm going to have to reconsider our entire friendship now."

I can't help but laugh with her, the weight of the past few weeks melting away, just for a moment. "Don't laugh, but I've heard that song before and I love it. I just thought it was by a Spanish singer. This is . . . this is a worse tragedy than when Marimar unknowingly ate her *gallina*."

"Ah, I've been there!" she says. "I hate when that happens. But this one's on you. The Smiths, Fer. The *motherfucking* Smiths!"

We laugh so hard that we almost forget that just a few minutes ago we were dying to go to sleep. We swap iPods and make a playlist for each other, sharing music we're passionate about. I introduce Alex to some classic rock en español beyond the radio hits, and she opens my eyes, or should I say my ears, to R&B, classic English rock, and some newer artists I haven't heard of before. It becomes our thing: every night, we listen to each other's recommended songs before we fall asleep.

❁✧❁✧❁

It's late, and The Bargain Bear is finally closed for the night. The air is thick with the scent of old books, like it's clinging to us after hours of shelving, organizing, and joking around. Alex and I are perched on the counter, munching on leftover cookies Charlie swiped from a café down the street before heading home. The quiet hum of the fluorescent lights fills the space, soothing in its own way.

"This place has a vibe," Alex says, brushing crumbs off her jeans. "Like, it smells a little weird, but it feels . . . cozy. Comfortably chaotic, you know?"

I laugh. "That's one way to put it. I think I'm just used to chaos. My high school was kind of like this place. Messy but full of heart."

Alex tilts her head, curious. "What was your high school like?"

I hesitate, trying to put it into words. "It was . . . relatively large. Definitely underfunded. But my teachers? They cared. Like, a lot. They fought hard for us to have as much as we could, even though it never felt like enough."

She nods, leaning back on her hands. "Yeah, my teachers cared too, but it was different. I mean, they had the resources to back it up. My school was mostly white and . . . let's just say 'comfortable.' We had everything—AP classes, sports teams for almost everything you could think of, a theater program, a pool. Hell, we even had a robotics club."

"A pool," I repeat, laughing softly. "You know, our principal promised us a pool once. Said we were this close to getting the grant for it. But, of course, it fell through. Same with the theater program they swore we'd have 'next year.' It never came, but they left the sign-up sheet in the office for months. Just sitting there, mocking us."

Alex winces. "That sucks. I guess I didn't really think about it, but . . . yeah. My school didn't have to hope for grants. We just . . . had things."

"Must've been nice," I say, no bitterness in my voice, just curiosity.

"It was," she admits. "But it had its downsides too. I was usually the only brown face in the room. The token Mexican kid. And yeah, my parents were doing well financially by then, but my classmates didn't let me forget where I came from. I remember once, in history class, the teacher started talking about immigration, and someone turned to me and said, 'Hey, Alex, is that how your family got here?' Like I was the spokesperson for all Mexicans. It wasn't even an ill-intended question either."

I grimace. "Yeah, that sounds about right. At least at my school, we were all in it together. Almost everyone was Mexican-American, so no one ever felt out of place like that. But . . . I guess it also meant we didn't have as much to aim for. No one really talked about college the way they should've. We didn't have counselors making sure we knew our options. Not that they didn't care—there were just too many of us and too few of them.

"For my friends who mostly had average grades, it was more like, 'Get through high school, get a job, help your family.' I always kept a high GPA, so for me, it was a little different."

Alex looks thoughtful, her expression softening. "You made it here, though. That says something. A lot, actually."

I shrug, but her words hit something deep in me. "Yeah, but sometimes it feels like . . . I don't know. Like I'm playing catch-up. Like everyone else already had a head start, and I'm just trying to figure out how to keep up."

"You're not playing catch-up," Alex says firmly. "You're climbing.

And climbing is harder, yeah, but it also makes you stronger. You're not here by accident, Fer. You earned this."

I smile at her, grateful for the reassurance. "Thanks. And you're not the token Mexican kid anymore. At least not while I'm here."

She laughs, her eyes bright. "Damn right. Now I'm just the cool one."

"Debatable," I tease, nudging her shoulder.

As we laugh, the differences between us shrink. They become a little easier to bridge. And I'm grateful to know I'm not playing catch-up alone.

Nothing Comes Free

Al que quiere azul celeste, que le cueste

AURORA

I'm not sure why today felt like the right day to tell them. Maybe it's because I was feeling better than I've felt since my chemo, less drained, less weighed down by the constant exhaustion. Or maybe I was just tired of holding it all in.

So, I called my children.

I had practiced the words in my head for days, but when the moment came, they still got tangled on my tongue. I could hear the way my children's voices tightened, like they were swallowing back tears, trying to stay steady for my sake. But they took the news better than I had feared. No panic, no desperate reassurances, just quiet understanding.

They, of course, offered their support, reminding me I don't have to do this alone. And maybe they were right. Segundo was right too, telling me I've always carried too much on my own. I've never quite known how to let others share the load, but today I finally did it, and it felt good to let it all out.

Letting go, even just a little, is an adjustment. But I am learning.

After all, adjusting is something I've done my whole life. I adjusted to moving in with my abuelos, then to leaving Huejosquite, to working for strangers, to carving out a life that belonged only to me. It wasn't easy then, and it's not easy now, but I've had to learn how to survive, how to keep moving forward even when the path ahead is uncertain.

It took a few months, but I slowly adjusted to my new life in the capital.

Working for Don Eulalio and Doña Constanza had been, in a way, easier than I imagined. It was simpler to be invisible in this new place, where everyone seemed to live their lives without even noticing me, than it ever was in Huejosquite, where I had always felt like a burden to my abuelos. Neither place offered a home I could call my own. The loneliness, though, was something I hadn't expected. It was a quiet ache that followed me around the grand house, from the tall, gleaming windows that looked out onto the bustling streets below, to the lavish marble floors that echoed with the sound of my footsteps as I cleaned.

I missed my mother terribly. I hadn't seen her face in months, not since the day I left Huejosquite, not since I'd hugged her goodbye at the bus station, knowing that my only chance at freedom was in the city, even if it meant I had to work as a maid. I longed to hear her voice, to see her smile.

But more than anyone, I worried about Pepi. What happened to her haunted me every day—the thought of her being swept away by a vile man, forced into a life she didn't ask for. I promised myself I wouldn't let that be my fate, but as I moved through the days in this strange, cold house, I wondered if Pepi would ever find a way out.

I still felt deeply guilty about having gotten away while Pepi couldn't. Logically, I knew there was nothing I could have done differently for her if I'd stayed in Huejosquite, but that knowledge provided little relief. But one thing I could do differently now that I was in the city was send my mother money that was just for her— money that my abuelos didn't know about and therefore couldn't take away. It felt great to be able to give her at least a small sense of independence.

Even though life with Don Eulalio and Doña Constanza was better than I had feared, it wasn't without its own complexities. The house was large and ornate, everything polished and immaculate, but I was little more than a shadow in their world.

Don Eulalio, with his thick mustache and ever-present cigar, had always been respectful. There was an indifference in his eyes that made it clear I was nothing more than a servant to him. Doña Constanza was distant and aloof. She had a grace about her, always moving with purpose, and yet she rarely spoke to me beyond what was necessary. They expected little from me beyond making sure the house was spotless and that their meals were on time—mindless tasks similar to those my abuelos had expected from me at their home and store. I knew that, even with their polite indifference, they saw me as little more than a fixture in the background of their elegant lives.

The evenings, though, were the hardest.

Don Eulalio occasionally had friends over for dominoes, mostly men in law enforcement. That was when the house would fill with noise, with laughter and shouting, the clinking of glasses, and the smell of cigars. Keeping Carmen's advice always present, I would stand at the edge of the room, pretending to be busy—dusting the furniture or organizing the kitchen—while the men argued about politics or the best way to play dominoes. I wished I were free to go to my room instead of having to stand around waiting in case someone needed another drink.

I tried not to listen, but sometimes I couldn't help it. Their words were harsh, often filled with disdain for the poor or for anyone who wasn't as wealthy as they were. In those moments, I tried to be as invisible as possible, keeping my head down, staying out of the way.

There was one man in particular that made me uneasy—Manuel.

While the rest of them engaged in conversations that revealed their classism, their machismo, and all those other *isms*, none of them conducted themselves the way Manuel did. He was a good-looking man who seemed to take pride in his appearance. His thick, jet-black hair was always perfectly slicked back, and his mustache neatly trimmed. His shoulders were broad, yet he had an athletic body.

I could see how the ladies "were all drawn to him," as he constantly bragged to the other men. Yet, the way he carried himself made me certain that none of them wanted to stick around him any longer than he wanted to stick around them.

There was an air of arrogance to him, always making jokes at the other men's expense, leading me to believe that he might be a recurring invitee to domino nights because of his position of power rather than genuine popularity.

The thing that made my stomach twist every time I saw him arrive, though, was the way he spoke to me—like he owned me, rather than me simply working at the place where he was a guest.

When he was there, I tried to spend as much time as possible in the kitchen instead of the dining room where they would usually have their gatherings. I would hear the laughter and chatter in the other room and wonder what my mother was doing.

Was she sitting alone, waiting for something, for someone to come home and give her life meaning again? Was she crying, the same way I did, wishing for a way out?

I don't know how many times I stood by the window at night, looking out over the city lights, clutching the small bundle of letters I had received from my mother.

I'd rip each new letter open, hoping to hear news about Pepi or about Paco. And every single time there was no news, I thought about running back—about gathering my few belongings and just returning to Huejosquite where I could at least be with her.

But I stopped myself.

Three things held me back.

The first was the thought that my grandparents would never take me back after having left behind their back. My letters to my mother had to be delivered through an intermediary, someone who would hand them off to her with no questions. To my abuelos, I was dead.

The second was my mother and Segundo. They had sacrificed so much, and their hopes for my future were bigger than any other person had ever given me credit for. I couldn't let them down.

And then there was Paco, tucked there safely in a corner of my mind and my heart. I admired the way he had taken a chance—leaving everything familiar behind to seek better opportunities for himself and his family. If I ever hoped to have a future with him, I knew I had to find the courage to do the same.

I didn't know what lay ahead, but I knew one thing: I couldn't go back.

Not yet.

I had come to Mexico City to escape my fate, but every day proved that I was only running in circles.

Where There's Smoke, There's Fire

Cuando el río suena, agua lleva

PILAR

It's hard to remember the details of that day. Everything is so far away, like a dream, like something that happened to someone else. But I can still feel the weight of it, that tension in the air, like the city itself was holding its breath, waiting for something to break while I was stuck there, running in circles.

The protests had been building for months, and even though I didn't fully understand it all, I could sense the change. The city was alive with rumors and slogans, everyone talking about the Olympics—which were now only ten days away—about the government, about what was happening in the streets.

My father tried to hide it from me, tried to pretend it wasn't happening at all. But I could see the way he would glance at the news reports, the way his jaw would tighten whenever the topic of the students came up. He said it was nothing to worry about, that it was all just noise. But I knew he was lying. We all did.

He was more irritable than ever, and I'd overheard him and some of his police friends complaining about the extra work all the manifestations were causing them.

That morning, the morning of October 2, 1968, I remember the stillness in the air as I got ready for the day. My brother Meño, usually so full of life, was quieter than usual. He seemed on edge, his eyes darting toward the door, like he was waiting for something.

I didn't understand it then, but looking back, I think he was waiting for Dad to leave so he could go too. Same destination, different reasons.

Our father had told me not to go out, to stay inside. But at the time, I thought it was just another one of his senseless prohibitions. He'd always been like that. He often forbade me from doing things, but he was never one for explanations.

There was something in his eyes, though, a flicker of something I hadn't seen before. Fear, maybe. Or guilt.

I didn't ask questions. I didn't know what to say.

I'd known he was working that day, so I'd invited Julia and Ofelia over. We hadn't seen each other in the four days since the quinceañera, and we had so much to talk about.

I was surprised when Chava showed up with Ofelia. It was supposed to be one of our usual girls' days of magazine cutouts and gossip.

Before I could ask about it, Meño stood up and announced that he and Chava were going out. "If Dad gets home before me," Meño added as he opened the front door, "tell him you don't know who I went out with."

Although Meño hadn't given me a straight answer when I'd asked, I could sense that when it came to politics, he sided with Chava. Seeing them head out together that day, after the particularly tense morning we'd had, filled me with uneasiness.

The world was moving too fast for me to keep up.

Julia headed back home around five in the afternoon. Neither Meño nor my father was back home by then, so Ofelia stayed longer to keep me company.

Around six thirty, we started hearing the commotion outside. The sirens. The neighbors stepping outside, trying to figure out what was going on. The rumors of gunshots.

And then, the news started to spread.

The government had opened fire on the students.

Ofelia's mother showed up at my door shortly after. After confirming that there was no one else home with us, she directed me and Ofelia to go with her back to their home. I didn't even think about Dad instructing me not to go out; the look on her face—a look I couldn't explain even if I tried to—made me do as she said.

"I'm not sure what happened yet, but I think it's really bad," she said as she sped-walked home, Ofelia and me in tow. "I think Chava and Meño were there."

I can't remember how I got from hearing Ofelia's mother's words to being seated in her living room, along with Ofelia and Don Rafael, Ofelia's father.

We huddled together with both the radio and the television on, worried sick about Chava and Meño.

Nothing.

No news.

It was unbelievable.

By nightfall, the names started trickling in, but not from the media. A group of women was now gathered in Ofelia's house, while Don Rafael and the other men had gone out in search of answers.

When some of the men returned, Chava's was one of the first names I heard.

"He was right there, at Tlatelolco," someone murmured. "He didn't make it out."

Ofelia's mother fell to her knees. The sound that escaped her was unlike anything I'd ever heard before. Raw, guttural—something that was not a scream exactly, nor was it a cry. It was something in between. A haunting wail that seemed to tear free from the deepest part of her soul and claw its way into the air, filling the room with a grief so profound it seemed to silence everything else.

It wasn't just a sound.

It was a physical embodiment of heartbreak.

A noise that carried the weight of every shattered hope and unanswered prayer.

Ofelia fell to her mother's side, and they remained there, on the floor, wrapped in an embrace that seemed to be the only thing helping them cling to life.

I barely had time to process it before panic gripped me from the inside out. If Chava hadn't made it out, did that mean Meño hadn't either?

Just then, Meño walked in.

His face was pale, almost gray, as if the blood had drained from his skin and left him frozen in time. When his eyes met mine, his lips trembled slightly, parted like he was trying to speak, but no words came out.

I rushed over to him and wrapped my arms around him, clinging to him like my life depended on it.

I couldn't breathe. It was like someone had reached into my chest and ripped out my heart. How could he have come that close to being gone? And how could someone like Chava—so full of life, so passionate about a better future for the country—just disappear like that?

His face. His laugh. His stories about the future.

Gone.

Just gone.

Emphasizing what I'd known ever since I could remember—that some absences echo louder than words ever could.

My mind kept circling back to the moments we'd shared just a few days back. To the moments I last saw him—smiling, laughing at some stupid joke we made or at the fact that I couldn't avoid stepping on his toes in my attempt to waltz along with him.

I couldn't wrap my head around the fact that he was gone. That he wouldn't be there to laugh again, to joke about everything that didn't matter.

When we got back home that night, my father said nothing, not even to ask where we had been.

He was sitting on the couch, his face pale, his eyes dull, like he had seen something that had broken him. Maybe he had. Maybe he had been a part of it. I didn't know then, and I still don't.

But when he looked at me that night, I saw something cold in his eyes—something that scared me more than anything else.

We didn't exchange a single word, but in my father's house, silence that deep didn't mean peace. It meant survival. Regardless, I didn't want to know.

Meño walked straight to his room, neither one of them acknowledging the other's presence.

And then, the next morning, my father was gone. No goodbye. No note. Just vanished, as if the city had swallowed him whole. No one had seen him. No one knew where he'd gone.

The opened, scattered drawers in his room made one thing clear—he had no intention of coming back. At least, not anytime soon.

Family sticks together, no matter what.

So much for all that bullshit.

The world had fallen apart, and so had I.

But it wasn't just me. Ofelia's family was packing to leave the city, trying to escape the pain, the reminders of everything they had lost. Ofelia's parents had already made up their minds. They couldn't stay in the city anymore. It didn't feel safe for anyone, not with everything that had happened.

I think they were running from the memories, from the images of Chava's face during his last moments that would haunt them forever.

I didn't blame them for it, not really. I just followed, numb, silent, not knowing where I was going—just knowing that I couldn't stay there.

But it was hard to let go of everything.

Hard to leave the city that had been my home for so long.

Hard to leave behind everything I had ever known.

Meño and I—we didn't have much of a choice.

Both parents had abandoned us.

We didn't have the means to stay in the city on our own, two unemployed minors. What else could we have done? Go to the family our father had kept us away from?

Most of all, I think we were both just trying to get away from the pain, from the memories that had carved themselves into our souls.

The day I told Julia I was leaving with Ofelia's family was one of the hardest days of my life.

"You don't have to leave," she said in a pleading tone. "I can talk to my parents, I can convince them to let you and Meño live with us. At least until your father returns."

My friend, who was usually so feisty, looked so broken. Tears were running in an endless stream down her cheeks.

"I hate that we're both leaving," I admitted, my own voice breaking. "It's always been the three of us. I hate the idea of being away from you. But Meño hasn't been the same since that day. Whatever it is he witnessed, it wakes him up at night. Sometimes his own screams wake him up. Ofelia's mother thinks that putting distance between him and the place that has caused him such torment will be good for him, and I agree."

Julia didn't try to convince me otherwise. She had seen what the massacre had done to Meño, and to Ofelia's family. Instead, she hugged me tightly, and we both promised to stay in touch.

As we rode in the back of Don Rafael's car, I kept thinking about my father. About how he had disappeared, just like my mother.

Maybe he had been a part of it. Maybe he had known more than he let on. But knowing would probably hurt me more than not knowing.

Everything was just so broken. We were leaving the city behind, but I couldn't see how it would ever leave us. How it would ever stop haunting us.

And all we could do was keep moving forward.
Keep breathing.
Keep surviving.
Even when it felt like there was nothing much left to hold on to.

Don't Air Your Dirty Laundry in Public

Los trapos sucios se lavan en casa

FER

I'm sitting in my second favorite class this semester—Women's Studies 101. It would be my absolute favorite if it weren't for the fact that Alex isn't here with me. She's in another class this hour, which means I'm sitting here with a bunch of strangers, holding on tightly to my pen while I daydream about what it would be like if she were by my side.

"Raise your hand if you've seen your vagina in a mirror," Professor Myers asks with a smirk that's somehow both mischievous and completely at ease.

She's one of those professors you can't help but admire. In her late forties or early fifties, she has wild blonde curls that bounce with every movement, free and untamed, just like her energy. She sweeps a strand of hair from her blue eyes, scanning the room for any sign of a raised hand, and an unexpected flush spreads across my cheeks.

The question blindsides me. My family never openly discussed genitalia or anything remotely related to it. Even the thought of it makes me tense, and I instinctively shrink into myself as if trying to disappear. The only woman in the room who doesn't hesitate to raise her hand is an older student, probably around my mom's age. She lifts her hand as though it's no big deal, and I'm just sitting here, about to combust with awkwardness.

I can't help but think about my mom. She'd rather die than admit to something like that in front of a class.

I remember the time, when I was seven or eight, I saw a box of tampons in the shopping cart of the woman ahead of us at the store. My curiosity was piqued, and I stupidly blurted out, "What are those?"

My mom's face turned red as she whispered, "I don't know," in such a rush that it made me drop the subject right then and there.

It wasn't until middle school, well after my first period, that I figured out what tampons were. Everything I learned about sex came from online searches or from giggles and whispers from friends. No one had ever sat me down and said, *Here's the deal*, like they had with my friends—not even the "birds and bees" version.

Back then, I thought I was lucky to avoid the cringe-worthy conversations, but sitting in this class, I'm wondering why such topics are still considered so taboo.

After a few more awkward seconds of no one wanting to raise their hand, three other students make half-assed gestures.

I've definitely seen my vagina in a mirror.

But raising my hand now is an impossible task. So, I keep gripping my pen tightly and avoid eye contact, wishing the floor would open up and swallow me whole.

Professor Myers stands at the front of the lecture hall, her voice clear and confident.

"It's important to know our bodies," she says. "Just like no one's ashamed to look at their hands, there should be no shame in looking at your vagina or any other part of your body. Men touch their penises every day with no one batting an eyelash, so why is it we're taught to hide from our own bodies?"

She pauses, letting the words settle, then adds with a sly smile, "And it's not all just pussy either."

The room bursts into laughter—the kind that comes from relief after a moment of intense tension breaking like a dam.

As we shift into discussing the reading, my focus wavers. Her words linger in my mind, circling back to the mirror question she posed.

I think about the first time I'd had sex—how confusing it had been, how much easier it might've been if I'd known my own body better.

My thoughts wander somewhere they shouldn't.

Alex.

I can't stop myself from wondering: Is her body like mine? Does it look the same, or is it different in ways I can't picture? Does she like to be touched the same way I do?

The thought sends an involuntary shiver up my spine, and I shift uncomfortably in my seat.

I can't help it. My mind is a whirlwind of questions and ideas I've tried to ignore ever since that moment in the stockroom.

Did we almost . . . ? Was that what happened? Or am I imagining it?

That moment keeps replaying in my head, tangled up with emotions I can't quite name. No matter how hard I try to suppress it, the memory won't let me go.

It's been several weeks now since what I've come to think of as *the almost-kiss* with Alex, and it's been bugging me—like a nagging question I can't answer.

Things between us haven't been weird. There's no tension, no awkwardness, but I replay that moment over and over in my head. Every time I think about it, my stomach flutters, and I feel like I missed out on something.

It's strange because I've always known that Alex is bi.

She told me as much during one of our first walks to The Bargain Bear. She made a casual comment about avoiding the Koala Coffee cart because of some "summer drama" with a blue-haired barista, and that's when she revealed it.

"So, you're . . . ?" I asked, trying not to sound too obvious.

"I'm bi," Alex said before I could finish my sentence.

"Caffeine deprived, is what I was going to ask," I joked, laughing to deflect.

"More like love deprived," she replied with a dramatic flourish. "What about you? Seeing anyone?"

I gave her the quick version about Three and somehow didn't scared her off with the more personal details of my life. She limited herself to listening and nodding when I told her about my dad's affair.

Now, sitting here in class, being forced to confront questions about my body and my sexuality, I think about Alex's honesty.

It makes me question everything.

Back then, I'd self-identified as straight. But now?

Now I'm not so sure.

That near-kiss in the stockroom keeps coming back to me. If Charlie hadn't walked in, I'm pretty sure Alex would have kissed me.

I would have kissed her back.

I don't know what's scarier—admitting to myself that my feelings for her are more than friendly or realizing that I have no idea how to deal with it. I'm used to considering myself an ally of the LGBT community, not a part of it.

Coming to terms with this realization? Imagining having to confront the members of my family who claim to be "neutral" yet use terms like *raritos* and *those type of people*? Not to mention, how would I confront the members of my family who don't even claim to be neutral?

It's not something I expected.

It's not something I wanted.

But these feelings are here, and I don't know how long I can keep pretending otherwise.

You Can't Force a Square Peg Into a Round Hole

A fuerza, ni los zapatos entran

AURORA

The doctor warned me that after the second session, my hair would most likely start falling out. It thinned out after the first one. It's strange how, now in my seventies, that thought makes me sad.

When I was younger, I never thought I'd care so much about something so vain, but I do. I enjoy waking up, brushing my hair, putting myself together—looking presentable, even if I have nowhere to go.

Funny, how something as simple as brushing my hair now feels like defiance. Back then, I would've shaved it off myself if it meant he'd stop looking at me.

I remember that night so clearly.

It was one of those Friday evenings when Don Eulalio would host his friends for their usual domino game. I'd been working as his maid for a few months by then, getting used to those gatherings, quietly staying out of the way, only stepping in when someone needed more food or another drink.

The house was warm and buzzing with conversation, the clink of dominoes mixing with the sounds of laughter and loud voices. I was in the kitchen, doing the dishes, trying to keep busy, trying to stay unnoticed. I had learned by then that being invisible was the safest way to be.

But then, I heard his voice.

Manuel.

He was usually drunk by the end of the night, but that night he'd shown up already drunk.

"Aurora," he called from the other room, his voice low and thick with alcohol.

I froze. My heart pounded in my chest. I knew this tone. It was one I dreaded.

I tried to ignore it, but then he called me again, louder this time.

"Come here."

I did as I was told, my feet practically moving against my will. When I stepped into the dining room, the weight of their eyes landed on me.

Manuel stood, his hand on the back of his chair, a sloppy grin plastered on his face.

"Bring us another round of drinks," he ordered, his voice too casual, too commanding. "What are you standing around for?"

I swallowed, trying to push the unease down.

"Of course, Señor Manuel," I said, forcing my voice to stay calm, even as I felt the familiar tightness in my chest.

I turned to gather the bottles, but as I did, I felt his presence behind me. He was standing much too close now. I could smell the alcohol on his breath, feel the heat of his body. I ignored the impulse to step away. I wasn't supposed to step away. That wasn't my place.

"You know," he said, his voice lowering to a near whisper, "I think you're getting more beautiful every time I see you."

His words hung in the air, thick with something unspoken.

"A woman who knows how to stay in the background . . . you could come out of the shadows a little. What do you say? A drink with me? A little conversation?"

His words felt like hands reaching for me, but I knew better than to let them touch me. I forced a smile, hoping he would go away, but instead, he stepped closer, his body blocking my path.

"You're a grown woman, aren't you?" he added, his eyes scanning me as if I were some kind of prize to be claimed. "No reason to be so shy."

I tried to step back, but his hand shot out and grabbed my wrist— too tight, too insistent. I was acutely aware of his fingers digging into my skin, but I couldn't make myself move. I had to stay calm. I had to keep control.

"I . . . I have to get back to my work, Señor Manuel," I said, my voice barely a whisper.

His grip tightened, and a smirk spread slowly across his lips.

"Come on," he said, his voice rising slightly. "You don't have to be so cold. Just a little drink. Just a little company."

Somehow, I managed to jerk my wrist free from his grasp. My breath was coming in short, panicked bursts now, but I stood my ground. I couldn't let him see me break. Not here. Not like this.

"I have work to do," I said, louder this time, trying to make it clear that I would not play along.

Manuel blinked, his smirk faltering for a moment, but then it returned, even wider, more mocking.

"Fine," he said, raising his hands in mock surrender. "No need to get upset. But I'll be waiting, Aurora. You're a woman, after all. You'll figure things out sooner or later."

He turned back to his friends, leaving me standing there, heart racing in my chest, every muscle frozen.

I felt small. Like nothing more than a shadow in the corner.

But I wasn't invisible anymore.

Not to him.

I turned and hurried back to the kitchen. My mind was whirling, my thoughts a blur of confusion and anger. I felt sick to my stomach.

He'd crossed a line, but worse—he didn't even see it.

It was all just a game to him.

I felt the walls closing in around me, trapping me in a world where I was nothing more than a servant to their whims, a shadow to their light.

And I would always be just that.

Until I could find a way to escape.

Again.

Whether it meant working for a different family or trying my luck in a different city, I didn't know.

All I knew was that Manuel had started to pay too much attention to me.

And staying there wasn't safe anymore.

There's None So Blind as Those Who Will Not See

No hay peor ciego que el que no quiere ver

PILAR

Alone in my room, after discovering my father had left, I opened the bottom drawer of my dresser and reached to the very back where I kept her tucked away safely.

My doll.

She wasn't much to look at anymore. Her once-blue dress had long ago faded to a pale grayish hue, and there was a small bald spot where her yarn hair had fallen off. But she was mine.

I picked her up gently and ran my fingers over the stitched name under her dress. The letters were pretty but uneven, clearly stitched by hand, and I knew exactly who had stitched them.

My mother.

I couldn't understand it. How could the same woman who'd once cared enough to sit down and carefully stitch letter by letter on this doll, giving her a name, be the same woman who abandoned the child this doll was meant for?

I held Mary against my chest and sat down on the bed. Many times throughout my childhood, my father had tried to take her away from me. But apparently, even as a baby, I'd clung to Mary like my life depended on it. I vaguely recall how her scent, faint and warm, was the only thing that kept me from crying at night when I was younger.

My father had grudgingly let me keep her, but as I got a little older, I figured out that it was better to keep her out of his sight.

In that moment, she wasn't just a doll.

She was proof that, at least for a little while, one of my parents had thought of me. Proof that maybe I hadn't been so easy to leave behind.

Now they were both gone, yet Mary was still with me.

She was one of the few belongings I took with me when we left Mexico City.

❁✧❁✧❁

We arrived in Tijuana a few days later, though it felt more like a lifetime.

It was Saturday, October 12, 1968—inauguration day for the Olympics. Tijuana was nothing like the Mexico City we'd left behind. It was bright and noisy, its streets alive with the sounds of vendors yelling, children playing, and cars honking as they crawled through the streets.

The Zonkeys, striped donkeys painted to look like zebras, stood proudly along the sidewalks, offering tourists the chance to snap a picture. They were a quirky symbol of the city's wild, whimsical side.

But for all the vibrancy of Tijuana, it felt as though I was looking at it through a fogged-up window, as if it were a place that existed in someone else's world, not mine.

A world someone else had escaped to.

The city was overflowing with life—people hustling and bustling, exchanging goods, talking animatedly in a mix of Spanish and English, even some Spanglish thrown in for good measure. The neon signs along the streets flashed constantly, advertising everything from tequila to the best tacos in Baja.

The rhythm of Tijuana was a fast one, much faster even than Mexico City, though at the time I hardly noticed the difference. My mind was still back in that cold, empty home in Mexico City, still haunted by the names of the students who had died, still trying to make sense of the hollowness that had settled deep within me.

Even now, days after fleeing, the pain of everything we had lost—Chava, our home, the city we'd known—lingered like a silent force holding me down. I could almost hear the gunshots in my mind, picture the faces of the students as they gunned them down in Tlatelolco. I still felt the shock of the news in my bones.

133

I couldn't escape it.

In the car, as we drove away from the memories, I heard Ofelia's parents talking, though their voices were low, as if they thought we were all asleep in the back seat.

They whispered about what had happened.

About *La Matanza de Tlatelolco.*

They said it like it was a name that didn't belong to anything real. The events felt surreal, even in my memory. The wound was still fresh.

I could imagine the voices of the protesters in my mind. Chava among them. Their cries for freedom, for the future, cut short by the sound of gunfire.

How many had died? No one really knew. Some said it was a few hundred; others whispered it was worse.

Doña Carmen's voice trembled as she spoke. "I don't understand how they can just move on, Rafa. The whole city knows what happened. The soldiers killed them like animals, and now . . . now everything is about the Olympics. How can we pretend it didn't happen?"

"No one's pretending, Carmen," Don Rafael replied, his voice quiet but full of anger. "But they've buried it. They've buried the truth. The Olympics are their distraction. They don't want the world to see the blood they spilled. But we saw it. We lived it."

I sat there, pretending to sleep, with Solovino resting on my lap, but every word they spoke felt like it was being carved into my chest.

I thought about Chava again. About how he was no longer with us.

He was just one name among hundreds of others, their stories silenced, their deaths hidden under a veil of government lies and control of the media.

And here, in Tijuana, I was adrift among people who were untouched by the place I had left behind. People who didn't know what it felt like to watch someone who was like a brother to you die in the name of something that was supposed to be right.

Here, life went on.

People were already talking about the Olympics—about the athletes, the opening ceremonies, the medals. No one talked about the students. No one wanted to remember them. It was as if they were just an unfortunate footnote in a much larger story. A story that didn't need to include their blood, their struggle. The tears of those of us left behind.

The government tried to cover it up. Make it disappear. The world had its eyes on the games, and everything else seemed to be forgotten.

We later learned about the heavy censorship—the way they smothered the truth. Journalists stayed silent, too afraid to defy the regime. In Mexico City, the massacre didn't exist on paper, in broadcasts, or in headlines. Everything we knew came from whispers, from the raw, terrified voices of those who had seen it firsthand.

In Tijuana, I wasn't even sure people had heard about it at all.

And yet, while Díaz Ordaz declared the games open, while the world marveled at Enriqueta Basilio—the first woman in Olympic history to light the cauldron—the massacre clung to those of us who had suffered its aftermath.

It refused to be erased from our minds. From our hearts.

Chava refused to be erased. He was just a kid. A little older than me.

I wanted to scream. To shake the world awake. To force it to see what had happened.

Instead, I let the helplessness swallow me whole.

Every Love Has Its Song

Cada amor tiene su canción

FER

As the weeks go by, Alex, Charlie, and I slip into a comfortable routine.

Alex's birthday comes and goes, followed by Charlie's. We celebrate his at a nightclub he somehow manages to get us into, hers with a small bonfire at the beach with some friends.

When my birthday arrives, I'm surprised to see a friend from high school actually show up at the apartment—one I haven't kept in touch with as closely as we promised each other we would.

At all three parties, we have Dr. Pepper mixed with vodka and a *mystery ingredient*—Charlie's concoction, which he dubbed our signature drink. Neither Alex nor I are fans, but we pretend, clinking our glasses together with forced enthusiasm before slyly dumping it when no one's looking.

It's a small, guilty pleasure to share that secret with Alex. One more among the many little rituals that have slowly been helping me drown out the pain of the past.

My mom called the night before to wish me an early happy birthday and to ask if she could have a breakfast cake for me at home, something we've done every year since I can remember. Mom and I are both breakfast and coffee people.

When I told her I wouldn't be able to make it, she sounded sad, but she didn't ask why and didn't insist.

I think she knew I just didn't want to go back home and deal with Dad.

❁✧❁✧❁

As for school, I'm starting to find my rhythm. I'm no longer drowning in confusion, but I do get a C on my second essay in Professor Johnson's class.

It's not a disaster, but it certainly won't boost my GPA.

Still, I'll pass, and that's all I really care about for now.

Charlie will be off doing his own thing the weekend before Thanksgiving, so two weeks before the holiday, the three of us host a small Friendsgiving in our apartment—turkey sandwiches and our signature drink.

I decide to skip the frat party they're going to afterward. I've let Charlie drag me to one before, and I'm pretty sure it's just not my scene.

Then, just as I'm settling into the couch, warm cup of coffee in hand, cozying up for a quiet movie night, Alex decides last minute that she's too tired and will stay in with me instead.

The plan: watch *You've Got Mail.*

I've seen it at least a hundred times, and even so, the last scene always makes me tear up. And, of course, I don't want Alex to see that side of me, so when the time comes, I start snacking on Hot Cheetos like my life depends on it.

At first, I think we've reached for the Hot Cheetos at the same time.

But then I realize Alex is holding onto my hand, not the chips.

Our fingers are intertwined, and it's like everything inside me goes still for a moment.

We've been roommates for a while now, so it's not unusual for us to end up in tangled limbs on the couch, laughing or watching trash reality shows.

But this?

This feels different.

The world around me spins in slow motion, and I wonder—just wonder—if she's experiencing it too.

Alex shifts slightly, using her free hand to grab the chip bag and place it on the coffee table, clearing the space between us.

But her hand doesn't leave mine, and my heart races.

I try to focus on the movie, pretending I'm not acutely aware of her touch, but as Meg Ryan says, "I wanted it to be you so badly," the familiar lump forms in my throat.

"Hey," Alex says, breaking the silence.

She turns toward me, and I freeze.

"Remember that day we were stocking books?" she asks softly, her eyes searching mine, like she's trying to figure out something I'm not sure I even understand yet.

"Which one?" I ask, though I know exactly which day she means.

The day I'd been upset about my essay grade, the day Charlie had barged in just when I thought something else might happen between us.

"The one we never talked about after Charlie barged in," she adds, and I can hear the unspoken words between the lines.

My heart skips a beat.

She's asking.

After weeks of wondering, she's asking.

I look down at our hands, tangled together.

There's no denying it now.

Her fingers are warm, her skin soft, and the line between us is blurring.

"I think you know I was about to kiss you," Alex continues, her voice low, tentative. "But I've been wondering . . . would you have kissed me back?"

I don't get to answer, because before I can even process her words, I'm leaning in.

Her lips are soft and warm, slightly spicy from the chips, but it's perfect.

In this moment, in this apartment, with our hands tangled together in a quiet connection that's both grounding and electric, nothing has ever felt more right.

Whether or not I was ready to admit it, I've wanted this.

I've wanted it so badly.

⚘✧⚘✧⚘

I wake up alone on the couch. Half a throw blanket is tangled around my legs, and my mouth tastes like Hot Cheetos. My brain's trying to remember where the hell last night ended.

Oh. Right.

I kissed Alex.

Suddenly I'm fully awake. The blanket hits the floor as I sit up, wide-eyed, heart tap-dancing in my chest like it's auditioning for a rom-com and a horror movie at the same time.

Charlie shuffles past me looking rough, which can only mean one thing: he had an epic time last night and an equally epic hangover to show for it this morning. I lift my hands in surrender as he collapses on the couch.

I don't speak, and neither does he. We have an understanding: he is not people until there's caffeine.

I creep to the bedroom. Alex is halfway through changing—shirt tossed on the bed, sports bra, sleepy grin. She sees me, and it's instant. That stupid fluttering feeling, like my lungs just remembered they exist.

"Evacuation code," I whisper, pointing at the living room.

She chuckles, pulling on a hoodie. "That bad?"

"Category five."

We make a silent agreement to make a quick exit and grab some coffee, leaving him to battle his hangover in peace.

❁✧❁✧❁

As we sit on a bench outside with coffee and bagels, Alex takes a breath, her fingers fidgeting slightly around her cup.

"So, about last night," she starts, glancing at me with a small, hopeful smile. "I really like you. I'd like for us to be something official. But I know this is new for you, so if you don't feel the same way or if you'd rather just be friends, I totally get it."

Her words strike a revelation within me.

This year has been so full of change, and most of it has felt so out of my hands. But last night? That was different.

It was our choice, and even with the uncertainty of everything, it felt real, like a step toward something I actually wanted.

The thought of putting all of that into words seems impossible, though. I don't know how to tell her that she makes me feel safe, or that last night felt like something I hadn't known I was missing.

So, of course, I end up blurting out the first thing that comes to mind.

"I don't want to be friends," I say, realizing immediately how wrong it sounds.

I see her face fall, a flash of hurt in her eyes.

"Wait, no," I correct myself, shaking my head. "I mean, I don't want to *just* be friends."

Her eyes soften as she takes that in. "So, are you saying . . . ?"

I repeat it, slower this time, making sure every word is clear. "I'm saying I don't want to be *just* friends."

Then I lean in and kiss her, letting the gesture finish the thought.

When we pull away, Alex is smiling, her eyes lighting up. "My mom's going to be so excited about this," she says, laughing. "Don't be surprised if she insists on calling."

A slight panic builds inside me at the thought. I've only spoken to her mom once, over the phone, after she insisted on meeting the new roommate. She is a talker, the kind who can easily carry a conversation without me saying a single word.

Alex is more reserved, but I can tell she's inherited her mom's kindness and straightforwardness. Still, the thought of Alex's mom calling me sends my stomach into a nervous knot.

Alex must notice my expression because she adds gently, "This doesn't mean I expect you to tell your parents or anyone, for that matter, until you're ready. No pressure. My mom's just the type who would figure it out anyway the second I showed up for Thanksgiving."

The relief is immediate, and I give her a grateful smile. "Thank you. I'm actually not going home for Thanksgiving this year, so no family announcements for me."

It's true; Thanksgiving isn't exactly a major tradition for us. My parents, both raised in Tijuana, didn't grow up celebrating it. But we've spent the last few Thanksgivings at a family friend's house, celebrating with a big meal.

This time, though, the thought of sitting at a table with people who only know the polished, idealized version of us sounds exhausting. I don't want to keep up the charade, to pretend we are still the perfect family. Let my parents explain my absence however they want. I know they'll simply brush it off. Say I'm busy with schoolwork. Keep up appearances like always.

A lightbulb moment shines in Alex's eyes. "Hey, I know this is super last minute, but if you're free . . . why don't you come with me?"

Between a Rock and a Hard Place

Entre la espada y la pared

AURORA

These last few days of feeling well have left me questioning everything. For the first time since my first round of chemo, I've had energy—real energy. Enough to sit outside and delight in the sun's warmth on my face, enough to enjoy a full meal without nausea creeping in. Enough to feel like myself.

And now, I wonder.

Do I really want to keep going through this? Do I want to endure the exhaustion, the sickness, the slow, creeping loss of the body I once knew? Or do I want to take what good days I have left and make the most of them?

I spoke to my children over the phone about it, testing the waters. They listened, though I could hear the unspoken words, *please don't give up,* in the way they held their breath before answering. They really want me to try at least one more round. I understand why. If I were in their place, I'd want the same.

So, I agreed.

One more round.

And then we'll see.

That was the plan I settled on last night. But the truth is, I've been making hard choices my whole life, and not all of them have felt like actual choices at all. There was a time when deciding my own fate was a privilege I couldn't afford.

Exactly a week after my uncomfortable interaction with Manuel, as I finished setting out the morning tray, Don Eulalio called me into his study, his face stern and eyes cold. I stood there, hands clasped, waiting for whatever instruction he had for me. His words hit me like a slap.

"Aurora," he said, voice low, "I'm afraid your services here are no longer required. You are to gather your things and leave by Monday noon. We won't be requiring your help this weekend, so feel free to use that time to pack."

For a moment, I was sure I'd misheard. I'd done everything he'd ever asked of me. I kept to myself, worked harder than anyone else, and never complained.

"I don't understand," I stammered, searching his eyes for some hint of reasoning. "Did I . . . was there a mistake?"

He didn't meet my gaze.

"No mistake. I've made my decision. That's all you need to know."

There was no softness in his tone, no room to plead. He looked past me, already ready for me to be gone.

It made no sense. I knew I could try to reason with him, but something in his expression told me that no words of mine would change his mind.

I lowered my head and stepped back, murmuring, "Yes, Señor." I went to the room I'd been occupying to gather my belongings, stuffing my few possessions into a small bundle. The clock ticked, marking each passing second as I packed up my life in silence. Two days to figure out my next step didn't seem nearly enough.

Then I left my room and made my way to the back door with one mission: to find a job. There was no way I could return to Huejosquite with nothing to show for my months of absence. Manuel was standing in front of the door, leaning against the wall with his hands in his pockets, watching me. The way he stood there, a faint smirk playing on his lips, told me he already knew. He must have known this was coming long before I did.

"So, Aurora," he said, voice low and soft, "it seems you're in need of a new arrangement."

His gaze weighed on me, his eyes lingering a little too long, reading into things that weren't there. My stomach twisted, but I stayed quiet, unsure of what he would say next. He pushed himself off the wall, stepping closer.

"You shouldn't have to go back to that little town of yours, not after you've made it this far," he said. "There's no future for you there, you know that. But here, with me . . ." He paused, letting the words sink in. "Well, a woman like you could have a stable life—a good life."

I thought back to those last few weeks in Huejosquite, to Pepi, and to my mother's frantic efforts to shield me from a similar fate. The weight of the choice before me pressed down, heavy and unrelenting, making it hard to breathe.

"Excuse me, Señor Manuel, I'm running late to meet with a friend," I lied and rushed past him.

"Just think about it!" he called out. "You'll never lack anything by my side."

I continued walking away without turning back.

I briefly considered asking Carmen for help, but she'd already done enough for me, and she had a young baby to take care of. I knew she'd been struggling with everything that being a first-time mother entailed. It hardly seemed like the time to add my problems to the list of things she was dealing with. On top of that, her husband, although much nicer, ran with the same circle as Don Eulalio, and I didn't want to cause them any problems. So I spent all day Friday and Saturday walking through the streets, searching for a job, finding door after door closed to me.

Sunday morning, I made one last desperate attempt. I went to the few other girls I'd made acquaintance with, asking for referrals. Girls who, just like me, were maids who came from small towns. That's when I realized that even though the city was big, it was still a small world when it came to word-of-mouth recommendations for maids. Manuel, with his reach and influence, had made sure no other family would welcome me in their home.

The thought of returning home, back to Mamá, back to that place where all my hard work would be reduced to whispers of failure, if my abuelos even took me back . . . it left me hollow. What could I say to them? That after running away, ignoring what they'd done for me, I'd only returned to be another mouth to feed?

But Manuel? Moving in with him would mean giving up the life I'd wanted, the life I'd struggled to keep mine. The thought that it also meant giving up the possibility of a happily ever after with Paco was almost unbearable. Still, if I went with him, I could keep sending money back to Mamá. I could make sure she had enough. That thought, more than any other, settled like a weight in my heart.

Sunday afternoon when I returned to the Vegas' home, running out of time and still not knowing what my next move would be, Manuel was right outside the fence.

"Have you thought about my proposal, Aurora? Many women would love to be in your place, and I'm not used to rejection."

I looked up at him, taking in the faint smile on his face.

"If I accept . . . you promise I'll be able to keep sending money to my mother?" I asked, weighing my options.

"Of course," he said, as if it were the simplest thing in the world. "You'll have everything you need, and more. You'll be taken care of, and so will my future *suegra*."

How would I tell my mother that I'd fallen into the very situation she'd tried to help me avoid? I decided I wouldn't. What she didn't know couldn't break her heart. If Manuel stayed true to his word about allowing me to send money, I could make my mother think that I'd found a better job. That I was happy in the capital. That her dreams of a better future for me were coming true.

With a sigh, I nodded, accepting Manuel's offer. I told myself it was a choice, that I could leave whenever I wanted. But deep down, I knew better.

While Some Cry, Others Sell Handkerchiefs

Mientras unos lloran, otros venden pañuelos

PILAR

Along with Ofelia's family, Meño and I settled in the city. The house in Tijuana was smaller than we had expected, especially for someone like Ofelia, who was used to larger, more comfortable spaces. Back in Mexico City, her family had lived in a spacious house with fine wooden furniture and curtains that always smelled clean. Now, our world had shrunk to walls of faded blue and a backyard more dust than garden. But at least it felt safe, and in that moment, that kept us from unraveling.

Meño had found a job almost immediately, working as a vendor at a downtown clothing stall where he started learning the basic English necessary to interact with the endless stream of American tourists. The little time he spent at home, he kept to himself, barely speaking, his gaze always lost in some distant point. He wasn't the same anymore. When his screams came at night, either Ofelia's mother or I would rush to his side and hug him until he'd fall back asleep. I wasn't the same either. But I said nothing, just kept trying to make sense of what little I could in a world that no longer did.

Ofelia and I shared a room. Our beds were nothing more than a couple of secondhand mattresses. One night during our first week in Tijuana, she plopped down on one of them, and it instantly sucked her into the center as if she'd fallen into a trap.

"Don't sit on that corner," she warned, standing up and pointing at the mattress. "It sinks like quicksand. I think it swallowed one of my socks."

I couldn't help but laugh for the first time in days.

Those first weeks in Tijuana, I spent my time exploring the city in search of a job that would allow me to contribute to our new home. I walked through colorful streets, past bustling markets where people sold everything from fresh fruit to trinkets, feeling like a ghost. My thoughts were still in Mexico City, trapped in memories of chaos, spilled blood, and the unknown fate of my father. It was easier to let the city around me fade into the background, to pretend I wasn't here, that I hadn't left everything behind. I found a job quicker than I expected, as a cashier at a small souvenir shop near Meño's work. While the pay wasn't much, it provided the perfect opportunity to spend time alone with my brother on our commute to and from work —one of the few moments he couldn't retreat into his room and shut out the world the way he did at home.

As the months went by, Ofelia's parents spent most of their days trying to organize their new life. Don Rafael, who had worked for years as an accountant for wealthy families in Mexico City, now took any temporary job he could find, from assisting at a workshop to unloading goods at the market.

"It'll take some time to rebuild my clientele," he'd said. "But it'll happen. Meanwhile, I want to be careful with our savings."

They never complained, but you could feel their pain for the past and their worries about the future in the silences that filled the nights.

"I don't understand why they're not trying to sell their house in Mexico City," I confessed to Meño one night.

"When something is so painful that you need to leave it behind, sometimes it's best to not look back," he replied.

I understood then that I should stop asking him about our mother. Meño had been ready to leave the past behind for a long time, yet I kept forcing him to look back.

As for me, I was still trying to adjust. My father's disappearance had left me feeling something between unease and resentment that I didn't know how to quell. Thankfully, Ofelia's family had taken in Meño, me, and even Solovino as if we were their own. But I knew our plight wasn't the same. They were facing their own struggles, dealing with their own pain, and I tried my best not to be another burden.

Although Ofelia understandably had her moments of crying over Chava, she didn't let the situation completely bring her down, as it nearly did for the rest of us.

One morning, she dragged me to the local market with the promise of finding "treasures." Among the stalls of used clothing and boxes of second-hand toys and other trinkets, she found a floral dress and tried it on over her clothes.

"Look, Pilar," she said, spinning in front of me, "don't I look like a movie star?"

"Of course," I replied with a smile. "Like Dolores del Río in her latest premiere, *Sunday Flea Market Bargains.*"

Solovino, who had followed us as usual, chose that moment to leap onto Ofelia, leaving a huge dirt paw print on the dress. She let out a theatrical scream, flailing her arms as if she could shake the stain off with the air.

"Solovino! This dress, sale price and all, costs more than your week's worth of food," she exclaimed.

"I think he's saying you're not as glamorous as you think," I said, laughing.

Ofelia tried to frown but ended up laughing too. "He knows nothing about fashion."

At night, the heat in the room was so intense it could've made the walls melt. We lay on our sheets, talking in hushed voices while the sounds from the patio, a lost cricket or Solovino's persistent scratching, filled the silence.

"Pilar, what are you going to do when things get better?" she asked one night, turning to look at me from her bed.

"When things get better?" I replied, staring at the ceiling. "I think I need to know what I'm doing right now."

Ofelia let out a small sigh, and even in the dark, I could almost see her rolling her eyes, not out of disdain, but habit.

"Well, I already know. I'm going to open my own clothing store, full of dresses like that one," she said, and I caught the shadow of her hand pointing to the floral dress hanging in a corner. I envied her for that, for her ability to dream despite everything. But I also knew that even though I couldn't imagine the future, I needed someone like her. Someone to push me to see it differently. Though everything was far from perfect, Ofelia kept teaching me, day by day, that even in the darkest moments, there was always room for laughter.

Little by little, Tijuana seeped under my skin. The smell of carne asada and tortillas on the comal filled the air. The quick, determined strides of its people reminded me of my life before everything had fallen apart. Not a life I could return to, of course. At that moment, all I had was the weight of the present and the uncertainty of the future. Even so, there were moments when I could almost see a glimmer of hope. Tijuana had its own rhythm, a rhythm that didn't care about what had happened in Mexico City. Here, people moved forward, or at least pretended to. They had their own concerns, their own lives to live, and they didn't care about the pain we carried from the past.

The conversations at the market weren't about protests or massacres; they were about bus schedules or which nightclub had the best music that night or about which stores across the border had the best deals. It was as if the world had simply kept spinning, indifferent to the broken pieces it had left behind. And, in a way, that was comforting. It was a reminder that life could go on, even when everything you've ever known vanishes in an instant.

To Give and Receive Is the Way to Live

Dar y recibir es de sabios convivir

FER

My last class before Thanksgiving break starts at two in the afternoon, but when I get to the door, there's a note taped up that reads *Class canceled. Enjoy your holiday!* Not one to argue with fate, I head back to the apartment. By 2:45 p.m., I've packed, unpacked, and repacked my duffel bag three times. Each time, I add something I'll probably never use, like a flashlight and a thick winter jacket—just in case. With the bag squared away, I wait for Alex to get back from her class so we can hit the road. Thinking of the weekend ahead is so exciting. It's a reminder that no matter what life throws me, there will always be something to keep me going on.

We're supposed to leave at six, a strategy Alex insists will help us avoid the "pre-Thanksgiving apocalypse" traffic and get to her parents' around midnight. But with three hours of downtime, I'm in this weird state where I can't relax but also can't focus. I wander around the apartment, sitting in random spots and pretending to look busy, but mostly just counting down the minutes.

Finally, at 3:42 p.m., Alex strolls in, instantly reading my restlessness.

"Okay," she sighs, flopping her bag on the floor. "I don't think my pre-drive nap will happen with you vibrating around here like a swarm of bees. Let's just go now."

The second she says it, I'm out the door, practically dragging my duffel bag with me.

"I can drive part of the way," I say eagerly, bouncing on my feet. "Or all of it, if you'd like. I have enough energy for an Olympic marathon."

Alex just grins, sliding into the driver's seat. "Thank you. I promise I'll let you know if I get sleepy enough to swerve off the road, but I actually kind of like the night drive. Now, on the way back? You're totally driving."

For the first hour and a half, we belt out everything from "Wannabe" by Spice Girls to "El son del dolor" by Cuca, like a couple of road-trip pros. But as the hours go by, we settle into a quieter vibe, each of us taking in the darkening landscape with snacks and the occasional bit of conversation.

Around ten p.m., we make a pit stop for coffee. The break somehow shifts the whole vibe—now the car is cozier, more private. I sip my half-cocoa, half-coffee creation and glance over at Alex. This moment is too perfect to disturb. But I'm not great at silence, and the quiet is taunting me. Staring straight ahead at the moonlit road, I blurt out, "My grandma used to make up games to keep my cousins and me entertained when we'd spend the night at her place. Wanna try one?"

I glance over, and Alex raises an eyebrow, curious but amused.

"Which one?"

"One of my all-time favorites is called *The Best and the Worst*," I explain, shrugging. "It's silly, but it was always fun—probably because my cousins and I could never keep it serious."

Alex perks up. "I'm intrigued."

"It's pretty simple. One person names a random thing, and everyone has to say the best thing and the worst thing about it. And you get bonus points if you make people laugh."

"Sounds perfect. You go first."

"Okay . . . sporks."

We go back and forth, picking random things like cats, Q-tips, and stairs. Each new topic brings out a story—like the time I had to have a Q-tip removed from my ear at urgent care, or the time Alex got her head stuck in the stair rail for a solid hour as a kid. By the time we're on to "the night," we're grinning, snacking, and laughing so much my cheeks hurt.

"The best part of the night?" Alex muses. "It's when you end up in those deep conversations that only happen after midnight."

I nod, impressed. "And the worst?"

"Definitely those all-nighters where you're so tired you want to face-plant on your bed, but you have to keep working."

I laugh. "Yeah, that's dead on."

Then, after a pause, Alex throws out, "Love."

I take a moment. "The best? Old couples who still hold hands, I guess. Something about it that kind of makes me feel like maybe love is worth it."

She smiles, a softness in her eyes. "Good one."

"And the worst," I add, "is that weird in-between time where you know it's over but haven't actually broken up yet. Torture."

We fall silent for a minute, the weight of that statement hanging between us.

"So, what was your worst breakup?" Alex asks softly.

"Oh, easy. I had a boyfriend named Angel towards the end of my senior year," I say.

"Oh, you can just stop there, everyone knows an Angel rarely lives up to their name," she says with a brief chuckle.

"He was actually with me when I caught my dad cheating on my mom. So, yeah, heavy stuff." I pause, gathering my thoughts. "That same night, he became my first . . . you know." I feel myself flush, but I keep going. "Anyway, he broke up with me by saying he wanted to 'explore' his options at community college. Then, get this, he still asked if he could sleep over since it was 'too late to walk home.'"

Alex gasps. "Please tell me you threw him out the window. Naked."

"I wish. No, I let him sleep on the floor." I cringe at my own confession.

She shakes her head, laughing. "Wow. That is . . . a whole new level of audacity."

I shrug, laughing with her. "True. But he didn't lie, at least, so I guess that's something. Anyway, what about you?"

Alex's face softens. "I haven't told a lot of people this," she starts, her voice barely above a whisper. "But... when I was fifteen, I got pregnant."

She doesn't look at me. Just keeps staring at her coffee like it might answer for her.

"He was older. A senior. I thought he was—" She lets out a breath. "Well. I thought wrong."

She smiles, bitter. "He dumped me the day I told him. Told me to 'handle it.' Like I'd misplaced a sweater."

I squeeze her hand, offering silent support as she continues. "He told me I should get an abortion. I thought about it, but then I had a miscarriage a few weeks later. When I told him, he said, 'What a relief.' It was like a punch to the gut. He felt 'relieved,' while I felt everything else."

I'm blinking back tears, amazed by her strength. I give her hand another squeeze. "I'm so sorry, Alex. That's . . . unimaginable."

She lets out a long breath, giving me a small smile. "It's okay. I'm in a better place now. His family was . . . well, let's just say they weren't jumping for joy over him dating a Mexican girl. His dad would say stuff like, 'Hola, señorita,' with this over-the-top accent, or sprinkle in random Spanish phrases every time I was around even though he knew my English is way better than my Spanish. He'd always ask when I'd make them 'authentic tortillas,' like that was somehow part of dating their son." She shakes her head with a slight laugh.

I can't help but laugh at how ridiculous it sounds. "Let me guess. He never actually tasted your cooking, right?"

She bursts out laughing. "Right. And lucky him too! Charlie still won't let me live down the time I melted cheese all over the stove trying to make quesadillas." She lets out a long breath. "Back then, it was hard. People talk, and even though I lost the baby, I still felt like I had this label I couldn't shake. That's when Charlie and I became best friends."

Her eyes light up, and she lets out a soft laugh. "He was a senior, and he was already my friend, but one day, he really surprised me. "He showed up the next day with this stupid serious look and said, 'We could say I'm the dad, if that helps.'"

She laughs, shaking her head. "I told him no one would believe that. But honestly? It helped. Just knowing someone was willing to stand next to me in the hallway."

"That's amazing," I say, shaking my head in awe. "No wonder you two are so close."

She nods, a fond smile spreading across her face. "That's Charlie for you."

The rest of the trip feels lighter, filled with goofy stories, laughter, and shared memories. By the time we pull into her parents' driveway, I feel closer to Alex than ever, the bond between us growing with every mile we traveled together.

When we finally roll up to Alex's parents' place at a fashionably late 12:05 a.m., I'm greeted by a two-story home with a yard so manicured it could win awards, despite it being larger than any yard I've seen in

San Diego. It's close enough to one of the country's priciest cities that it feels like we just pulled up to a celebrity's house. And that's when the reality hits: we did not grow up in the same universe. I'm suddenly self-conscious—my parents' small, single-story, two-bedroom house is a step-up from the trailer where we lived my first thirteen years.

I have never felt this way around Alex before. Her mom had been super sweet over the phone last week, even made Alex hand me the phone just to say how excited she was that I'd be tagging along, but now, standing here with my overnight bag, I feel . . . well, out of my element.

Inside, the house is quiet, and all the lights are off, signaling everyone's already in bed. We creep through, and I ask, "So . . . where am I crashing?"

"My room, of course," she says, as if it's no big deal.

"Your room?" I whisper-yell, totally taken aback. Of course, Alex's parents know we share a room back at the apartment, but so far we've still stuck to our own beds. I don't imagine there's an extra bed in Alex's room, being that she's the only daughter. "Are you sure your parents are okay with that? I'd really rather not start off on the wrong foot here."

Alex laughs and whispers back, "As long as you don't get me pregnant and dump me, we're good." Honestly, I don't think there's anything Alex can't joke about. "Plus, my parents expect me to be smarter now. Trust me, I got the 'birds and the bees' PowerPoint with bonus slides on 'good decision-making' last time. Very detailed." She grins.

I relax a little at her humor, and we both crawl into her bed, exhausted. In the morning, Alex's parents finally emerge after we've already had two cups of coffee and cleaned up our breakfast.

Her family is warm and friendly, putting me at ease instantly. By dinner, I even forget that their house is about three times the size of the one I grew up in. I meet her brothers, who are both hilarious and kind of remind me of sitcom characters, along with their girlfriends, who Alex privately tells me are cool but probably won't make it to the next family dinner based on her brothers' dating records.

On Friday, we spend most of the day playing board games with her parents and brothers. As a kid, I never felt like I missed out on having siblings. I had enough cousin drama for a lifetime and I never had to fight over TV remotes. But seeing how much fun Alex's family has together, I wonder if I've missed out on something special. Later, as we settle down to watch a Christmas movie, Alex leans her head on my shoulder and wraps her hand around mine. It's such a simple gesture, but it brings on that warm, fuzzy feeling that makes me crazy about her.

❁✧❁✧❁

Saturday morning, we say our goodbyes, and Alex gives everyone a round of bear hugs, promising to be back for winter break. We won't head back to San Diego until tomorrow because Alex has planned an entire day of sightseeing with a surprise overnight stay near LA to make the drive back easier. First up? Crossing the Golden Gate Bridge, an item I'd had on my bucket list.

"So, what do you think?" Alex asks once we're across.

I give her a little shrug. "Well . . . it was . . . a bridge." We both crack up because, yeah, it was just a bridge, and I guess I thought it would be more exciting?

"Way to sell it," she says, laughing.

"No, I'm glad we crossed it together! But I think I might've just put it on my bucket list because it's what people do. I've never been particularly passionate about bridges . . . or anti-bridge, you know?" I'm rambling, and she's looking at me like she's studying my brain through an imaginary magnifying glass. "What I'm saying is," I try again, "the bridge itself was meh, but being here with you? Not meh."

She smiles. "Well, I can guarantee the rest of today won't be underwhelming."

From there, we head to Fisherman's Wharf, where I insist on getting a caricature done because I can't resist being a cheesy tourist. We share a clam chowder bread bowl I devour despite my long-standing mistrust of clams. Then, we stroll through Chinatown, snapping a picture of us kissing under paper lanterns, and finally land at a tiny, cozy restaurant with the most mouth-watering food I've had in ages.

"This shrimp and pork siu mai might actually challenge my loyalty to carne asada fries," I say, eliciting a mock gasp from Alex, who's well aware of my obsession for the cheesy, meaty, spicy, holiday-in-your-mouth, San Diego staple.

"Oh, I didn't realize I'd be bringing a traitor to my secret family spot," she jokes. "My brothers will flip if they find out I brought you here without them."

"Pinky promise I'll keep it quiet," I say, extending my pinky.

We finish the night with pastries and coffee from a Chinese bakery before setting off toward LA. My stomach is so full it's a wonder I can walk, but I wouldn't trade it for anything.

We reach the hotel a little past nine, worn out and stiff from the road, but not even close to sleepy. After a pit stop at the 7-Eleven across the street, we've got a pile of snacks spread across the bed as we mindlessly scroll through channels until we finally land on an episode of *Hell's Kitchen*. The contestants are in some challenge where they're blindfolded and trying to guess what they're tasting.

"I bet it looks easy, but you'd totally blank if you tried it," Alex says, laughing as one poor contestant is humiliated after guessing "pork" when given a taste of chicken.

"Unless they hand out one of Charlie's infamous drinks, I'd recognize that anywhere." I joke.

"Please, I'd have amnesia and still remember that horror," Alex adds. We're both cracking up when I get an idea.

"Why don't we try it?" I gesture to our snack spread, grinning.

She starts by handing me a Hot Cheeto. Easy. I get it right. Next up, I feed her a peanut M&M. She nails it. We're on a roll. Take that, Chef Ramsay. Then she hands me another Hot Cheeto.

"Hey, come on, trying to trick me?" I laugh.

"Why wouldn't I give you your favorite?" she says, smiling that flirty smile of hers.

"Oh, I'm definitely kissing you now, and not because that line worked on me—it's purely to prevent further cheesiness." I lean in to kiss her, both of us blindly pushing snack bags aside as we move closer. The lingering spice from the Hot Cheetos makes the sweetness of her chocolaty kiss even better, and I try to place the bag of chips on the nightstand behind me without breaking away. I'm acutely aware of my breathing, shaky and uneven, as I lean into this unfamiliar territory.

"Leave it," she whispers against my lips, guiding my hand back down and gently taking the bag away as her fingers trace up my arm and under my shirt. In no time, our shirts are off, tossed somewhere into the snack pile. Her skin sends waves of warmth through my body, and I can't tell if I'm panting or hyperventilating, or both, as her hands explore, sending little shivers through me. My heart pounds with a mix of excitement and anxiety, every movement is new and overwhelming in the best way possible.

Then—oh, wow—there is a sudden, searing heat somewhere very much not intended.

"Oh! Ow!" I yelp, flinching back.

Her eyes go wide with alarm. "Did I hurt you? Are you okay?" she asks.

"Yes, I mean, no, I mean . . . yeah, but it's . . . Hot Cheeto fingers!" I stammer.

We lock eyes, horrified, before bursting into laughter. We're both red-faced and still giggling as we make a beeline for the shower, stripping off what's left of our clothes. As soon as the burn subsides, Alex's hands find their way back to me, her mouth following close behind, until I'm a trembling, breathless mess. I can barely stand, but somehow she steadies me, her lips moving to mine. The intensity of our passion clings to her, and I'm wrapped up in it. My heart's racing, and a nervous thrill washes over me—it's my first time doing something like this, but I want nothing more than to explore all of her.

I shut off the water, and we make our way back to the bed, where I explore every inch of her with the same attention. A nervous flutter fills my chest, making my breath catch as I try to focus on her. My hands tremble slightly, betraying my inexperience, but I can't pull myself away from her. I don't want to. She pulls me closer, and we spend the rest of the night wrapped up in each other, losing track of time as we drift in and out of sleep. Falling in love with her is like letting go of the ground beneath me: freeing, unknown, and impossible to turn back from.

The next morning, sunlight sneaks through a tiny crack in the curtain, hitting me right between the eyes. Groggy but content, I smile at the memory of the night. Alex grabs her laptop and cozies up next to me, scrolling through our weekend pictures and uploading them to Facebook, including one of us kissing under the lanterns in Chinatown. From the way she looks at the picture, I know it's not just about the beautiful setting, it's about us and how much it means to have me here with her.

I only have MySpace, and our friend groups don't really overlap, but I wonder if maybe it's time to change that. Alex doesn't bring it up, though, just squeezes my hand, her gaze still soft on that photo.

Time and Tide Wait for No One

No hay fecha que no llegue ni plazo que no se cumpla

AURORA

My second round of chemo is coming up in just a few days, and before the exhaustion takes hold of me again, I want to write. I want to get more of my story out while I still have the energy, before the chemo pulls me under again.

The first year with Manuel was a mix of joy and pain. Our son, the little boy we named after him, was everything I could have ever dreamed of. A beautiful, sweet-tempered baby. I had dreaded having a child with Manuel, but now that I had one, he was perfect.

That was the joy.

But along with the joy came a lot of pain.

❀✧❀✧❀

I remember that morning, right after our son was born, June 3, 1951. Manuel was grinning, proud to be a father, and he pulled me close, pressing a kiss to my forehead.

"I'm gonna go celebrate with my compadre," he said, eyes sparkling with excitement. "The father of a *machito* deserves a little celebration, you know?"

I nodded, trying to hide the knot in my stomach. I didn't love him, not the way I had once hoped for love. Marrying him had been a desperate last resort in the first place. It felt like no matter how hard I tried to escape my destiny, I was never fast enough. I accepted it, but it didn't mean I had to like it.

"Should I have dinner ready?" I asked, my way of asking if he'd be out late. He waved me off, already heading toward the door.

But the hours turned into days. Two days that slowly squeezed the hope out of me, that maybe becoming a father would transform Manuel into someone better. I wasn't worried about him, not in the way most wives would have been. I didn't care if he was out there drinking or with whoever he'd found at the bar. What worried me was how I would care for my baby alone, how I would manage without any help. My son needed me, and I had to figure it out.

Manuel had left me alone with the baby, and I wondered how long I could keep pretending this was all okay. When he finally stumbled through the door, reeking of alcohol, I didn't feel relief. I felt . . . nothing. He didn't apologize, didn't offer any explanation. He just mumbled something about needing to blow off steam. I wasn't angry that he'd left. I didn't care enough for that. But the cold reality settled in that, once again, he'd left me with everything: the baby, the house, the weight of it all. While he disappeared into his own world. It wasn't the first time, and I had no reason to believe it would be the last.

And in his world, there was no space for me to have one of my own.

Manuel didn't like me having friends. He never said it outright, but he liked me depending completely on him. He made it so difficult, so exhausting to keep in touch with Carmen, the only close friend I had in Mexico City, that eventually it just became easier to let the friendship fade into the background.

Loneliness settled over me like a second skin, and the only warmth I had left was my son. My sweet, perfect little boy who smiled up at me like I was his universe. And I loved him more than anything. More than I thought possible.

I hadn't told my mother about him.

Not because I was ashamed of him—I could never be. But because I could still hear her voice, soft with hope, telling me to dream as big as I wanted. Telling me that her biggest dream, a dream that had once been my father's too, was for me to accomplish my own. Despite our harsh circumstances back in Huejosquite, she believed I would become a nurse, that I would help people, that I would somehow escape the limitations society had placed upon us. Every time I looked at my son, I saw my future shifting further away from the dreams she had held onto for me. Nevertheless, the truth I was hiding made my chest heavy with guilt.

❀✧❀✧❀

Then there was the other part. The part that twisted in my stomach when I thought about the things Manuel had done, the things he had said. The night of our first anniversary was one of those nights. He'd promised me he would be there, that we would make it special. Instead, he came home late, stumbling through the door. I could smell the alcohol on him before I even saw him. He tried to smile, but it was forced, crooked. I'd briefly considered asking where he'd been, but his silence made the question dangerous. Then, he had hit me.

After a while, I'd learned to read the cues, to know when the slaps were coming, but when he showed up after days of celebrating our son's birth, the slap came so fast; I didn't see it coming. I didn't even have time to cry out before Manuel was pulling me to the floor, his hands gripping my arms, shaking me as he yelled.

"You don't even care to ask where I've been, do you? You just sit here, waiting, acting like everything's fine!" His voice was raw, full of anger. "My father was a lowlife who couldn't have cared less if my mother or any of his children starved to death, yet I'm out there, doing everything I can to give you a good life, and this is how you repay me? You appreciate nothing."

My chest tightened, my breath grew shallow, and I didn't respond. There was no point in saying anything. I didn't ask where he'd been, because it wasn't the first time. Only this time he'd left me alone with our newborn baby for days, and now he was angry because I hadn't begged him to come back.

I wanted to scream, to shout at him it wasn't fair, that he had left me with all of it: the baby, the house, the empty promises. I wanted to say I was done. But I couldn't. I didn't. I just stayed quiet, held back the tears, and tried to protect our baby as best as I could. He was still so small. How could I tell him what was happening?

The one thing Manuel kept his promise about was sending money to my mother. Not much. Not nearly as much as I had hoped. But it was something.

$$\text{❀✧❀✧❀}$$

The letter from my mother came just a few weeks after my baby was born. Pepi was with Segundo now. He'd taken her to the city after her father refused to let her return home. Naturally, my abuelos were furious when they found out that most of Segundo's time and money were going toward building a life with Pepi. To them, he was as good as dead—and even though she never said it, I could see how that left my mother more vulnerable and alone than ever. She now had to communicate with both of us through secret letters.

I read that letter so many times, it almost tore apart in my hands. I wrote to Pepi and Paco once, but when they wrote back asking how I was doing, I didn't have the heart to reply. I wanted to be like Pepi. I wanted to be free. But I couldn't. I had to stay. However, deep down I had a feeling that if things with Manuel continued going down the same path, I might not survive much longer.

THE THIRD STRAND: The flowers of our roots.

No matter how fast you run, fate will catch up

El pasado alcanza hasta al más veloz

PILAR

Tijuana moved fast, and I pretended to keep up. Back then, I thought change meant progress. It didn't. Sometimes change just means running in place somewhere new.

Two years after arriving, I had found a job at the department store where I still worked. At first, it had been a relief: steady hours, a paycheck, a way to carry my weight in the house where I still lived with Ofelia's family. But that relief had long since faded. The job wasn't fulfilling in any way that gave my life meaning, but it was easy. Predictable. And somehow, I had let the years slip by, staying in the same place.

Don Rafael and Doña Carmen had rebuilt everything they had lost after we left Mexico City. All the material things at least. Don Rafael's business was thriving again, and the family was doing well. Meño had moved to San Diego after falling in love with a girl from there who he'd met at a nightclub in Tijuana. They had just had their first baby, and though he still visited often, he belonged to a different world now. But he was happier than ever, and I was happy for him.

And Ofelia—she had never stopped. She was studying design, making plans, dreaming of the boutique she would open soon. She had a vision, a future, something to reach for.

I used to dream like that.

Back then, I thought freedom would fix everything. I didn't know freedom came with bills, stomach knots, and a creeping sense of failure when nothing changes. Turns out, wanting more isn't enough. You have to know how to ask for it. I never did.. I had pictured a life full of adventure, of choices made on my own terms. But now that I had the freedom I had once craved, I didn't know what to do with it.

Don Rafael and Doña Carmen had never held me back. If anything, they encouraged me. They had always been kind, always treated me as one of their own. If I had wanted to go back to school, they would have supported me.

But I had done nothing.

Instead, I had let the department store become my routine, my days blending into one another. I had stopped asking myself what I wanted.

✿✧✿✧✿

That evening, I arrived home from another long, unremarkable day at work. The familiar smell of food filled the house, and the murmur of conversation came from the kitchen.

As I stepped inside, Don Rafael and Doña Carmen were already waiting for me.

"Pilar, take a seat," Doña Carmen said, her voice unusually serious.

I glanced between them, trying to figure out what was going on. Ofelia was there too, standing near the table, her expression was neutral, but we were too good at reading each other. Something was wrong.

Don Rafael cleared his throat, looking down at a slip of paper in his hands.

"We got a call today. From someone in your family," he said carefully.

I stiffened. I had never been close to my family when we lived in Mexico City. Now in Tijuana, I hardly ever remembered I even had one.

"Your aunt called," Doña Carmen said. Her voice was too calm. I already hated whatever came next.

Don Rafael pushed a slip of paper toward me like it was a bomb.

"She said it's about your father."

I didn't touch the paper. Just stared at it, like maybe it would self-destruct and take the past with it.

I swallowed hard, trying to steady my voice. "Did she say anything else?"

Don Rafael shook his head. "Only that you should call back."

The silence stretched between us. Their eyes were on me, as if waiting for a reaction, but I didn't know what to say.

My father had been a shadow in my life for so long, a figure from a past I had tried to outrun. Whatever this news was, I wasn't sure I wanted to hear it.

But I also knew that I couldn't ignore it.

Ofelia walked over to me, reaching for my hand. "Whatever it is, you don't have to face it alone."

I reached for the piece of paper with a hand that felt too unsteady. "I'll call her," I said finally.

The Devil Knows More From Old Age Than From Being the Devil

Más sabe el diablo por viejo que por diablo

FER

As soon as I pull into my parents' driveway, I can tell by my dad's face that something is off. He's staring at me with narrowed eyes, his lips drawn into a thin, tight line as he waits for me to finish parking and get out of my car.

When I step out of my battered 2001 Camry, which I recently purchased from one of Charlie's friends, I see what my dad has in his hands: the cartoon of Alex and me at Fisherman's Wharf.

"Can you explain this to me?" His sharp tone tells me that, rather than an explanation, he's just seeking confirmation of what he already figured out. In the cartoon, I'm kissing Alex's cheek, and there are hearts all around us.

For a split second, I consider lying—telling him we're just friends and that the cartoon is just exaggerating our friendly love for each other. Those cartoons are meant to be funny anyway, aren't they?

I am not prepared to have this conversation today. Not when I'm just getting used to being around my parents again. Over the past school year, I rejected several invitations from my parents to come spend the weekend at their home. I had some conversations with my mom over the phone, always initiated by her, but the idea of going back home and seeing Dad just brought up the anger in me. However,

165

Alex and Charlie are home for the summer, and I somehow ended up letting my mom convince me to come spend the summer with her and Dad.

"You can't stay mad at your father the rest of your life, Fer," my mom had said. "Please, just come for a few days, and if you're really miserable with us, you can go back to your apartment. We both miss you so much."

To my surprise, when I told Alex and Charlie about my mom's invitation, Charlie was quick to side with her. "I'm not trying to justify your dad, Fer, but you haven't seen the man in an entire year. Your mom still invites you all the time, despite your constant rejections. Do you really plan on staying mad at him forever and punishing your mom along the way? I'm just saying, if my parents tried so hard to have me in their lives, I'd give them a chance."

Part of me had wanted to be mad at Charlie, to tell him to mind his own business. But deep inside, I knew he was right. Also, I had brought him into my business; I couldn't be mad at him for not saying what I wanted him to say.

"When I left home and was living in my car, my parents didn't reach out to me even once," Charlie adds, his voice cracking and his eyes brimming with tears. "Eventually, I caved and reached out to them."

My face flushed with shame at how entitled I must have seemed to him.

When I finally accepted my mother's invitation to spend the summer back home, Alex brought up that the previous summer they'd subleased the apartment, and since none of us were staying there, we could do it again to save some money. The idea of not having the apartment to fall back on made my stomach twist, but not wanting to be selfish, I accepted.

Now, the look in my father's eye makes me think I made a huge mistake by caving in and coming to their home for the entire summer. In retrospect, a visit here and there on the weekends would've made more sense, but here we are.

"What does it look like to you, Dad?" I try to sound firm, but inside, the possibility of rejection is almost more than I can handle. Why the rejection of the man I've avoided for a year terrifies me, I don't know.

"In our family, we are not like that, Fer. What will people say if they find out *que andas con tus cosas*?"

Mom peeks her head out the door. "Come inside. There's no need for the neighbors to hear you arguing."

I follow Dad in, my pulse hammering in my ears. "What things, Dad?" I press. "Weren't you so concerned before about what people would think that I live with a man? Alex isn't a man, so what's your issue now?"

Dad scoffs. "Don't play dumb, Fer. You know exactly what I'm talking about. So, this means what I think? She is your *novia?*"

The anger boiling inside me drowns out my fear. "Yes, she is my girlfriend, Dad. Has been for months. We're in a committed, faithful relationship."

Mom stiffens. She hasn't said a word since we walked in, but the pain in her eyes tells me my jab at Dad hit her too.

Dad's voice rises. "Yes, I made a mistake, Fer, but that doesn't mean you get to blame me for every poor decision you make."

"Alex is not a poor decision," I fire back, matching his volume.

"Well, I won't have that kind of thing around me. If this is who you're choosing to be, maybe you were right to stay away."

"You don't have to worry about that, I'm out."

I storm to my old room before he can reply. My heart pounds as I shove clothes into a bag, my hands shaking too much to zip it properly. Thankfully, my laptop and other school materials are still in the car.

When I rush back through the living room, Mom is in tears. Dad asks her if she knew about me and Alex. None of it matters. The front door is still open, and I step through it without looking back.

With no apartment to go back to, and the two people I'd usually go to five hours away for the summer, I drive toward the one other person I can always count on.

Thirty minutes later, I parallel park in a spot right in front of my grandma's house. The timing couldn't be more perfect. Just as I turn off the ignition, Rubén's voice trails off with the last line of "Esta Vez." I've played the song on repeat the entire drive, letting it sting a little deeper each time. I'm weirdly fascinated by these tiny, perfect moments—like arriving at my destination just as a song ends. It's like the universe gave me this one sliver of perfection, and yet, time can still be such a brutal jerk. Case in point: if I hadn't overslept exactly ten minutes this morning, I wouldn't have been in such a rush leaving my parents' house, I wouldn't have been late to class, earning myself a door practically slammed in my face. Most importantly, I wouldn't have been in such a hurry that I carelessly left the caricature of me and

Alex out in plain sight, and I wouldn't have had that dreaded conversation with Dad forced on me, rather than having it on my own terms. Funny how one minor delay can throw your entire life into chaos. Now here I am, staring at my puffy red eyes in the rearview mirror, wondering how I'll sneak those past Abue without her noticing. What excuse will I make if she does?

I ring the doorbell outside her front gate and start picking at the chipped yellow nail polish on my fingers. Yellow felt like a cheerful color just two days ago. Now, it's the most ironic detail of my day. Abue appears at her door with a soft smile.

"*¿Y eso, que nos visitan las estrellas?*" she greets, always making me feel like some kind of celebrity.

I manage a weak chuckle, not sure how to answer or even explain why I'm here. As she fiddles with the gate, I study the latch intently, avoiding her gaze. She opens the gate, and I throw myself into a hug before darting past her, praying she won't ask questions.

Thankfully, Abue's never been one to pry. She's the queen of minding her own business. *Zapatero a tus zapatos*, she always says, and she seems to live by it. Instead, she dives into her usual list of dinner options, reciting them like a poet on open-mic night: "Tortitas de papa, chicharrón with warm tortillas, nopalitos . . ."

My throat tightens as I force back a sob. "Thanks, but I'm not really hungry," I say, plastering on the most cheerful tone I can manage. "Just wondering if the stars could crash here for a while."

I don't need to say anything else. Abue is already nodding in agreement. She takes me upstairs to the guest room and simply tells me to come down for dinner when I'm ready.

I set my laptop on the dresser, intending to email the professor who nearly broke my nose with the classroom door. The injustice of it—she slams the door in my face, and I'm the one who has to apologize? But I can't afford to fail this class, not when I've worked so hard. I've barely opened the laptop when a cluster of old photos wedged under the dresser's glass top catches my eye. There's a shot from my high school graduation, a few candids of my cousins and me as little kids, and even a black-and-white photo of Abue, young and beautiful. She's holding a baby, and there's a kid, maybe two years old, standing next to her. The kid looks a lot like Mom, but my aunt Marta, the middle child, is ten years younger than Mom, so I'm not really sure who's in the picture. There aren't many pictures of Abue when she was young or of Mom as a kid, so I make a mental note to ask Abue about this one later.

Among the photos are random magazine clippings and faded newspaper ads. One announces a wrestling match featuring El Perro Aguayo. Another is a cutout of a famous Mexican actress, the kind who always played a rags-to-riches heroine. I smile, remembering the days when my biggest concerns were avoiding the *agüita de riñón* pee-filled bottles the wrestling fans hurled at each other, or protesting bedtime before the novela ended.

My stomach growls, snapping me back to reality. Today, I've survived on nothing but coffee from the Koala Koffee cart I grabbed on my way back to my parents' this morning. The email can wait. I toss my only change of clothes into a drawer and head downstairs, where Abue has set the table with tortitas de papa, tortillas, and a plastic bag of chicharrón. She hands me a cup of instant coffee—it's not my favorite, but at her house, it somehow tastes different.

"Do you remember when we were kids?" I ask, my voice soft with the nostalgia of those days. "How we'd always stay over at your place?"

Abue chuckles, her eyes lighting up with the memory. "Of course. Your abuelo and I used to invite the whole crew over when one of your parents went out and needed babysitting. It always filled us with so much joy to have a noisy house with all of you running around."

I smile, leaning back as the memories flood in. "Saturdays were the best. We'd all pile onto the couch to watch those same Pedro Infante or India Maria movies on Televisa."

She laughs again, a little more loudly this time. "Oh, yes! And then I had to convince you all that the first one to get up and smack the TV when it went static was the winner, or else none of you would want to get up. Remember how the picture would freeze, and you'd have to smack it just right?"

I nod, laughing too. "You'd think we would've learned to do it sooner, but nope. Everyone waited until the screen was all blurry, then it was a race to see who could get to it first. Good thing you've always known how to turn everything into a game."

Abue shakes her head, still amused by the memory.

"*¿Quién le da un chingadazo?*" I say, imitating the way Abuelo would ask who'd get up and fix it.

I think back to the first time Abuelo told me his and Abue's love story. We'd just watched *La de la Mochila Azul* for the millionth time when he sighed, "*Qué triste cuando el amor se va.*"

"But you have Abue," I'd told him, always the little smart-ass. "I don't think she's going anywhere. And she's kinda slow, so you'd probably catch her even if she tried!"

He'd laughed, then told me how he and Abue had known each other since they were kids but had lost touch for a few years.

"Pero a donde el corazón se inclina, el pie camina," he'd said. "So, once I found her again here in Tijuana, I knew I couldn't let her go. Little by little, we built this house together. You wouldn't even imagine what it looked like when we first started living here. And well, the rest is history."

I glance around, thinking about how true that is. Abue's house is beautiful, and I can't imagine it ever being anything else. Her eyes always glimmer with pride when she talks about how my abuelo built it with his own hands—for her, for us, their children and grandchildren. I'm so thankful for it because it holds most of my best childhood memories.

"I miss him," I sigh, the words slipping out before I can stop them.

I instantly regret it, but Abue only sighs too, then shakes her head. "If they still show those same few movies on channel twelve, your grandpa's probably making the rounds, whacking every TV in heaven."

We both giggle.

After dinner, I head back upstairs and sit down to write that dreaded apology email. I attach the assignment I was supposed to turn in this morning, promising to show up on time for the rest of the summer. I'm about to close my laptop when Abue taps softly on the open door, holding a box of cookies.

"There are toiletries under the sink if you need any. And are you sure you're warm enough with that blanket? I can grab another just in case."

"Thank you, I'm fine," I say, but my voice wavers, and before I can stop it, a tear slips down my cheek.

I turn away, cursing myself for being such a crier.

"It's about Alex," I blurt, and Abue sits beside me, her box of cookies in her lap.

"Did Mom tell you she convinced me to spend summer break back at home?"

"Yes, because your roommates went home for the summer?"

I take a deep breath. "Sort of . . . Abue, Alex isn't just my roommate. She's my girlfriend. Dad kicked me out after I told him. He kept asking how he's supposed to explain it to the family. Mom . . . just said nothing."

Abue looks at me, her eyes warm. "You know you're welcome here as long as you need. You did nothing wrong, mi estrella."

I wipe my eyes. "Just until the semester starts," I reply. "You're not disappointed in me?"

Abue squeezes my hand. "I could never be disappointed, especially not for being honest about someone you love. I only wish I'd been that brave when I was your age. Your parents will come around, you'll see."

"Why does being honest about who I am have to be an act of bravery?" I whisper.

She sighs. "Only God knows, but one day you'll see it all makes sense."

I don't really believe that, but I don't have the heart to say so. I just nod, trying to hold onto her comfort.

"Sometimes the things that take the most strength to hold on to, are the ones that mean the most to you. But you know what would always cheer me up?"

She pulls a few cookies from the box, stuffs them into her mouth, and, to my surprise, starts singing "El Noa Noa" by Juan Gabriel, completely garbled with crumbs. I can't make out a word, but I'd recognize that tune anywhere. I have a hunch Abue chose that song because Juan Gabriel famously said *Lo que se ve no se pregunta* when questioned about his sexuality, and *El Noa Noa* is one of his most iconic songs. This is her telling me my sexuality is nobody's business but my own. I join in, singing through my laughter. Things may be a mess right now, but with Abue here beside me, it feels like maybe, just maybe, it'll be okay.

❀✧❀✧❀

The next morning, my throat feels like it's been roughed up by sandpaper, a mix of singing my emotions out last night and the leftover ache from crying myself to sleep. I check my phone and spot two texts from Alex:

10 pm: *I miss you. How'd it go with your essay?*

12 am: *Please text back, I just need to know you're okay. I tried calling, but the dial tone sounds like you're in Mexico, so I'm assuming the stay at your parents' didn't work out after all. Are you at your grandma's?*

I text back: *Crappy signal. I'll call you later. I'll be ok. Love you.*

When I get downstairs, Abue is already in the kitchen, stirring a pot of oatmeal on the stove.

"I'm gonna go pick up some of my stuff, but I'll be back this afternoon if that's okay," I tell her.

"Of course it is," she says, taking a copy of her house key out of her pants pocket and pressing it into my hand. "Will you be alright?"

I can't quite say "yes," so I shrug, giving her a quick hug before heading out.

❀✧❀✧❀

As I park outside my parents' house, my heart races so loudly that I'm convinced the couple across the street can hear it, their dog pausing to look in my direction. With trembling fingers, I text my mom: *Is he there?*

In less than ten seconds, her face appears at my car window. Her eyes are hollow, shadowed with a grayish tint I've never seen before, as if sleep has completely abandoned her.

"Your dad's not here," she mumbles. "I thought you might come to get some things, so I packed a few bags. You can come in and get more if you want. Your grandma told me you're staying with her."

Yesterday, I'd thought Mom's silence meant she agreed with Dad, that she had nothing to say in my defense. But now, seeing her here, her invitation to come in while he's gone, I realize it's not that she's disappointed in me, she's just not willing to stand up to him. Somehow, that hits even harder.

I hadn't brought too many things from the apartment for my summer stay at my parents', so I just throw whatever Mom packed into the back seat, hoping everything I wanted back will be in there, and I drive off with a simple, "Thanks, bye."

❀✧❀✧❀

On the drive back to Abue's, my anger flares in every direction: at Dad, at Mom, at myself, even at that rickety fuckity Koala Koffee cart and that dingus-twat blue-haired barista. I scream, not caring that my window is down due to lack of A/C in my car. The couple in the car next to me at the red light looks at me like I'm crazy, and maybe I am, but I don't give a flying fuck.

I keep thinking of how I waited so long to come out to my parents. To myself. How I never truly spoke up about who I am. Isn't that just as bad as not standing up for myself? My eyes are more swollen and red than they were yesterday, but I don't even care anymore.

When I walk into Abue's with my new key, she's not downstairs to notice. I go straight to the fridge, planning to make myself a toast with butter and sugar—one of my go-to comfort snacks—before going up to let her know I'm back. I open the butter container, but instead of butter, I find a mound of beans. And that's it. My last shred of composure is about to haul ass out of my body. If I don't laugh, I'm going to cry over the butter container full of beans.

I dig around and find at least two more containers with beans, plus one Nutella jar holding tomato sauce. I decide on strawberry jelly for my toast and start heading upstairs. Near the top, I overhear Abue on the phone.

"I'm sorry it took me so long to tell you all of this, and I'm sorry to do it over the phone, but you're still in time to reach out to her. Don't make the same mistake I did."

I don't know what she means by "mistake,"—as far as I'm concerned, my Abue is the most perfect human being on the face of the earth, but I think she's talking to my mom. My stomach twists. There's a history here I've never asked about. I pause for a second before calling out, "Abue, I'm here!"

"Come in, mija," she replies, and I walk into her room holding my toast.

"I can go make you one too if you want," I offer.

She waves me off, smiling. "No, thank you. Now, tell me, how'd it go?"

I sit down and tell her everything.

"I just don't get why my relationship is anyone else's business, why anyone but me and Alex even cares. Alex's parents are so cool with it. I wish my parents could be the same."

Abue listens, nodding, then says, "You know, I just finished talking to your mom. She called to ask how you're doing. She was concerned that you drove off angry. I told her she has to reach out to you. But, mija, there's something I need to tell you that you might not want to hear. I know someone else who's been angry over someone else's decisions about their relationship. Can you guess who?"

I cross my arms, already feeling defensive. "This is different, Abue."

She tilts her head, patient as always. "Is it?"

"Yes! What my dad did—he broke our family. That wasn't just about him, it was about all three of us. He didn't just betray her, he betrayed me too. And I don't see why I have to pretend like that didn't hurt me."

"No one is saying it didn't," Abue says gently. "But your mother—whether or not you think she was right, decided to forgive him. It's not your father's cheating that's tearing your family apart, mija. It's the anger you're still carrying."

I shake my head. "That's not fair. I'm not the one who ruined things."

"No, but you are the one who won't let them heal."

I look away, jaw clenched. Alex would understand. She was the one who had my back when everything fell apart. She was the one who said it wasn't just one mistake, that men like my father don't change.

"It wasn't the first time it happened, Abue. He'd cheated before; he'll do it again. And I don't want to sit around watching Mom get hurt over and over."

Abue sighs, her face softening. "That's exactly what your mother said about you and Alex."

I blink. "What?"

"She told me people judge. That they'll hurt you for it, that she didn't want to see you suffer." She shakes her head. "Mija, we can't stop the people we love from getting hurt, but we can be a gentle presence standing next to them, reminding them they're never alone in their healing."

I inhale sharply, suddenly feeling like the wind has been knocked out of me.

I've spent so much time being angry, convinced Mom was weak, that she was letting Dad walk all over her. Wondering why she couldn't see that she was going to get hurt again if she continued down the same path. But hadn't she felt the same way about me? She wasn't ashamed of me—she was afraid for me. And what have I done in return? I've shut her out, treated her like the enemy. For over a year now, I've been furious with Mom over Dad's choices. I turned my back on her, convinced she'd betrayed herself by forgiving him, but I never stopped to think about what she's been through. Not only did she have to bear the shame of Dad's cheating—why is it that the betrayed person ends up carrying the shame anyway?—but she's also had to deal with me, cold and distant when she probably needed me most. I even went back to her home for the summer while barely speaking to her! How entitled have I been, yet she still welcomed me back in and accepted what little crumbs I was willing to throw her way.

My cheeks burn with shame as I remember how close we used to be. Maybe we weren't "besties" like Alex and her mom, but we were close. I hug Abue, thank her, and ask to use her landline. I hardly get any signal in Tijuana, so I'm thankful her old phone still works. Abue steps out, giving me privacy, and I dial the number, crossing every finger and toe that Mom will pick up, not Dad.

"Bueno?" Mom's voice sounds over the line, and I feel a swell of relief.

We agree to meet tomorrow at Artemio's, our old spot for breakfast burritos and coffee. There's so much I want to say to her: apologies, stories about school, details about Alex. And I want her to tell me about everything that's been going on in her life. For once, I want to stop being angry and listen.

Where There's Life, There's Hope

Donde hay vida, hay esperanza

AURORA

I told Rosa. Protecting her from the same shame and regret I've carried for years finally gave me the strength to let it all out.

I sat in the quiet of my room, the phone pressed to my ear, my hands trembling slightly. It was the conversation I'd been avoiding, the one I'd known I needed to make. The kind of conversation where the words never come out easily, tangled in the chest like a knot that can never come undone, where they catch in your throat and leave a bitter taste behind. But it was time. Rosa needed to hear it.

The second I picked up, I could hear the heaviness from the previous day lingering in her voice.

"Rosa," I said softly, trying to steady myself. "I've got something to tell you."

And just like that, I let it all out. The past I'd tucked away for so long. How the diagnosis hanging over me like a dark cloud had been casting a shadow on everything I thought I still had time for.

"I left them, Rosa. Your siblings. I left them behind," I whispered, my voice shaky as I spoke into the phone. "And I don't know if I'll ever be able to make it right. I'm afraid I won't even get the chance to."

There was a long pause on the other end. I could hear her breathing, as if she was processing what I had just said, her silence heavy with questions I could never have answered before. I winced, feeling the weight of her silence. I hadn't told her, not because I didn't want her to

176

know, but because I wasn't sure how to explain it.

"I never knew how to say it. I left them behind when I thought I couldn't give them the life they deserved. But I've carried the guilt every day, and now I'm afraid it's too late."

Her voice came through, soft but strong. "Times have changed, Mami. There are ways now that you can find them. Things that didn't exist before. It may be possible to track them down, and I'll help you do it. I promise."

A small spark of hope flickered in my chest, but fear quickly smothered it. What if it's too late? What if they've lived all these years thinking I didn't care? What if I've already failed them?

"I'm not looking for forgiveness," I said, my voice trembling. "I just don't want them to carry the 'what-ifs' after I'm gone. I want them to know I never stopped thinking about them, even if I couldn't be there."

On the other end of the line, I heard Rosa's voice, stronger now, full of conviction.

"You'll find them. We'll find them. You've got more time than you think, and you've got me with you every step of the way. You can't let fear hold you back. It's never too late to make things right."

But even as she said the words, a lingering doubt stayed with me. The years I'd lost felt like an impossible gap to bridge, and the fear that it might be too late to find them clawed at me from the inside.

"I don't want you to make the same mistakes I made," I finally said. "You need to hold on to what you have. Your relationship with your daughter. I've let fear make too many decisions for me. I ran away from things I should've faced. And now . . . now I can't go back in time and change everything. You still can. I'm sorry it took me so long to tell you all of this, and I'm sorry to do it over the phone, but you're still in time to reach out to her. Don't make the same mistake I did."

I'd just hung up the phone when I heard Fer's voice calling out to me.

"Abue, I'm here!"

Time Is the Best Doctor

El tiempo es el mejor doctor

PILAR

The air in Mexico City felt different than I remembered, the streets more crowded, the buildings taller, the faces more hurried. It was as if the city itself had transformed, but some things had remained the same. I hadn't planned on returning, not after all those years. But when I heard my aunt's voice on the other end, changed everything.

"Tu papá falleció," my aunt said, the words hitting me harder than I expected. "Cirrhosis," she added. Confirmation that he had continued spiraling down the same path, a path that made it a wonder he had survived that much longer.

I hadn't spoken to him since he left, but a part of me still needed to be there. I felt the pull of something I couldn't ignore. Ofelia had come with me, as she always did, understanding the unspoken things no one else could.

Meño hadn't come. I had called him, but his response had been flat, without hesitation. He made it clear he wouldn't be part of that chapter, not after everything that had happened.

"I'm not going to the funeral, Pilar," he'd said, his voice distant. "I've got nothing left to say to that man."

I paused, unsure how to respond. I had expected nothing different from him, but hearing it still stung.

"I've moved on. You should too."

Meño lived his life with no need for closure. I both envied and

178

admired him for that. But for me, this had felt like something I had to face, something I needed to acknowledge. So, I flew back to Mexico City, stood in front of the man who for better or worse had been my father, and said goodbye.

After the funeral, I sat in a bustling café, the noise of Mexico City washing over me again, and I felt the strange, bittersweet weight of the moment. The city had changed, but the ghosts of what we'd lived through still lingered in the air.

Ofelia sat across from me, stirring her drink with a small silver spoon, her eyes scanning the café and occasionally lingering on the door. A bell jingled, and I felt the air leave my lungs. I looked up and saw Julia standing at the entrance. Her eyes widened, mirroring the same mix of excitement and uncertainty I felt. We locked eyes for a moment before she broke into a smile. I rose instinctively to meet her.

"Julia!" My voice cracked as I embraced my childhood friend.

"You look exactly the same," she whispered, pulling back slightly but keeping hold of my arms, as if convincing herself this was real.

We sat down together, laughter bubbling up as we exchanged small stories about the trip, but lighthearted chatter soon gave way to something deeper.

"I almost didn't recognize you," I admitted, studying her. Her once perfectly styled waves now fell loose and straight, though no less elegant.

"Time doesn't pass in vain," she replied with a soft smile, tinged with something like nostalgia.

Ofelia and I had spoken often about how much we missed Julia. But life had pulled us in different directions, and we hadn't kept in touch as much as we had intended. At first, grief and change kept us apart. Then, after a few exchanged letters, our communication tapered off.

Ofelia had reconnected with Julia a few months before my father's passing. When I had asked about her, Ofelia had given me a knowing look.

"If you want to know about her, you need to make the effort to reach out."

She had been right. But guilt and time had created a distance I wasn't sure how to cross.

"We have so much to catch up on," Ofelia said as we settled in. "How have you been?"

Julia took a sip of the coffee we had ordered for her before answering. "Well, I won't lie. After you left, there were moments I felt left behind. But over the years, I came to understand that we were just kids. You didn't have much of a choice. If we're honest, you two got the worst of it. But that didn't make me miss you any less. Or any less envious that you still had each other."

That honesty—straightforward and raw—was just like Julia.

After a pause, she continued, "I got married a few years later. Ricardo was a good man. We had a son together." An intense pang of guilt and sadness hit me, how had I let myself miss out on so much of Julia's life?

"And then?" I prompted, noticing the slight shift in her expression.

She set her cup down. "Then work and routine caught up with us. No big fights, no betrayals. Just distance. One day, we realized we had stopped being a couple."

"But you still keep in touch?" Ofelia asked gently.

Julia nodded. "Our son has always been our priority. Ricardo visits him often, even though he's started a new family. We are cordial. He's a good father, and I'll always be grateful to him for that."

"I'm sorry I wasn't there for you," I said, trying to imagine what she had gone through.

Julia shrugged, a calmness settling over her. "At first, I resented you. But I also could've put in more effort. That's in the past. I've learned to value peace above all else. My divorce taught me that not every story has a villain and a heroine. Just people, doing the best they can. I never thought I'd be a single mother at twenty-five, but despite it all, I'm doing okay. My son is healthy. I have a good job as a dental assistant. It's not the life I dreamed of, but it's a good life. And for now, that's enough."

I looked at her in silence, overcome with relief and admiration, feeling the guilt I had carried for years slowly dissolve."

"You've always been so level-headed, Julia," I said. "Even in the hardest moments."

"Except that time you gave that girl a piece of your mind—and fists—for messing with Pili," Ofelia added, making us all laugh.

Julia grinned. "Not always. But life teaches you." Her gaze drifted to the window. "So much has changed. The city, us. But somehow, we're still here."

I nodded. "We are."

Ofelia exhaled. "We've had to change too. But little by little, we've learned to live with it."

"Sometimes, it feels like we never really left," I added.

Julia studied us, her expression serious. "I can't imagine what that must have been like. I tried to pretend things weren't broken. But they were. You never really leave, do you?"

I shook my head. "No. You just learn to carry it."

For a long moment, we sat in silence, the weight of history pressing on us. Then, Julia smiled. "I'm glad you're here."

I reached across the table, squeezing her hand gently. "Me too. And I don't want to let time or distance get in the way again."

Ofelia nodded in agreement. "We made it through so much already. Maybe now, we can make up for the time we lost."

Julia exhaled, a warmth settling over her expression. "I'd like that."

The moment hung between us, quiet yet full of unspoken understanding.

Then Julia's face lit up mischievously. "Okay, Ofelia told me that Meño just became a father. I want to hear every detail about your nephew! How's dad-life treating Meño? And how's auntie-life treating you?"

Laughter bubbled up again, the weight of the past giving way to something lighter. For all the changes, for all the things we had lost, one thing remained: each other. And that, at least, felt like something worth holding on to.

Before leaving the café, we looked each other in the eye and promised that, no matter how many kilometers were between us, we would never again let physical distance cool the bond we had built together. Because, in the end, our friendship wasn't about proximity— it was about the effort to stay present in one another's lives.

He Who Has Roots Grows Wings

Quien tiene raíces, tiene alas

FER

I get to Artemio's five minutes early and spot Mom already sitting toward the back, nervously stirring her coffee. She looks about as anxious as I feel. My legs go weak, and I keep repeating to myself, *Don't cry, don't cry, don't cry*, as I make my way to the table and slide into the seat across from her.

"I didn't know what you'd want for breakfast, but I got you coffee," she says, nudging a cup toward me. "*Es de la olla*," she adds, seeing me reach for a sugar packet. I put the sugar back, taking a sip of the rich coffee, the piloncillo and cinnamon warming my throat as I try to gather my thoughts. This is harder than I thought it would be.

I take a shaky breath. "When I went to Abue's after telling you and Dad about Alex, I thought . . . I thought you were mad and disappointed in me too. And that hurt, because I've always wanted to make you proud. But then, after seeing you again when I went to pick up my stuff, I wasn't so sure. I thought maybe you weren't disappointed, maybe you just wouldn't stand up for me with Dad. And somehow, that hurt even more." The tears start before I can even finish.

Mom's eyes are soft, filling with her own tears as she listens. "I'm so sorry I made you feel that way, mija. I'll be honest, it'll take me some time to wrap my head around everything. But I am not mad or disappointed. I'm just scared for you. I don't want you getting hurt or

182

judged. This is something that's new to us. To our family."

"That's the thing, Mom," I say, swallowing hard. "After talking to Abue, I realized that I've been doing to you the same thing you're starting to do to me. I owe you an apology. I was so angry about Dad's cheating, and when you forgave him, I couldn't understand it. I was so scared he'd hurt you again that I ended up hurting you even more. And I am so, so sorry."

We sit in silence for a moment, letting it all settle.

"I should have reached out to you first. I promise I'll do better. I'll talk to your dad, remind him it's my house too. You're welcome back anytime, whether or not he likes it." She reaches across the table, placing her hand on mine.

"I'm not ready to see him yet, so I think I'll stay at Abue's for the rest of summer break. But I'd like us to stay in touch more. I've missed you," I tell her, and I really mean it.

"Oh, mija," she whispers. "I've missed you too. I understand you do not want to see him, and I'll respect your decision to take all the time you need. And I know this doesn't excuse what he did—he overreacted, said some hurtful things he shouldn't have said, and I should have stopped him. He's scared too, though, even if he's got a pretty terrible way of showing it. I'm sure he'll come around, eventually," she adds, her hand giving mine a squeeze.

"That's what Abue says too, but . . . I'm still so mad at him I don't know if it even matters."

The next week passes quietly and, honestly, pretty nicely. Aside from the hour-long wait to cross the border each morning on my way to class. In the evenings, Abue and I sit together and talk. We reminisce about Grandpa, swap stories from when I was a kid running around with my cousins, and she even lets me in on some hilarious stories about Mom's childhood. Turns out, my mom wasn't always so calm and collected, like the time she tried to "bake" mud pies for Abue and set the oven on fire, or the time she cut off a chunk of the curtains because she wanted to make a dress for her doll.

Midweek, my professor emails back, accepting my essay and calling it "impressive." Turns out, maybe I was exaggerating a bit when I said she nearly knocked my nose off with that door. Because this is a remedial summer course, I get to replace the D+ I got in Professor Johnson's class with the A I earned this summer.

❀✧❀✧❀

The day I finally head back to my apartment, I get there before Alex or Charlie. I let myself fall onto the couch with a loud sigh, thinking about how I'm only a few weeks away from my first anniversary living here. This one year has somehow packed in more drama than all eighteen years before it.

A couple of hours later, Charlie bursts through the door, looking frazzled and immediately exclaiming, "Don't ask!" I don't ask, of course, but that doesn't stop him from diving into a complete play-by-play of his summer drama, only pausing once to inhale mid-rant.

Right before sundown, Alex arrives. I ignore the fact that I'm at least twenty pounds heavier than her and throw myself on her like a koala. When we're done showing all the PDA Charlie can handle without puking, he naturally launches right into his story all over again, even though—just for the record—Alex didn't ask him either. To his credit, the details remain consistent and he's probably the only person in the world who could tell me the same story a million times and I would still find it amusing.

"By the way, if my mom calls and asks if you liked the snickerdoodles she sent you, you loved them. I ate them on the way, sorry," Alex tells me, and I try to make an angry face, but burst out laughing.

As the sun sets outside, a lightness settles over me. The year's been hard, sure, but with Alex and Charlie here, I realize I'm not alone, and maybe this is exactly where I was meant to be all along. The distance between my mother and me is finally starting to heal too. After everything, we're finding our way back to each other, piece by piece. It's not perfect yet, but there's a sense of peace in knowing that things are on the mend, and that we're both slowly learning how to be there for each other again.

Over the next couple of months, I fall into a pleasant rhythm. My classes this semester feel a lot more manageable, and I'm loving my Chicano Studies course. On the first day, Professor López strides in, does a quick intro, and then throws out the question, "So, who here can tell me what 'Chicano' means?"

As soon as the word leaves his mouth, there's a spark of recognition. It's the first time I've been in a classroom where my identity isn't something to justify. Here, it's acknowledged, celebrated even. I realize how important it is to see yourself reflected in what you learn, to know that your story, your culture, is worthy of being studied and understood. Something clicks inside me, a sense of belonging.

One guy, sitting right in the front row, raises his hand confidently and blurts out, "The Mexican gangsters who wear, like, baggy pants and bandanas and stuff?"

For a second, the entire class is silent as we collectively try to figure out if he's joking. I can feel the collective cringe rolling through us. A girl sitting near me gives me a look that silently asks the same question I am, and a guy in the back mutters, "Oh, no . . ." under his breath. I stifle my own urge to facepalm, though I'm realizing there's a lot about my culture that I'm still learning too.

Professor López doesn't miss a beat. "Not quite," he says, smiling kindly. "But I'm glad you're here with us—one thing we'll do in this class is debunk some stereotypes and explore the Chicano movement along the way. For example, did you know thousands of Chicanos fought in WWII alongside other US citizens?" And just like that, we're off to a great start.

Lately, I've been talking to my mom more often, calling her most evenings and seeing her as often as I can on weekends. I'm excited to tell her everything I'm learning, things I never heard a word about in high school. She even joins me on two required field trips—one to Chicano Park and another to Balboa Park. As we wander through each park, admiring the murals and architecture, with Professor López explaining the reframed histories and the symbols of resistance embedded in every corner, I feel this quiet ache thinking about how I spent an entire year angry at her. But I can't go back; I can only appreciate how lucky I am to share a piece of my education with her now—and feel grateful that she made all of this possible. In those moments, I see more clearly how the roots of migrant and diverse cultures have shared not just these parks, but the country we live in today. And even though I've felt out of place in college, something about being here—learning this with my mom—makes it easier to see where I fit.

Mom and I have been making regular trips to Tijuana to see Abue. After Mom and Abue sat me down to tell me about Abue's cancer, I've been making it a point to spend as much time with Abue as possible. After her second round of chemo, it took her body too long to recover. The third round was even worse and a midpoint scan determined that the chemo wasn't helping as much as they'd hoped. So, although it was difficult for the rest of us to accept, her doctor supported her decision to stop chemo and go on alternate treatment with quality of life as a priority. Luckily, she's been doing relatively well despite everything, and the cancer is progressing slower than the doctor initially expected.

I love to spend entire days with my mom and Abue, taking long strolls on the beach, visiting different cafés, and just catching up on everything we missed during those months I stayed away. I invited Alex to join us once, and now she comes with us almost every time. Abue and Alex are practically obsessed with each other. Abue taught Alex how to braid flowers into my hair the way she used to do for me and my cousins all the time when we were little and pretended to be princesses. Last time, I actually caught them conspiring about something in hushed giggles like kids at summer camp. Having my mom, Abue, and Alex all together, sharing a meal or watching an old movie, is a happiness I can't quite put into words. It's like I'm reliving the night I met Alex's family, except this time, it's my family making her feel like one of us.

Then one night, after another day with Abue, Alex and I get back to the apartment, and she finally convinces me to join the rest of humanity on Facebook. MySpace has been on life support lately, and apparently, everyone's making the jump. She sits next to me while I set up my profile, and for my first post, I upload a picture of us from earlier that day: Abue, Mom, Alex, and I smiling at the camera, the ocean behind us, all holding up our cups of coffee. I caption it, "Nothing beats a beautiful day at the beach with a great cup of coffee and even better company. So grateful to spend the day with my grandma, my mom, and my girlfriend Alex." I hit send and my pulse jumps—like I just launched myself into some unknown space.

The second the post is live, Alex leans over and gives me a quick, proud kiss. She's beaming, and I realize that this is the first time I've publicly called her my girlfriend. In one little click, I'm out.

"Hell yeah mis queer lovers favoritas!" Charlie yells from his room across the hall, and I know he's seen my post.

Several months later than I would've wanted to, but I'm out. And for the first time in a long time, my life, though still not perfect, is more than good enough. It's pretty damn amazing.

You Made Your Bed, Now Lie in It

A lo hecho, pecho

AURORA

Three rounds of chemo. Three cycles of exhaustion, nausea, and waiting for results that never came. At my last appointment, the doctor's face told me everything before she even spoke. Not enough progress.
The words didn't shock me. I had felt it deep down in my body—the way the exhaustion settled in faster, the way I wasn't bouncing back the way I should. I listened as she laid out the options, as she explained to me and my children what more treatment might look like, but in the end, I already knew my answer.
I've decided to stop.
It wasn't an easy choice; I didn't want my children to think I was giving up. But it's a choice I'm at peace with. I have spent a lifetime fighting. Fighting to survive, to escape, to create something better for my children. Now I just want to make the most of the time I have.
Rosa will travel with me to Mexico City while I still have the strength to go. There is one last thing I have pending.

I've put off telling this part of my story for so long, kept it buried, thinking it was better left unsaid. But there's no more hiding from it now.

❁✧❁✧❁

187

I had been so careful, slipping money into the hidden compartment under the bed, holding onto the bus ticket like it was my lifeline. I had saved every cent, little by little, for months. A few pesos here, a little more there. The ticket was for a bus leaving the next day. I'd recently gotten news that my mother had developed chronic bronchitis. Whether my abuelos were willing to take me back or not, I wanted to be near my mother, to take care of her. This, along with the possibility of getting away from Manuel, away from his quick hand and his short temper, had given me the strength to try to return to Huejosquite.

I heard his voice before I saw him.

"Aurora."

I froze, my chest tightening as I slowly turned toward the bedroom door. There he was, standing in the doorway, looking at me like I was a stranger. His eyes were dark, narrowed, and I could already see the storm brewing behind them.

"What's all this?" he asked, his tone sharp.

I swallowed, trying to find my voice, but it caught in my throat.

"I . . . I was just going to take the baby to my mother's for a few days," I stammered, the lie tasting sour as it left my mouth.

He didn't move at first, just stood there, watching me with that stony expression. Then, his eyes flicked to the hidden compartment under the bed. The one with the money. The one with the bus ticket.

"Aha," he muttered, his lips curling into a sneer. "So, you needed to hide money under the bed just to go 'for a few days.'"

My stomach sank. My pulse pounded in my ears as I watched him take slow steps toward me. Before I could react, he pulled out the money and the bus ticket. He held them up in front of my face, his eyes flashing with anger.

"You think I wouldn't notice?" he said, his voice low and dangerous. "Did you think I'm so stupid I wouldn't notice you squirreling away money behind my back? You really thought you could just disappear, didn't you?"

I tried to take a step back, but he was too quick. He grabbed me by the wrist, his grip tight, painful.

"Where do you think you're going, Aurora?" he spat, his breath hot against my cheek. "You think I'll let you take my son? You think I'll let you leave like you've got some right to walk out that door?"

"I . . . I wasn't . . ." I tried to speak, but the words caught in my throat. What was the point? He wasn't listening. He never listened.

Manuel's eyes filled with something darker now, something I had seen too many times before. A possessiveness, an entitlement. He didn't just want me to stay; he needed to control me. Needed me to need him.

With a sudden, violent movement, he shoved me backward, pushing me onto the bed. I gasped, struggling to breathe as I landed hard on the mattress, the air knocked out of me. Before I could recover, he was on top of me, his hands holding me down with an iron grip.

"I've been good to you, haven't I?" he said, his voice eerily calm. "I've given you everything. And this is how you repay me? Trying to leave with my son?"

I said nothing. What was the point? What was there to say?

His hands moved roughly, pinning me down, and I closed my eyes, trying to block out the sound of his voice, the feeling of his weight on top of me. I could hear him breathing heavily, each exhale coming out as a growl.

"I'm not letting you go, Aurora," he whispered into my ear. "I will not lose you. Not like this."

I couldn't fight him. He knew it, and so did I.

That night, despite everything—despite my will to leave, despite the plans I had made for my freedom—our second child was conceived. A daughter I hadn't planned for, hadn't wanted. Who would want to bring a girl into this world? Not when I had learned, in the cruelest way, what Mexico did to its women: how it silenced them, broke them, used them without mercy. I couldn't bear the thought of another innocent soul born into a life where her body might never truly belong to her, where injustice lurked in every shadow, where her worth would always be questioned, her voice dismissed.

And in that moment, as I lay there, trapped once again, I realized I had lost. Not just my fight to leave but my hope for something better. For myself, and for her.

❀❖❀❖❀

Then came the day everything changed, the day I found out I was carrying another child, just four months after having given birth to my daughter. By then, Manuel's physical violence towards me had become the bread and butter at our home. I couldn't see myself living like that. Getting me pregnant seemed to be Manuel's way of keeping me dependent on him, and while he'd never laid a hand on our children, it was breaking me to raise them in a home where they'd constantly witness violence towards their mother.

So I finally worked up the courage to go to the police station. I had thought perhaps someone there would listen, that someone would help me before it was too late. But looking back now, I see I was just as naïve as the girl who'd first arrived in the city, believing she could make a life of her own there.

I remember the way the officer's face twisted into a mocking grin when I spoke Manuel's name. He leaned back, crossing his arms, eyes gleaming with amusement as he glanced over at his buddy behind the desk. They shared a laugh as he said, "You really want us to lock up Manuel? What's he done, come home a little late?"

He didn't even bother to hide the disdain in his voice. I pleaded, trying to explain the things he'd done, the things he'd threatened, but they just shook their heads, laughing under their breath.

Then one of them muttered, "Maybe we should tell him you stopped by," and I felt my blood turn to ice.

I walked out of there with my head down, the weight of what I had to do settling like a stone in my chest. There was no help to come, not from them, not from anyone there. I had to leave. I had to get my children away from him.

The weight of my sleeping daughter pressed softly against my shoulder as I took careful steps out of the police station, my heart pounding with each beat. I held my breath, afraid that if I exhaled, I'd lose the fragile thread of resolve keeping me from collapsing. They'd laughed at me in there, smirking and whispering as I pleaded my case, as if every word I spoke was some twisted joke. I'd watched their faces, Manuel's friends, loyal to him in ways I couldn't fathom, practically daring me to push any harder.

I'd gone back to the house with a plan, just enough of one to get the three, soon to be four, of us out of the city. I packed only what we needed, moving as quickly as I could, trying to ignore the sickness clawing at my stomach, the sickness that told me this was real, that I was truly on my own.

Home, of course, wasn't the word I'd have chosen for the place where Manuel held his power over me, where each night became another test of patience and prayer, where my son's cries were becoming quieter, more frightened, and where I'd learned to stop looking him in the eyes whenever he asked me why his papá shouted so much. I couldn't let them stay there, I knew that now with certainty.

And as hard as I'd tried to plan for another escape, another option, Manuel's reach, his threats, the suffocating certainty that he would always find me . . . it kept me there, trapped, day after day.

But that night, after the laughter of those men at the station despite my black eye and swollen lower lip, after the thought of their words reaching Manuel's ears, I knew I couldn't wait. My hands trembled as I packed, ignoring the ache of my back, the gnawing fear that I was already too late, that at any moment I'd hear Manuel's heavy footsteps outside the door.

I had just wrapped my son in his little jacket and grabbed my daughter's blanket when I heard the unmistakable creak of the front gate. My heart stopped, freezing every muscle as Manuel's heavy footsteps came up the path. He was early. He was drunk. And he was angry.

My pulse hammered in my throat as I glanced at my children, wide-eyed and confused, sensing the shift in the air. There was no time to hide what I'd done, no time to shove the hastily packed bag back into the closet or come up with an excuse for why we were all dressed and ready to go. The keys jingled in the door, and I knew I couldn't risk staying, couldn't stay and face what he'd do if he saw me ready to leave.

I crouched low, "Stay here with your sister, mijo. Mamá has to go." I whispered to my son, forcing a steady voice.

"Mamá . . ." he whimpered, clinging to me, fear filling his little eyes. I pried his hands off gently, giving him one last hug. I quickly tucked Mary under Pili's arm.

Please help me take care of them, I silently asked the doll. My father. Both.

"Stay quiet, Meño. I'll come back for you, I love you," I murmured, even though I didn't know if I could keep that promise.

Just as I started making my way toward the back door, the front one burst open, Manuel's figure casting a dark shadow in the doorway. His eyes landed on the packed bag on the floor, then flicked to me, realizing in an instant what I'd tried to do. His face twisted with rage, mouth curling into a snarl, and in that moment, I knew he was capable of anything. Capable of ending my life and that of the baby growing inside me.

"Aurora!" he roared, stumbling toward me with murder in his eyes. "You think you can just leave me?"

There was no time to think, no time to explain. I turned and ran, tearing through the door and out into the night, my footsteps pounding down the alley as his shouts echoed behind me. I didn't look back, didn't dare risk even a glance to see if he was following. All I could hope was that he continued to focus his rage on me and not the children.

When I reached the bus station, I was breathless, my face streaked with tears I hadn't even noticed spilling down. Huejosquite was no longer an option, I couldn't risk Manuel finding me. The first bus leaving the city was bound for anywhere but there, and that was all I needed to know.

With shaking hands, I took out the pesos Carmen had slipped into my pocket and bought my ticket. I climbed aboard as if my life depended on it, because for all I knew, it did. Each step away was one less chance for him to find me.

As the bus pulled away, the city lights faded into the distance. I pressed my hand against the window, praying my children would be safe until I could bring them to me. Carmen's words echoed in my mind, her voice firm but kind as she made her promise.

"Go, Aurora. Do what you need to do. I'll look out for Meño and Pili until you can come back for them. They'll be safe with me. I swear it."

Stopping by her house had been a risky move, but her reassurance was now the only thing keeping me from breaking down completely. Yet, the guilt gnawed at me, consuming me with each passing mile, though I knew deep down I had made the only choice I could at the time.

I gently cupped my hands over my belly, the soft curve a reminder of the life I was carrying. Silently, I promised myself I would find a way to bring Meño and Pili back to me, no matter what it took. For now, I had to trust Carmen's promise and keep moving forward.

❁✧❁✧❁

I stepped off the bus in Tijuana, the rough hum of the city buzzing in my ears as I felt the weight of what I'd done pressing on my chest. The streets were blindingly bright, neon lights blinking in every direction. But none of it mattered. I didn't care about the noise or the surrounding chaos. I had one goal: to stay hidden and survive until I could find a way to recover my children.

With only enough money for a night at a cheap motel, I found the first one I could afford and sank into the bed. The musty sheets clung to my skin as if they could swallow me whole. I barely slept, my mind too busy, the images of Manuel's face, twisted with fury, replaying over and over in my head. The overwhelming guilt of having done one of the most despicable things a mother could do.

But morning came, and with it, the harsh reality of what I had to do next. I couldn't rest for long. I had to keep moving, keep building something for myself and the baby growing inside me.

By the time I walked down the street, the sun was already high in the sky, the heat of the day pressing in. My stomach growled, reminding me just how little I had. But as I passed a small diner, the *Help Wanted* sign in the window caught my eye. I didn't hesitate. I walked in and found the owner, a woman with too much makeup and a voice that matched the harshness of the city. She didn't ask too many questions. After I explained I was new in town and needed work, she just handed me an apron and told me to start immediately.

Waiting tables wasn't a simple path out of the mess I was in—definitely not what I had dreamt I'd be doing at twenty—but it was work. I kept my head down, moved quickly, and did my best to avoid speaking too much. The tips were small, the hours long, but it was enough. Slowly, day by day, I built a routine. My belly grew, a constant reminder of the baby I'd soon need to care for as a single mother. As the months passed, the exhaustion weighed heavily on me, but there was also a strange sense of pride in knowing I was surviving on my own, with no one to tell me what to do or how to live.

Then one afternoon, as I was wiping down a table near the window, a familiar voice caught me off guard. I froze. My breath caught in my throat.

"Aurora?"

I turned, and there he was.

When One Door Closes, Another Opens

Cuando una puerta se cierra, otra se abre

PILAR

The sun was setting as I stepped out of the airport, back into Tijuana. The orange glow of the horizon spilled across the streets. I didn't look back when the taxi stopped in front of us and the driver waved us in. I was done with looking back.

The city had, in recent years, started to feel like home, in its own rough, resilient way. But today, as I passed through familiar roads, it felt different—like I was coming back to something, but not quite the same. I hadn't realized how much I'd still been carrying with me until now.

The funeral had been the closure I needed, and now, it was time to move on. My father's death hadn't been a surprise, not really. I hadn't spoken to him in years, not even when I found out he'd returned to the city. And yet, standing there in front of his casket, I'd realized how much of him still lived in me.

I stared out the window, watching the city unfold before me. Tijuana hadn't changed much since that first day we'd arrived, but I had. I felt a lightness I hadn't known in a long time, like the first deep breath after holding my breath for years.

"Are you okay?" Ofelia's voice broke through my thoughts, gentle, as always. She hadn't said much during the trip back, just letting me be, letting me process it all in my own time.

I nodded, glancing at her.

"Yeah," I said, and for the first time ever, I truly meant it. "I'm okay."

She smiled, her hand reaching to grip mine, and I could see the relief in her eyes. We didn't need words to understand each other. We never had.

As we pulled into the neighborhood, the familiar sights of Tijuana greeted me. The dusty roads, the small shops, the buzz of life that never seemed to stop. I could already hear the sounds of children playing, the distant hum of a radio, and I felt a pull in my chest. This was where I'd build my life, where I'd find a way to heal, to grow, to make something out of the brokenness. It was time to leave my comfort zone of working at the department store I'd been at for the past eight years and build something I could be proud of.

I reached for my bag as the taxi pulled up in front of the home I still shared with my chosen family. A wave of nostalgia hit me as Doña Carmen, Mom, rushed out to greet us, but not in a heavy way. More like a quiet invitation to move forward, to embrace what came next.

I closed my eyes for a second, letting the memories of Mexico City fade into the distance. Letting the echoes of my father's passing settle somewhere deep inside me, where they belonged. The past would always be a part of me, but it didn't have to define me anymore. I was ready for something new, something that belonged only to me.

I walked inside, my heart lighter than it had been in years. And for the first time in a long time, I didn't feel like I was carrying the weight of the world on my shoulders. I had come to Tijuana to escape the past, but now, I was here for something else . . . my future, waiting for me to take it.

What Time Brings, It Can Take Away

El tiempo todo lo trae y todo se lo lleva

FER

It's Friday afternoon, and I'm walking into The Bargain Bear, feeling the familiar buzz of excitement for the weekend. Yesterday, Facebook reminded me it's been a year since I publicly came out, and Alex asked me to meet her after her shift so we can go celebrate. My day's been good, productive even, since I finished all my homework from yesterday's class. Alex is supposed to be here by now, but I don't see her. Maybe she's in the stockroom.

When I open the door to the back, I'm hit with something that I can't process right away. Alex is sitting on the floor, her body trembling as she wipes her eyes. She looks like someone just ripped the world from under her. My heart stops in my chest, a tight knot in my throat. Alex never cries.

Before I can say anything, she scrambles to her feet and throws her arms around me, her voice barely above a whisper, shaking with every word.

"I'm so sorry, Fer, it's your abue. There was an accident. She . . . she didn't make it."

The world stops spinning, but I hear nothing. Everything is muffled, just a ringing sound buzzing in my ears, like a faraway alarm I can't silence. I don't feel the urge to scream or cry or even ask questions. It's like my body is frozen in time, not sure how to react to a loss this sharp, this incomprehensible. I can't even breathe.

Alex must have taken care of everything because ten minutes later, Charlie walks in, covering my shift without a word. He just gives me that look, the one that says, "I got this." Alex helps me to the car, and without a word between us, she drives us to the hospital. I know Alex has never driven in Tijuana. Hell, driving here is like a game of "how many rules can you ignore and still make it through alive," but somehow, she's navigating it with a determination that matches my own silent panic.

The ride is a blur. I'm barely aware of the world outside, just trying to keep my feet planted firmly on the ground while Alex's hand grips mine like a lifeline.

When we finally arrive at the hospital, I find myself in a slow-motion nightmare. My feet are walking through hallways, but I'm not fully there. The door swings open and there they are, my family. My mom and dad are standing in the corner of the room furthest from the entrance, arms wrapped around each other in some fragile version of comfort. My aunts, uncles, and cousins are gathered around the bed, all their faces too blurry for me to recognize at first. Abue's body is there, still, lifeless, but the pain in the room . . . that pain is alive.

I see Tía Abuela Pepi cradling Abue's hand, her head resting on Tío Abuelo Segundo's shoulder. Tío Abuelo Segundo, who's like a second grandfather to me, is rubbing her back gently, the only comfort he can offer.

I feel my mom's gaze before I turn to face her. She lifts her head, and then, like he's waiting for permission, Dad slowly steps forward and pulls me into his arms. The hug is tight, almost suffocating, but I don't care. I need it.

I hear snippets of what happened. Abue was crossing the street, got hit by a car that ran a red light. She was alive when they brought her in, but unconscious. At first, I'm almost numb, but a surge of anger flares up inside me when I hear tía Lucía whisper, "She's resting now."

Rest? Rest? That word stings like a betrayal. My abue never stopped moving, never stopped talking, laughing, or living. Not even the cancer had managed to dim her light. At first, we'd insisted that she needed to take it easy, but my abue was stubborn. Eventually, we all realized it was best to let her be. Just last weekend, she had us doubled over with laughter telling stories about her first days in Mexico City.

"Once, the wind blew my skirt over my shoulders while I was getting on the bus. It covered my eyes, and I almost fell right down the steps. The people behind me had to pull me back up!" She laughed, eyes twinkling.

"Oh man! I would've wished for the bus to run me over instead," I joked, making her laugh even harder.

And now that image, that laugh, that moment—its sweetness turns to something sour in my mouth, and the guilt rushes in. Did I cause this? Did I somehow jinx her with my joke? How could I have known that the last time we laughed together would be the last time we'd laugh together?

I'm pulled out of my thoughts by tía Marta's loud sobs, and I remind myself grief takes different forms. Some people cry in torrents, some mutter clichés to dull the pain, some bury it inside. We're all just trying to survive this in the only way we know how.

Eventually, we're all forced to leave the room so Abue's body can be prepared to get moved elsewhere. I will never see black sheets the same way again after I see them roll her body away wrapped in one. I fucking hate black sheets. I hate beds with stupid little wheels too.

Later, Alex drives Dad back home so that Mom and I can keep the car they came in. The night at Abue's is a blur of phone calls and funeral arrangements, the air thick with the weight of decisions that have to be made in a time like this. My cousin Nora and I are tasked with putting together the obituary booklet. As we comb through the old photos, I stop at a picture that catches my eye—Abue with two young children. I don't know who they are, but I recognize the picture. Of course, it's the one I meant to ask her about the day Dad kicked me out, but I never did.

"This one's cute," I tell Nora, pointing to it. I still don't know who the kids are, but it's one of the very few photos we have of Abue when she was younger.

She shrugs, unsure, but agrees, and we decide to add it to the booklet. It's strange, deciding which pieces of Abue's life we will share with everyone. The woman was everything to me, and now she's just a collection of moments in photos and words.

After a sleepless night, we head out to get copies of the obituary made. Nora spots a little shop, Papelería Pili. We walk in, and the smell of old paper and something sweet fills the air. A young girl behind the counter is coloring a puppy with a purple crayon. With a bored glance, she calls out, "Grandma Pili, customers!" A couple seconds later, a woman steps out with a warm smile and offers to help.

Despite being so distraught, I can't help but notice how fashionably dressed she is, her outfit matching the beautiful aesthetic of the shop.

She says she'll prioritize our copies, and I give her my name and number. The weight of everything grows heavier with every minute that passes. It's all too much. Too fast. Yet, I keep moving, because that's all I can do.

Where There Was Fire, Ashes Remain

Donde hubo fuego, cenizas quedan

AURORA

I had to blink a few times to make sure it was really him, that my mind wasn't playing tricks on me. But no. It was him. The same boy I had loved, the man I had once imagined a future with. He looked different now, older, his face marked by time, but the same spark was still there, the one that had once drawn me to him. He was standing in the diner's doorway, his eyes wide in shock as they landed on my growing belly, and there was something about his presence that made the room smaller, more suffocating.

"Paco."

The word barely made it past my lips before I had to turn away, my heart hammering in my chest. I couldn't bear for him to see me like this. But he was already stepping toward me, his gaze softening as he reached the table where I stood frozen.

"You're really here," he said, his voice low. "I thought you . . . well, I thought I'd never see you again."

I wanted to say something. I wanted to tell him everything. To apologize for making it impossible to reach me the last few years, to explain, to say all the things that had been left unsaid between us. But I couldn't. Not now. I wasn't the same girl he had known.

"Paco," I whispered, finally meeting his gaze, "it's . . . it's been a long time."

He smiled, but it didn't quite reach his eyes. "Too long."

I felt the baby shift inside me, a reminder of what I'd left behind. But here he was. Paco. And for a moment, it was as if the years hadn't passed. It was like we were back in that time, that space, when we could have been anything, could have had everything. Together.

But life had changed. I had changed.

I wiped my hands on the cloth apron, trying to keep my composure. "You should sit down," I said softly, gesturing to the empty seat across from me. "I'll get you a coffee. It's the least I can do."

He nodded, his eyes still not leaving mine, as if trying to read something in them I wasn't ready to share. And for the first time in years, I let myself wonder what would have happened if I hadn't left Huejosquite. I shook the thought away, trying to focus on the present.

I handed him the coffee, my hands trembling slightly as I sat across from him. Paco cupped the mug in his hands, his gaze flickering between my face and the swell of my belly. Silence stretched between us, heavy with all the things we hadn't said in years.

"You're here, in Tijuana," I stated the obvious, breaking the silence, though my voice wavered, "I've got a lot to tell you."

He nodded, his expression somber. "I've been here a while now. The Bracero Program..." He trailed off, shaking his head with a bitter laugh. "It wasn't what I hoped it'd be. They worked us hard and paid us little. I couldn't save anything. So I came here, figuring I'd try my luck at the border before heading home empty-handed."

His words tugged at something deep inside me. I could see the weariness in his face, the disappointment of dreams unfulfilled.

"Huejosquite," I murmured. Just saying the name of the town where we'd shared that kiss so long ago, where we'd had to say goodbye, brought a flood of memories, both sweet and painful. "Do you still think of going back?"

"I don't know," he said, leaning back in the chair. "I've been trying to save money, not sure yet if I want to return to Huejosquite or bring my parents here with me. Two of my brothers are in Tijuana as well."

I looked down at the table, unable to meet his eyes. "I've been saving too," I said softly. "Not to go back but to bring my mother here. She's sick, Paco. I don't think she has much time left."

My voice cracked, and I pressed a hand to my belly, willing myself to stay composed. "I want her close, so I can take care of her. I want to save enough to get her here before it's too late."

His eyes softened, the harsh lines of his face melting into something gentler. "Is she strong enough to travel?"

"If I can get her here quickly, she still will be. I want to give her the opportunity to live away from my abuelos. Let her have at least a little bit of happiness before . . ." I let the sentence trail off, I couldn't finish putting into words what was on my mind. It was too painful.

"Aurora," he said, his voice quiet but steady, "you've always been the strongest person I know. If anyone can do it, it's you."

I wanted to believe him, but the weight of everything—my children, my mother, my unborn baby—felt suffocating.

"It doesn't feel that way. Every day, I wake up and wonder how I'm going to make it work. I'm scared, Paco. Scared I'll fail," I admitted.

"You won't," he said firmly, reaching across the table to take my hand. His touch was warm, grounding, and for a moment, I let myself hold on.

"I've never forgotten about you, Aurora," he added softly. "Not once."

His words hung in the air, and I didn't know how to respond. I hadn't forgotten him, either, not truly. But life had carried us in such different directions, and now we were here, sitting across from each other like ghosts of what could have been.

His eyes drifted back to my belly. "Does he make you happy?"

"He's not in the picture anymore . . . I still think about Huejosquite sometimes," I admitted, pulling my hand back gently. "About the life we could've had if things had been different."

Paco nodded, his gaze steady. "But they weren't. And we're here now. Maybe that means something."

I didn't know what to say. All I knew was that in that moment, sitting with Paco, the noise of the diner faded, and for the first time in a long time, I felt something like hope.

❀✧❀✧❀

The morning sun filtered through the frayed curtains, illuminating the faded edges of the small wooden table that sat in the tiny space that served as both our dining room and living room. Our little house in Tijuana, with its cement walls painted a worn-out yellow and its corrugated metal roof that creaked in the wind, wasn't much, but it was our refuge. The corners smelled of dampness covered up with off-brand lemon-scented floor cleaner, but Paco always said the real warmth came from the people who lived there, not the walls.

In the living room, Rosa was crying, her small whimpers rising and falling like waves. From the kitchen, as I stirred the beans in the pan, I called out affectionately, "Coming, Rosita!"

Before I could step away from the stove, Paco appeared in the doorway, his hair messy and his eyes still swollen with sleep.

"I'll get her, Aurora," he said, his voice hoarse with sleepiness, yet gentle.

"Are you sure? You just woke up," I replied, but he was already beside her, scooping her up with effortless ease.

Seconds later, I heard him singing a lullaby. It was the same one my mom used to sing to me when I was little, the one about picking an apple for God. Paco's voice was a soft whisper that seemed to calm not just Rosa but me as well. I kept stirring the beans as the sound enveloped me, grateful for the calm Paco brought into our lives, even in the hardest moments.

Paco returned with Rosa in his arms, her hair still disheveled from her nap.

"She's calm now," he said, planting a kiss on her small forehead. Rosa babbled happily in response.

"How's your mom?" he asked, settling into a chair by the table with Rosa still clinging to his shirt.

I sighed as I served two bowls of beans. "She had a rough night. She wouldn't stop coughing, so I got up to give her some syrup, and that helped a little, but . . ." My voice trailed off, as it always did when I thought about her.

"Aurora," Paco began, using the determined tone he took when he had decided something, "we could look for another doctor, someone who can give her better treatment."

I shook my head as I sat down across from him. "Paco, we're barely scraping by, and you work so much you barely sleep. I don't want you to take on more than you already do for us."

Paco took my hand with the patience he always showed me. "Aurora, it's not a burden. It's family. And I'll always do whatever it takes."

I stayed silent, something inside me cracked a little. I knew Paco meant what he said, but I also knew he was already working endless shifts at the plastics factory, coming home every night with sore hands and a hunched back. For my part, I sewed clothes and cleaned houses when I could, but the money barely covered Mom's medication, Rosa's diapers, and some groceries.

Later, while Rosa napped, Paco went outside to fix the fence. I kept washing clothes at the makeshift sink next to the water tank. The cool morning air was warming up, and with every garment I wrung out, my mind wandered to Meño and Pilar. I knew they were well taken care of financially, but that didn't stop me from missing them every day or feeling that unbearable guilt for leaving them with Manuel.

I should have done more. I should have fought harder, begged someone for help, found a way to take them with me. But I was pregnant, terrified, barely holding myself together, and the thought of Manuel turning his rage on the baby inside me—on all of us— paralyzed me. I told myself I was protecting one child by leaving, but in doing so, I abandoned the other two. I should have risked it. I should have stayed and endured whatever I had to, because what kind of mother runs for her life while leaving her babies behind? I should have been braver, stronger, more. And no matter how many times I replayed it, no matter how many ways I tried to rewrite that moment in my mind, the ending was always the same. I had left. And they had stayed.

"What are they doing now?" I murmured to myself, imagining Meño in his school uniform and Pili playing at some daycare. Meño always wore that serious expression, as if he carried the weight of the world on his shoulders, while Pili probably still had that lighthearted laugh, trying to make him smile.

It hurt to have left them behind, but I knew that here in Tijuana, with how little we had, I couldn't offer them the life they deserved. Paco had insisted we'd find a way to bring them here, but I couldn't do it just yet. It wouldn't be fair to him or to Rosa. If Manuel felt even half as proud of Pili as he did of Meño, then maybe it wouldn't be fair to them either. For now, all I could focus on was keeping afloat what we had.

That night, after putting Rosa to bed and making sure my mother was comfortable, I sat at the kitchen table with my notebook of expenses. Under the weak flicker of the bare light bulb, I went over the numbers again and again, trying to stretch them like dough for tortillas.

Paco came in, tired but calm, and sat beside me.

"What are you thinking?" he asked, glancing at the columns of numbers.

"I'm thinking I don't know how we're still managing," I replied, setting the pencil down.

He took my hand and squeezed it gently. "We do it because we're strong. Because, even with so little, we have Rosita, your mom, and . . . we have each other."

I leaned my head on his shoulder, closing my eyes as the day's exhaustion caught up with me.

"Thank you, Paco. For everything."

"Until the end, Aurora," he murmured, his voice like a warm whisper in the darkness. "Until the end."

❀✧❀✧❀

One afternoon, I was washing dishes while Paco worked on the sink. His attempts to stop the leak with a rag and a wrench were as stubborn as he was. From my mom's room, I could hear that cough again, a sound that had become so constant that at times we forgot about it, like a song that plays nonstop on the radio until you stop noticing it.

"How long do you think this will last?" I asked, more to distract myself than because I cared about the sink at that moment.

"A few days, if we're lucky," Paco replied, shrugging. But his voice sounded too calm, as if he was hiding something.

I was about to insist when I heard a car engine stopping in front of the house. I looked out the window and saw a green truck loaded to the brim. Then, I heard it.

"Aurora, come out, we're here!"

That voice. That voice hadn't changed a bit, even though it had been years since I'd last heard it in person. I dropped the rag and ran to the porch. There was Pepi, getting out of the passenger seat as if she had just arrived from a short outing instead of hours and hours of driving. She shook the dust off her shoulders with that attitude of someone who is always in charge. Behind her, Segundo got out of the driver's seat. His hat was tilted, his smile wide, but his eyes searched for mine with a mixture of joy and something else—something I recognized instantly: concern.

"I can't believe my eyes!" I exclaimed, putting my hand on my chest.

"SURPRISE!" Pepi shouted, opening her arms as she came toward me.

I wanted to run to her, but my feet felt heavy, anchored by the years that had passed since I last saw them. They had been long years, filled with the silences I, myself, had fed. I knew they had tried to reach me, insisted, but I couldn't. I hadn't wanted them to see what my life with Manuel had become, neither the visible scars nor the invisible ones.

"What are you doing here?" I asked, now looking at Segundo, who approached me with his arms open.

"It was time for us to be together again, sister," he said as he wrapped me in a hug. His strength was the same as always, the kind that made me feel safe when we were kids. "Mom needs us, we need each other . . . I had to meet my niece."

Rosita. His words hit me hard. Rosita, at almost two years old, had never met her uncle Segundo or Pepi.

"Thank you," I whispered, pulling away from him. I couldn't look him in the eye without feeling small, ashamed of the years I had let pass without reaching out. Of all the dark details of my life he didn't know . . . things I hadn't dared to share.

Paco appeared in the doorframe, his smile confirming what I already suspected.

"You planned this?" I asked, through tears.

"Of course. Segundo and I have been planning this for weeks. I knew you wouldn't do it."

Pepi put her hands on her hips. "How could I miss this? I wasn't going to leave you alone with all this on your plate. Besides, it's been way too long. How knuckle-headed can Segundo be to accept this distance?" she joked, winking at my brother.'

Segundo let out a laugh while lifting a box from the truck.

"Let's talk less and work more. Aurora, where do you want all this?"

Rosita appeared in the doorway, grabbing onto the hem of my dress with her tiny hand. Pepi bent down to her level, smiling warmly.

"Look at her! She's just like you when you were a little girl, Aurora." Rosita hid behind me, laughing nervously.

Segundo returned at that moment, and when he saw Rosita, his face changed. He bent down to her, arms extended.

"Come here, little one. I'm your Uncle Segundo."

Rosita hesitated for a second before taking a step toward him. Segundo lifted her easily and placed her on his shoulder. "I've been waiting a long time to meet you," he said softly.

Seeing them together filled my heart in a way I hadn't felt in years.

Later, while we had dinner in the living room, the atmosphere felt lighter, as if the years of distance were slowly fading away. Pepi was talking nonstop as she served enchiladas, Segundo and Paco were discussing the best routes to get around Tijuana, and my mom, from her chair, smiled weakly as Rosita played with the buttons on her blouse.

The Truth Always Comes to Light

La verdad siempre sale a la luz

PILAR

"Grandma Pili, customers!" I headed over to the counter at the call of Zuri, my granddaughter. Ofelia's granddaughter, really, but the bond between us knows no difference.

Two young girls, perhaps in their teens or early twenties, stand on the other side, their eyes heavy with something I know all too well—grief. The kind that doesn't show itself in tears but in the quiet weight that pulls at your posture, the kind that settles into your chest and stays there.

I greeted them with a smile, but it felt too thin, too forced. I'd seen this before, too many times. I knew that look. Grief takes different shapes, but it always leaves a mark.

One of the girls slid a booklet onto the counter. I caught a glimpse of it—an obituary. The words blurred in my mind for a moment as I wondered who they'd lost, what part of their life had been taken from them.

Despite the stack of papers in the queue, I promised to prioritize their copies before taking one girl's name and number, promising to give her a call as soon as they were ready.

I started the machine, the hum of the copier filling the room, but my mind lingered on the girl who was holding the booklet. There was something about her, something familiar, though I couldn't quite place it.

As I flipped the obituary booklet and prepared to place it back in the photocopier, I noticed the photograph. A woman holding a baby, a child standing next to her. The woman's smile was warm, her eyes full of life, though there was a shadow in them I couldn't quite place.

I squinted, leaning closer. My heart skipped a beat. I had seen that woman before. Her face, those eyes. For a split second, I was back in Mexico City, the day after the massacre, staring at the photo I'd just found hidden among my father's things. The photo of my mother holding me, Meño standing next to us. I felt my pulse quicken.

I placed the photo on the copier, pushing all the thoughts of my past to the back of my mind. The grief in the room, their loss, it felt familiar. The mother in the picture had abandoned me, the villain in my father's story, and at times, in my own. But to these two girls who had come into my shop just a few minutes earlier, Aurora seemed to have been someone completely different. To them, she was a mother, a protector, someone worth remembering. I could tell by the way they held the booklet, how tenderly they spoke about her, that she was someone very special to them.

A couple of hours later, as I handed them the copies, I found it almost impossible not to say something, not to force the answers to my lifetime of questions to spill out of them like a piñata. I wanted to ask who she really was, to know if there's more of her in me than I ever realized. But I couldn't bring myself to do it. They were still so young, and they didn't need me to add more weight to their grief. I didn't have the heart to make their day any harder.

They thanked me and left, and I couldn't help but wonder if, all along, my mother had been closer than I ever realized. If, perhaps, we'd passed each other by, exchanging fleeting glances, unaware of the deeper truth hidden behind the eyes meeting ours.

❀✧❀✧❀

Later that afternoon, after Julio, my nephew, had picked up Zuri, I sat behind the counter, carefully straightening the pens and notebooks, my hands moving on their own as my mind wandered. The walls, once bare, were now filled with postcards, stationery sets, and little trinkets I had picked up over the years—a tie to the beautiful moments

I'd shared with my friends when we were teenagers, poring over magazines and scrapbooking our dreams for the future.

My papelería had become more than just a shop. It had become a home of sorts, a place that, even though it was small and humble, felt like my very own.

The sunlight streamed through the window, casting long shadows on the worn wooden floor. I paused for a moment, running my hand over the edge of the counter, and thought about how far I had come. The past still had a way of creeping up on me, but as I stood there, in the shop I had worked so hard to build, I felt . . . content.

I thought about my biological mother, how I had grown up missing her, how much I longed for the tenderness she had never shown me. Her absence had shaped me in ways I didn't always understand, leaving a hollow space in my chest. For years, I carried that weight, believing it would define me. But in that moment, standing there in my little shop, I realized that missing her had somehow made room for something else, something I could never have imagined when I was younger.

There were days when I wondered how different my life might have been if I hadn't grown up with the kind of absence I'd known. What if I'd had the kind of mother who tucked me in at night, who encouraged me when I was scared? What if my father had been different, more present, instead of distant and cold?

But then, I looked around, at the walls filled with colorful cards and books, and I understood. If my life had begun any differently, if my past hadn't been so full of emptiness, I wouldn't be here now, running that shop, surrounded by a life that was mine. I wouldn't have grown close to the family I had chosen. The family that had chosen me.

The day Ofelia and I had arrived back to Tijuana after my father's funeral and our re-encounter with Julia, I'd gone straight to my room to look for Mary. I held her close to my chest for a long time as I released all the tears I'd been holding in all my life. The tears for all the could-haves, what-ifs, and should-haves that had weighed so heavily on me. As I finally set those tears free, I also freed myself of the unknowns in my past that hadn't let me move forward. At least not completely.

"I want you to have her," I had told Ofelia. "I know she doesn't seem like much, but all these years she's been the only physical tie to my mother. You are my family now, and I want to give you something as meaningful as what you and your family have given me."

She hesitated at first, but I used the words she once used with me against her: "You know this isn't really a choice, right?"

Ofelia smiled, I presume remembering the day of her quinceañera.

"She'll think you're rejecting her because of her bald spot," I added.

And with that, she reached for her, grinning wide. "Oh, I would never! If I love you," she teased, pointing at me in a circular motion, "of course I can love this beauty, with her little bald spot and all."

We both laughed, hugged, and let a few happy tears escape. "I'll take good care of her for you, Pili, and if you ever want her back, don't hesitate to ask."

Without all the pain, I wouldn't have made the friends I had, like Ofelia, who had stood by me from the very beginning, and Julia, who was still a constant in our lives despite the miles between us. The three of us had become not just friends, but sisters of sorts. We had shared our dreams, our struggles, and now, our successes.

Sometimes, when I closed the shop for the evening, I would sit quietly in the back and think about everything I had. I never married, but I knew I didn't need a husband to complete me. I had my brother, Meño, and his children, my nieces and nephews, and now even his grandchildren. They were my family. My heart.

I wasn't just their aunt; I loved them as if they were my own. I was the aunt who would always be there to listen, to laugh, to spoil them with treats, and to offer a safe space whenever they needed it. And I loved my business too. My little shop was a part of me now, just like they were.

Family isn't just blood, I thought to myself, a soft smile tugging at my lips. *It's the people who choose to stand by you, who fill in the gaps where the world left you empty.*

Ofelia and Julia, aside from their respective husbands and children, had found family in each other, and their businesses had thrived. I felt proud to be part of their journey, as they had been part of mine. Ofelia had her boutique in Tijuana, and Julia sent her clothes from Mexico City, while Ofelia returned the favor by sending American clothes to Julia. It wasn't just about the business—it was about the trust we had in one another, the bond we'd forged from years of friendship.

I gazed out the window, watching the people pass by on the street. It was a small life, a quiet one, but it was mine. The shop, the laughter of Meño's children, Ofelia's children, the shared meals with my chosen family. It was all enough. I had built this life from the ground up, and in many ways, I was thankful for the path I had taken, even if it had been a rocky one.

"I'm happy," I whispered to myself, a thought that had come to me slowly but now felt completely true.

Blood Calls

La sangre llama

FER

It's been two months and six days since the funeral. Some days are a blur, others feel like I'm stuck in slow motion. I think about Abue every day, but Fridays hit harder. That was the day I got the news, the one that stopped my world cold and turned it upside down. In some ways, it still feels like it just happened; it's fresh in my chest. Yet, all other aspects of my life seem to be coming together.

Thanksgiving's coming too, but tonight, I'm celebrating my anniversary with Alex. We decided to keep it low-key. Nothing fancy, just the two of us on the couch with snacks and a movie.

And, of course, Charlie. Because he's Charlie. He's been kind of a mess after a recent breakup, and as much as we joke about him being a third wheel, we love him too much to turn him away, even on our anniversary. So, he's with us on the couch, trying his best not to mope.

"I have dibs on Alex, anyway," he reminds me.

We try to convince him to join us in celebrating with our signature drink, and he surprises us by admitting he's always thought it was shitty, but kept making it because of how much we seemed to like it. We get a laugh out of him when we confess we've never liked it either, and we realize we've all been suffering through gulps of that god-awful thing for no reason other than our love for each other.

I end up bringing the entire pot of coffee over to the coffee table. Because that's how we're coping. Coffee and distractions.

This year, I won't be going to San Francisco with Alex for Thanksgiving. Charlie's making the trip with her, "to get away from it all," as he puts it, and I'm fine with that. I've decided to spend the holiday with my parents instead. Things aren't perfect with Dad, but we're working on it, and that is a win. I agreed to spend Christmas in San Francisco with Alex, and she'll be ringing in the new year with my family in Tijuana, in the house that was Abue's and now belongs to my aunts and my mom. There's a little comfort in knowing the house is still in the family and is still a location of constant reunions.

We're halfway through *Clueless* (which I'm all in for because, let's be real, Paul Rudd) when my phone rings. The area code is from Tijuana, and I'm not sure what to make of it, so I excuse myself and head into the other room to answer it.

"Hello, may I speak to Fer?"

"This is she. Who's calling?"

"Hi, Fer, this might sound strange, and I hope I'm not being inappropriate, but this is Pilar from Papelería Pili. You were here a couple of months ago?"

"Oh, right, oh my gosh! Did I forget to pay? I'm so sorry. I was, uh, pretty out of it at the time. How embarrassing."

"No, no! Nothing like that!" She laughs, warm and patient. "I'm actually calling about the booklet you brought in for copies. There was a picture inside, and when I saw it, something just . . . clicked. I think our families might be connected somehow. I don't want to make assumptions, but if you're open to it, I'd love to meet and talk. I know this isn't what you gave me your number for, and I really hope I'm not crossing a line, but . . . it would mean a lot to me."

I pull the phone away slightly, stunned. Pilar, from the copy shop? I barely remember that visit—I was too consumed by everything happening at the time. But a picture? A connection? My heart stumbles over itself. What could this mean?

I hesitate, then agree to meet her at the shop. And I decide to ask Mom to come along. I don't know what this meeting means yet. But I know I don't want to walk into it alone. If these past two years have taught me anything, it's that when your whole world might shift, having the people you love by your side can make all the difference.

I fix the tassel on my cap, a small gesture of triumph as I take my place among the rest of the graduates. The magnitude of all of this gets to me in a way I didn't expect. I've waited so long for this day, and now that it's finally here, it's almost surreal. I did it. I am the first in my family to graduate from college. It's an accomplishment I can barely process.

The auditorium buzzes with excitement as names are called, but I take a moment to look up at the stands, where my family is. They're waving a banner with my name on it, and for a split second, I feel like I'm in a movie. I catch Alex's eye first, her beaming smile lighting up the crowd. She's been here with me through so much, and seeing her face, proud and full of love, makes the moment even more real. Beside her is Charlie, who, just like Alex, graduated last year and has continued to be one of my biggest cheerleaders. His fiancé sits proudly next to him, the only other guy in all of San Diego who can rival Charlie's good looks and over-the-top charm.

Then I spot Pilar, my tía, sitting right behind them. I can't believe it's been two years since that fateful day Mom and I met with Pilar. Since the day soon after when Mom gave her Abue's diary, a piece of the mother she never got to know. A piece of Abue she could finally call her own.

"We haven't read it," Mom told her. "We thought you deserved at least this much to call your own. We hope you find in it some of the answers you've surely been searching for."

Tía Pilar has talked to us about her brother Meño; he hasn't felt ready to meet us yet, but we've met his children and grandchildren. Although at first, we were slow to get acquainted, we've grown closer to Tía Pilar over the past year. She's been there for all important family events, and I can see it in her face now, the way her eyes shine with pride, that our bond will only grow tighter.

And then there are my parents. Divorced for a year now—my mom's decision—but still sitting next to each other, for me. For this moment. They're both clapping, their faces soft with something I can't quite describe. Next to them, Tía Abuela Pepi, the closest thing Abue ever had to a sister, holds Tío Abuelo Segundo's hand up in the air to wave at me as if his arm were an extension of her own body.

At the sight of Tío Abuelo Segundo, a lump rises in my throat. Abuelo Paco isn't here. Not physically, at least.

It's been years now since we lost him, but there are still moments— quiet ones, unexpected ones—when I feel the weight of his absence pressing against me like a hand on my shoulder. Today is one of those moments.

For a long time after discovering our true bloodline, Mom and I struggled with what that meant—what it meant for us, for our history, for everything we thought we knew about our place in the world. But no matter what the truth revealed, one thing never changed: Abuelo Paco was there.

Through scraped knees and whispered bedtime stories. Through long afternoons spent fixing things around the house. Through every birthday, every heartbreak, every single moment that mattered. He wasn't connected to us by blood, and yet he never hesitated to claim us as his own. Never treated us as anything less than family.

That was the part we had to make peace with; not the discovery of our lineage, but the realization that love has never been dictated by DNA. Abuelo Paco wasn't my mom's father by birth, he was her father by choice. And what greater love is there than the one that is chosen, over and over again?

I take a breath, steadying myself, blinking against the sting in my eyes.

Seeing all of these people I love gathered here for me, makes me realize that the dreams I carry are not only my own—they are the whispers of those who believed in me long before I knew how to believe in myself.

My throat tightens, a mixture of gratitude and something else, something bittersweet. I wish my abue were here to see this. I can feel her with me, her voice in my head, telling me to keep going, keep pushing forward. To remember the dreams she had for me. She always told me I was destined for something big. The way she managed to fulfill her dream of becoming a nurse well into her fifties has been a constant reminder that dreams are worth chasing, and even though she's gone, this is just as much for her as it is for me.

Before I know it, the ceremony is over, and I'm standing with my classmates, cap in hand. The crowd stands up, clapping and cheering, but I'm already scanning the stands again. I throw my cap high into the air, watching it blur as it spins. When it falls back to the ground, I know I've made it. That we've made it.

I glance up at my family one more time, and even with all the noise, all the excitement swirling around me, there's this quiet stillness in my heart. I've done it. This moment is mine. And I know exactly who I'm doing it for.

I tug at the braid resting on my shoulder, a braid just like the one Abue used to lovingly weave with flowers in my hair as a child. I think back to the way she'd pull my hair through her fingers, weaving each strand together as if she were weaving the stories of our family: the sacrifices of those who opened a path for us, the brave decisions of those who found new routes, and the flowers that now bloom as the fruit of everything we've planted. Each twist and knot is a part of us. A braid that not only brings the past together but drives the future.

In that moment, I know that I've spent so much of my life judging the way my family does things questioning their decisions, trying so hard to be different, to find my path. I wanted to stand apart, to create something of my own, but now I understand something deeper. While I still believe in finding my voice, I realize there's a power in embracing the ties that connect us. My roots don't just anchor me, they've carried me forward, shaping who I am and who I was meant to become all along. The love, the sacrifices, the lessons, they've all shaped me.

And so, I decorated my cap with the phrase *"De tal palo, tal astilla"* and right under it, the closest English translation I could come up with, *"From the stem, the same bloom."* It's an homage to all the women before me, to everything they've done to get me to this point. Strong, resilient, and proud.

"Gracias, Abue, this is because of you." I whisper under my breath, and in that moment, I can almost hear her laughing beside me. I smile, knowing the strands of her love are still woven through me, through everything I've done, and everything I'll do.

ACKNOWLEDGMENTS

There wasn't a single second I spent writing this book without thinking about my abuelita María. Not only was she at the heart of this story, but when those "who do I think I am, writing a whole-ass book?" moments crept in, I reminded myself that she would've been my number one cheerleader through it all. So, abuelita, gracias, this is because of you.

A big thank you to the family and friends who were there from the beginning, reading through versions I thought were final… until they weren't. From making sure my characters didn't accidentally teleport, to helping me fine-tune every last detail on the cover, to nitpicking my font choices and placement—your support and encouragement have meant the world. Pepi, Ofelia, and Julia are a reflection of the incredible women I'm fortunate to be surrounded by.

Mami and sister, sharing my writing with you was the most vulnerable part of this journey. Your opinions have always mattered the most to me, and you know which parts of this book are based on our personal experiences. I can't put into words how much your receptiveness and support through this process has meant.

Thank you to my daughter whose mere existence has challenged me to deconstruct and rebuild myself. And to my husband, who got a lot less quality time with me—and a lot more of me sitting in front of my laptop for countless hours—yet never made me feel like this sacrificed time was in vain.

To my beta and ARC readers, thank you for dedicating your valuable time to reading my novel. Your feedback and kind words have given me the confidence to turn what started as a passion project into a published work.

Last but not least, thank you to Tais Macedo for the beautiful cover illustration (if I could insert a thankful cat gif here, I would), and to Gretchen Picklesimer Kinney for helping me shape this story into what it is today. Taking a chance on a stranger from the internet to be my editor was the best decision I could've made. I'm convinced every writer needs a Gretchen in their lives.